A ROUGH TUMBLE

Luke overtook the other rider just as he turned through a sparsely wooded area and headed for the gap in the hills leading to what had to be Rhoades's camp. Arm swinging out, Luke caught the other rider on the shoulder. That blow didn't unseat him, but it did make him veer away from the valley. Luke leaned in and his horse responded perfectly. It must have been trained as a cow pony. Using his knees, he steered the horse closer.

Both hands grabbed for the rider. He caught part of the duster with one hand as the outlaw reached for his six-shooter. A huge heave lifted the man from his horse and dumped him to the ground. Luke kept his balance and wheeled around. It was a foolish thing to do but he never thought about it. Arms outstretched, he dived from horseback.

The impact as he hit the outlaw made him see stars. For the outlaw it was worse. His six-gun went flying and he sat heavily.

Luke shook off the shock and started to draw. The other man tackled him, arms circling his legs and lifting. Crashing to the ground in a flailing heap, they swung and kicked and tried to connect with their opponent. Neither had any luck until the outlaw came to his feet. He reached to the top of his boot and yanked out a thick-bladed knife.

"I don't know who you are, but you're gonna spill your guts."

RALPH COMPTON

TIN STAR

A Ralph Compton Western by

JACKSON LOWRY

BERKLEY
New York

BERKLEY
An imprint of Penguin Random House LLC
penguinrandomhouse.com

ISBN: 9780593100639

First Edition: April 2020

Printed in the United States of America
1 3 5 7 9 10 8 6 4 2

Cover art by Chris McGrath
Cover design by Steve Meditz
Book design by George Towne

THE IMMORTAL COWBOY

This is respectfully dedicated to the "American Cowboy." His was the saga sparked by the turmoil that followed the Civil War, and the passing of more than a century has by no means diminished the flame.

True, the old days and the old ways are but treasured memories, and the old trails have grown dim with the ravages of time, but the spirit of the cowboy lives on.

In my travels—to Texas, Oklahoma, Kansas, Nebraska, Colorado, Wyoming, New Mexico, and Arizona—I always find something that reminds me of the Old West. While I am walking these plains and mountains for the first time, there is this feeling that a part of me is eternal, that I have known these old trails before. I believe it is the undying spirit of the frontier calling me, through the mind's eye, to step back into time. What is the appeal of the Old West of the American frontier?

It has been epitomized by some as the dark and bloody period in American history. Its heroes—Crockett, Bowie, Hickok, Earp—have been reviled and criticized. Yet the Old West lives on, larger than life.

It has become a symbol of freedom, when there was always another mountain to climb and another river to cross; when a dispute between two men was settled not with expensive lawyers, but with fists, knives, or guns. Barbaric? Maybe. But some things never change. When the cowboy rode into the pages of American history, he left behind a legacy that lives within the hearts of us all.

—Ralph Compton

CHAPTER ONE

"YOU BETTER HAVE a strong stomach, mister, if you want to poke around in there." The stagecoach driver kicked at a piece of charred wood that had fallen from the way station after it had been set on fire. Curls of smoke still rose from sections of the devastated way station, betraying the sources of the most disgusting stenches.

Luke Hadley coughed and tried not to let the rumble in his belly bring up what little he'd had to eat that morning before riding up to the destroyed way station a few minutes after the stage arrived. The nose-wrinkling smell wasn't even what the driver meant. That was bad, but the sight of burned bodies in the building's still-smoldering remains was worse. He hitched up the S&W Model 3 Schofield slung at his right hip. His fingers settled on the wood butt and tapped nervously. He had arrived too late again, and it tore at him.

"Do you know what happened?" Luke did. He wondered if the driver had guessed.

The man shuffled over and stared up into Luke's deep blue eyes. He stood about four inches shorter than Luke's five-foot-ten but somehow had a commanding air about him. Whether that came from years of herding stagecoach passengers or maybe being an Army noncom once upon a time didn't matter right now. He was deadly serious as he drew himself to attention and gave his report to a fool who asked.

"Murder, that's what it was. Murder most foul." The driver's chapped lips curled a little. "That's from Shakespeare. A ghost is complaining about how he got hisself killed. Those folks that tended the station won't be complaining to anyone, so I have to. It had to be the Rollie Rhoades gang. Word of them scavengers has been floatin' around for more than a month. Yes sir, got to be them. No Injun done this. No call for them to. They've been peaceable for nigh on a year."

Luke sucked in his breath and held it until he turned a little wobbly. Forcing himself to let it out caused him to reflexively suck in another breath corrupted with the stench of burned human flesh. He looked past the driver to the way station corral. The horses were gone. They might have kicked open the gate and run off when the fire started. If he were a gambling man, he would place every cent he had on outlaws stealing the horses. This is what Rhoades and his cutthroats would do. The senseless killing and arson were trademarks of the baby-faced, always smiling Rollie Rhoades and the road agents that he called his family. No pack of rabid dogs matched their ferocity.

Especially Rhoades's right-hand man, Crazy Water Benedict.

Luke's fingers curled around the butt of his six-gun so hard, the muscles in his forearm protested. He forced himself to relax.

"That's about what I thought."

The driver stepped close enough to bump chests. The reek of sweat and horses and trail dust rising from the driver almost overpowered Luke. It was still better than the smell of death.

"You're not one of them," the driver said forcefully. "My boss made sure I seen the wanted posters on each and every one of those varmints. You a lawman? You don't have the look of one, but . . ." He squinted at Luke, sizing him up.

Luke had encountered this attitude before and had prepared for it. He silently reached into his coat pocket and pulled out a stained piece of latigo with a battered tin star pinned to it. The driver squinted and reached out to run his finger over the embossed letters, then looked up. He nodded curtly.

"Wondered when the Pinkertons would be hired to catch Rhoades. That owlhoot don't much care who he steals from." The driver looked over his shoulder at the burned station. "Or who he kills." He wiped his lips and turned to the stage. "Got to comfort the passengers. They took it well enough when I told them they wouldn't get no whiskey here, but then one's a peddler and the other's a gambler from the look of his hands. No tellin' how they will react."

"You don't care if I sift through the ashes?"

"Go on. If your Christian charity moves you, go on and bury them, too. What remains of them." The driver heaved a deep sigh and wiped his mouth again with his filthy sleeve. "The Tomlinsons been married for ten years and ran the way station for the past eight."

"Anyone else?"

"You mean did they have young 'uns? No, thank the lucky stars. For them that was a continuing sorrow, but now it's a blessing. They had a stable hand, but he left a month back to marry the Willum girl. Ugly as sin, that one. The girl, not the hand. Don't know what he saw in her, but then I don't even recollect his name. That might have something to do with it. She noticed him and nobody else did." The driver shook his head and opened the stagecoach door. He pushed one man back in and started his spiel to keep the two passengers calm and in the coach.

Luke returned the tin star to his pocket, wiped sweaty palms on his pants legs and stepped carefully over some still smoking timbers. The way station had been a fair size. From the way bits and pieces of the roof scattered around, there must have been an explosion. Rollie Rhoades had been a Border Ruffian before the war and enjoyed blowing up buildings and bridges just to watch the blast. It wasn't much of a stretch to think of him planting dynamite and setting it off just to watch the destruction and hear the shrieks of the poor souls inside drowned out by the loud boom and rush of flames.

As he stepped on a plank, a sickening sound made Luke recoil. He kicked aside the board to reveal a man's charred body. It must have been Mister Tomlinson. Luke tried the best he could to roll the corpse into a singed blanket, but the cloth fell apart. A tarp pulled from under a box proved sturdier. He continued his distasteful task and dragged the stationmaster to a grassy area a few yards from the ruins. He returned to his heartbreaking hunt. His gorge rose when he found a woman's body not five feet from where he'd found the man's corpse.

"That there's Miz Tomlinson," the driver called from his position in front of the stagecoach team. He kept the horses calm in spite of the burned smells. "I never saw her when she wasn't wearin' that dress. Ugly pattern but she was partial to it."

Luke saw that the two passengers had exited the stagecoach and pointedly looked away across the Kansas prairie. Just because they didn't look didn't mean death and destruction hadn't occurred.

Perpetrated by Rollie Rhoades.

Since no one offered to help, he removed her from the ruins. He laid the woman's body alongside her husband and dug graves. His arms ached and his heart broke for the couple by the time he dropped the last spade of dirt onto the mounds. Luke said a silent prayer over the graves. That was all he could do for them, and he hoped it was enough.

Bringing in the gang who had murdered them was little enough justice. Luke added the Tomlinsons to the list of reasons for stopping Rhoades and Crazy Water Benedict and all the rest. The dead couple's spot on that list was far down and, truth to tell, near the bottom.

The stage driver finished watering his horses and had fed them grain found out back. He had to depend on tired horses to finish the trip into Preston. Tending them now was all he could do, but the man's antsy moves showed that the driver wanted to get back on the road soon. Luke didn't blame him. The sooner he delivered his passengers to the depot in Preston and gave the postmaster a couple sacks of mail, the safer he would be. Like a monkey, he climbed into the driver's box and took the reins.

Luke started to ask to ride along. He saw no reason to keep poking through the ashes. The stationmaster and his woman were properly buried. Luke had said a short prayer over their final resting places, then decided they deserved some sort of markers. Something personal from their belongings made sense.

"Give me a couple more minutes, and I'll ride along with you."

The driver nodded as if his head was mounted on a spring.

"That's much appreciated. Having a Pink guarding me and my stage'd give a real sense of comfort. To the passengers," he hastily added. "Yes sir, them passengers'll be relieved to have you with us, scouting for outlaws. But hurry up. I don't want to be on the road after dark, and this team's not got the spunk they had when I first harnessed them this morning."

"I'll be quick," Luke promised. He used a long stick to poke about deeper in the ruins, then stepped back.

"You said the only ones here were the Tomlinsons."

"I did. You find another body? Must be one of them road agents." The driver dropped to the ground, came over and stopped at the edge of the destruction. He kicked at another burned stick, doing his best not to look.

"It's not an outlaw, not unless a woman rode with the gang." Luke tried to take his eyes off the body and couldn't. The fire had reduced the body to little more than a blackened log, but the strips of dress and high-button shoes definitely identified a woman.

He swallowed hard. Crazy Water Benedict had stolen away Audrey during the wedding. Luke touched the wound in the middle of his chest. That had been the third shot the outlaw had taken. Looking up from flat on his back, the first slug having lodged in his shoulder, Luke saw nothing but a gun barrel so big he might have crawled into it. Crazy Water Benedict had laughed, pulled Audrey closer and planted a sloppy kiss on her protesting lips, then he had fired. Luke winced. The remembered pain went beyond the impact of the bullet in his chest. Saving Audrey from being kidnapped by Benedict and Rhoades and the others hadn't been possible.

Vision going dark, his last sight had been Crazy Water Benedict dragging Audrey away from the wedding bower and Rollie Rhoades shooting the handful of wedding guests one by one, smiling angelically as he committed foul murder.

"You all right, mister? It's like your body is here but your mind went roamin' somewhere far off."

"I have to be sure." Luke tried to move but couldn't. "Can you show me her face?"

To get a better look at the body, the driver kicked at a timber. It made a crunching sound. He wiped soot from his boot.

"What is it you want to be sure about? You Pinks got a missing person to find?"

"Yeah, a missing person."

His wife. His kidnapped wife!

"Well, the doc over in Preston is the county coroner. The undertaker, too. Ain't much call for any of his services. He's not that good a doctor. Folks get sick, they go to the vet. And gettin' buried in the town cemetery is something of a chore 'less you're a Mason. They got the best section all fenced off for their people. The rest of the cemetery is low-rent real estate, if you ask me, and it's better to get buried out behind your own house. That's what most of the folks around Preston do."

Luke shut out the voluble driver's torrent of words and forced himself to be as careful as possible rolling the woman's body onto another tarp. He dragged it free of the rubble and reached a level spot just behind the stage. A few quick turns securely wrapped the body.

"What're you fixin' to do?" The driver looked uneasy as Luke positioned the body under the rear boot.

"The only way the coroner'll look at the body is to take it to him."

"Not in my stagecoach!"

Luke said nothing. He faced the driver. The expression on his face spoke of trouble for anyone denying him. The way his gun hand moved restlessly. A small twitch in his eye. The set to his jaw. The driver saw a man ready to kill to get his way. So did the two passengers who came around to protest the long wait. They backed away and clambered into the coach. They slammed the door. The gunshot-loud sound made the driver jump a foot.

"Fifty cents. I'll pay four bits to put the body in the boot for the trip to Preston."

The driver turned cagey.

"That's not the cost of a ticket on this stage line, no sir."

"A dollar." Luke's cold blue eyes speared the driver.

"Done. But you got to load the body in all by yourself and take it out once we get to town. No way am I helpin' with that chore."

Luke fished around in his vest pocket and flipped a silver cartwheel in the driver's direction. The man snared it. With a move any gambler would envy, the coin vanished into a vest pocket. The driver untied the canvas flap over the boot. Two pieces of battered luggage were pushed to one side. Luke wondered if both belonged to the peddler or if the passengers each had a bag. Then the physical exertion of lifting the body, as light as the remains were, and placing it into the boot occupied his attention. He secured the body, tied down the canvas flap and stepped away.

"Mind if I ride up on top with you? I can fasten my horse to the back." Luke saw a flash of greed cross the driver's face. He had unleashed the avarice by agreeing to pay for the corpse. He headed it off. "You don't have a shotgun messenger. Like you said before, that'd make you a sitting duck for the road agents. Seeing two men in the box might convince them not to bother."

"Can't stop you from ridin' along, but up in the driver's box is another matter. Company policy, you know. No freeloadin' passengers allowed, no sir."

Luke's ire rose. The driver had already said he'd appreciate having a guard riding alongside. He pointed this out to the man.

"I know I said that, but you never said a thing about bein' in the box with me. The extra weight'd tucker out the team that much faster. Besides, two men'd hardly slow them owlhoots down. They'd have us outgunned three or four to one. However many they got ridin' with the gang is more 'n we can handle."

"I'm a Pinkerton. If I flash my badge, that'd drive them off. Not even Rhoades wants a posse of agents on his trail."

"You're already after him, ain't you?" The driver looked suspicious at the logic.

"Would he prefer one man or a company of agents? Chances are I might never run him to ground. Or the home office decides my time is better spent on some other job. But kill me?" Luke shook his head. "That's a surefire death warrant."

That made the driver laugh out loud. "Them back shooters got a dozen death sentences racked up against them. They're a dangerous bunch, but you know that. Ah, hell, climb on up. I can use the company. Won't be the first time I lied to the company about things that happened out on the trail."

The driver banged on the compartment door and warned his passengers they were moving out again. Luke tied his horse's reins to the back of the coach, then climbed up into the driver's box. The hardwood seat had been rubbed smooth by more than one guard riding alongside the driver. It took only a few seconds to realize a pillow under his backside would have been a comfort.

The driver pulled the reins off the brake, settled them in his left hand, then used the long whip to crack over the lead horse's head. The team protested and lurched forward. Once on the road they settled into a steady pull.

"Don't want to tire 'em out more 'n they already are

with a quicker gait," the driver said. "As much as I want to get to town, it's no good havin' them die in harness."

"Your team's lathered up already," Luke observed.

"I might have pushed them a mite hard when I saw the smoke risin' up from the way station. That was a goodly three miles down the road. I'm real sorry I done that now, but how was I to know? There's not been serious trouble since the Pawnee uprisin' four, five years back."

How was he to know? Luke didn't have a good answer, so held his tongue. The rattle of the wheels and the wheezing of the tired horses as they strained to pull the heavy stage drowned out much of what the driver said. It didn't matter. The man was less inclined to want conversation than someone to listen to him. That suited Luke just fine. He drifted with the roll and bump and creaking of the leather straps acting as springs and returned to the day.

That day. The day he married Audrey.

He hardly remembered the preacher's words. He was drifting in a world of shock and love and realization that he had finally found his heart's desire in the woman. So beautiful and she had taken to him right away, unlike any other woman he had ever met. He had seen her in the general store and had been too shy to speak, but she had been bold. Now the wedding dress accentuated her trim figure and turned her into an angel come to earth. His hand had shaken like he had the palsy as he slipped the gold band onto her finger. The preacher's words had come from a thousand miles away, as if through the roar of a Kansas tornado and Audrey laughing in delight at his shock. "Man and wife," the preacher had said. "You may kiss the bride," he had said.

Luke had. Audrey returned the kiss fervently and the world shattered around them. He remembered gunfire. Three of the guests had been cut down. Luke kept his arm around Audrey's waist and saw Rollie Rhoades, his smiling baby face and his six-gun blazing away. That vision distracted him from Mal Benedict.

Crazy Water Benedict, they called him, because of his fondness for whiskey laced with locoweed. He was worse than his boss when it came to wanton killing. He had rushed forward. Luke saw his best man slaughtered. He tried to push Audrey behind him when Benedict's first bullet crashed into his shoulder. A second slug knocked him flat onto his back so he stared up at the bower blocking the hot noonday sun.

He clenched his hands so tight he shook as he remembered how Benedict had kissed her and aimed the six-shooter at him and the muzzle flash and smoke and tearing pain in his chest. He pressed his hand against the spot.

"You all right?" The driver looked sideways at him. "You ain't havin' a heart attack or anything like that, are you?"

"An old war injury." Luke laughed but there wasn't a shred of humor in the sound. Rhoades had been responsible for saving him, though he didn't know it. Luke had hardly been fifteen in 1858 but his pa had sent him to Trading Post to buy seed grain. Charles Hamilton had led the Border Ruffians in what became known as the Marais des Cygnes massacre. Riding with him had been Rhoades and Benedict and other bloodthirsty killers. Rhoades had detonated an explosion that sent a piece of shrapnel into Luke's chest.

He had cursed the shrapnel for sixteen years, and yet it had saved him. Rhoades's buried shrapnel had deflected Benedict's killing bullet, even though the shard had slipped deeper into his chest.

"You for certain sure you're all right? You turned pale as a whitewashed fence post. Now, I know a man who sees what we just did can react later on. It's like a fuse burnin'. You not gettin' ready to explode because of what happened to the Tomlinsons, now, are you?"

"How much farther?"

"Not far." The driver sounded as relieved to declare that as Luke was to hear it.

Within a half hour, the prairie town of Preston showed itself and before the hour the driver drew rein on his exhausted team in front of the depot. The two passengers erupted from the compartment before the driver or Luke had a chance to warn them what they'd find when they retrieved their luggage.

Their reactions caused a ripple of laughter among the men gathered to greet the stage, but the silence that descended on them all when they saw the condition of the woman's corpse gave Luke the chance to drop down, heave the body over his horse's back and ask where to find the town doctor.

Several men pointed in the same direction. Luke headed that way. He considered asking for new directions when he turned the corner on the main thoroughfare and headed down a narrower street. Then he saw the badly painted sign swinging in the late afternoon breeze.

"'Doctor Payne.'" He smiled ruefully. If he couldn't take some amusement at that, he wasn't likely to ever find laughter in the world.

His horse let out a thankful whinny as he took the body from the saddle. The woman hadn't weighed much in life. In death she was only a pile of bones and charred flesh, but the horse's objection came more from the smell than the weight. Luke kicked open the door, swung about agilely and dropped his load on an examining table.

Seated at a desk across the room, a man with a shock of mussed gray hair looked up. He adjusted his wire-rim glasses and scowled.

"I'm not taking patients, sir. Especially not ones all wrapped up like a mummy."

"Don't rightly know what a mummy is, but this isn't a patient intended for a doctor. It's a dead body wanting a coroner's expert opinion." Luke almost choked. The stagecoach driver had said only the Tomlinsons were in the way station. This woman had been the same size as Audrey. The Rhoades gang might have shot her and left her to burn. Why bring her all this way was a mystery, but Rhoades and Benedict acted out of mad dog spite, not any kind of logic.

"You paying for the burial? I'm the town digger, too."

"Tell me what you can about her." Luke settled on the edge of the doctor's desk.

"You get on out of here and let me work."

Luke didn't budge.

Doctor Payne shrugged, ran his fingers through his hair instead of using a decent comb, grabbed a white coat and went to the examining table.

"Well, now, what do we have here? A burned body."

He rubbed his nose as the tarp fell away from the body. “A woman.” He poked and prodded and made a rude noise when an arm fell off.

“How old was she?” Luke wanted to hear that Mrs. Tomlinson’s grandmother had been visiting. That would explain the unknown extra female in the way station.

“Not old. From the look of her, not more than thirty. Less.”

Luke tried to swallow but a lump in his throat grew and choked him.

“There’s no way to ever know what she looked like when she was alive and kicking. The fire burned away her face. Even the skull is cracked from the fire. What caused so much heat?”

“It was likely an explosion.”

The doctor nodded slowly as he ran his index finger around the bare skull.

“That makes sense. The cheekbones are broken, but not from a beating. A stick or two of dynamite going off a few feet in front of her would cause this damage.” He made a quick grab as the arm fell off the table. He caught it before it hit the floor.

“Is that a wedding ring?” Luke wondered if the words even escaped his lips. His heart hammered so hard he barely heard his own voice.

“It is.” Doctor Payne broke off the ring finger and knocked debris away, cleaning off soot and charred flesh the best he could. He held it up, looked at it, then polished it with a cloth.

Luke grabbed it from him. He wanted Audrey’s wedding ring back. If he couldn’t have her, he’d treasure the ring forever.

Looking at it brought tears to his eyes. The initials etched inside the ring weren't hers—or his. It was a terrible thing to be grateful for another's death, but his hope that Audrey still lived flared bright and true, as bright and true as his love for her.

The doctor took it back and tucked it into his coat pocket.

"'Less I miss my guess, that's the ring Tommy Zinn gave Beatrice Willum. Those are the right initials. Not many *Z* and *W* folks in these parts and none of them would end up together inside a ring like this."

"Willum?" Luke had heard the name but was too numbed to remember when.

"Tommy worked at the way station until Beatrice took it into her head to marry him. He was a layabout, a good-for-nothing boy, but then she was hardly a prize. Their wedding was the talk of Preston a few months back. Where'd you find this body?"

Luke told the doctor/coroner/undertaker what he could.

"Sounds like she was visiting the Tomlinsons. Sorry to hear about them. They were good people. Some of the few in this forsaken town to actually pay up their bills when they came due." The doctor cleared his throat. "Are you going to ride out to the Willum farm and let Beatrice's folks know?"

Luke shook his head. "It's not good hearing this from a total stranger. You knew them, at least a little. I'm not too good with delivering such sorry news." Luke felt the itch to hurry on, now that he knew Audrey hadn't died in the fire.

"You have any idea where Tommy is? No, I reckon

not if you're just riding through." Doctor Payne turned the simple statement into condemnation.

Luke dropped a twenty-dollar gold piece onto the doctor's desk for the burial and left without another word.

He stepped into the sultry night and wished for a wind to kick up and dry the tears pouring down his cheeks. Like his luck, not a puff of air came his way.

CHAPTER TWO

LUKE HADLEY FELT apart from everyone around him. He bumped into a man and bounced away, hardly noticing. The man muttered something about drunks, but Luke's shock didn't require booze. Nothing mattered anymore. Preston, Kansas, was a decent enough town. It wasn't much different from the town he had grown up in, but everything struck him as hollow, empty, no longer the sort of place for anyone to make a home.

Audrey was gone and her kidnappers were still at large. Never in his wildest dreams had he thought the encounter with the Border Ruffians before the war would echo down through time to blight him now. At every turn they made his life a living hell. He had been so sure that the body in the burned-out way station had been his wife's.

"What if it had been Audrey?" He realized he spoke out loud when heads turned to stare at him. He hurried on. While he cared nothing about what the townspeople thought of him, he still felt embarrassed at acting this way. He lied to himself about getting tougher emotionally. If anything, every contact with the Rhoades gang opened new wounds. Giving up was the sensible thing to do. The easy trail. Just walk away. The chance that Audrey was still alive after so many months was less than drawing to an inside straight against a professional cardsharp. But a tiny spark of hope still burned in him.

Without knowing it, his steps turned toward the Drunken Cow Saloon and Drinking Emporium. Music playing badly on an untuned piano poured from inside. Bright lights spilled onto the boardwalk under the double swinging doors, and laughter reminded him it was possible to enjoy life.

"Others can enjoy themselves. There's no way I can, not without Audrey."

He stopped just outside the doors. The heavy clouds of cigar smoke and black fumes from the coal oil lamps engulfed him. He coughed, then heard the clink of glasses against the bar and the liquid gush of rotgut whiskey going into those glasses. Taking the doors one in each hand, he pushed them open and stared around inside the Drunken Cow. It lived up to its name. Three men were stacked like cordwood to one side, all passed out. Another man sprawled in a barber chair at the back of the room. Whether it was the barber sleeping off a long day of cutting hair or someone who found the empty chair comfortable and claimed it for his own hardly mattered. All that mattered to Luke at the moment was quenching his thirst—and letting the tarantula juice make him forget for a while.

The saloon keeper worked to keep the lined-up glasses filled with tarantula juice and the mugs topped with foamy beer. The sight drew Luke to the mahogany bar that ran the length of the room. He wasn't a drinking man, but he had built a powerful thirst from the instant he saw the destroyed stage depot out along the road.

"Welcome, mister. What's your pleasure?" The jolly barkeep twirled the tip of a well-greased mustache and grinned. Two gold teeth flashed in the light from the oil lamp overhead. He hitched up his canvas apron and moved so he could rest his protuberant gut against the back of the bar. "We got the finest bourbon whiskey in all of Kansas. Billy Taylor's, it is. Or if you want to do nothing more 'n wet your whistle, nobody's complained about our beer. It's brewed right here in Preston, just down the street. I ain't sampled it but customers say this batch is 'bout the best old man O'Malley's cranked out in months."

"They wouldn't dare complain," joshed the man next to Luke. "You'd cut them off." The man slapped Luke on the shoulder and explained. "The beer's awful but it's all we got in Preston. O'Malley's pa brews it himself."

"He does that very thing, and I take pride in the family business." The barkeep held up a clean mug so Luke could see the cut facets reflecting rainbows. He even caught sight of himself. "Whiskey or beer? Both will get you where you want to go."

"Beer," Luke decided. It didn't matter to him if Abe

Lincoln's ghost brewed the beer. He wanted it to be wet and he wanted to forget, if only for a few minutes. He dropped two bits on the bar.

"That's good for five mugs. You want change or should I keep the brew flowing?"

Luke tasted the beer. Then he drained it in a long draft and put the mug down with a click.

"Keep it coming."

"That's what I like to hear!" O'Malley refilled the mug and worked his way back down the bar, listening to sad stories and telling jokes and keeping his customers happy.

Luke wished he could share in that joviality. He didn't know any of them. He didn't care to. All he wanted was to be alone with his sorrow. It didn't matter if he wallowed in self-pity. Audrey was still captive.

For a moment he brightened at the notion she wasn't dead, that Benedict and the others held her captive. But that might be worse than being dead. They weren't men any woman should be forced to deal with.

He eventually lost track of how many beers he downed. He remembered dropping another fifty cents on the counter but never knew if he had polished off five beers before starting on another ten. Or if he got anywhere near what he'd paid for. The best part was that the men on either side left him alone. He drank and thought of Audrey and the life they had planned.

Then he just drank.

The saloon turned quiet as the men passed out or left. He had a full mug in front of him and lifted it, only to have his elbow jostled. He spilled the beer onto the bar. Irrational anger flared. Pivoting on his heel, he spun and faced a man an inch taller and fifty pounds heavier. There might have been an ounce of fat on his body, but where wasn't obvious. Luke faced a giant capable of ripping his arms off and beating him to death with them.

This enraged him even more.

He shoved the man so hard he took two steps to keep his balance. Spurs jingling, the man turned and squared off. His hand hovered near the Colt slung low on his right hip. He might not be a gunslinger, but he was no stranger to using the smoke wagon weighing him down.

"You're mighty clumsy," the man said in a voice so low it rumbled like summer thunder.

"You made me spill my beer." Luke put his hand in the frothy puddle on the bar.

"How'd you know? You're so drunk you can't see straight. Now tell me you're sorry you shoved me."

Luke lifted his hand and flicked beer droplets in the man's face. It was as if his brain had become detached from his body. He floated a few feet away, watching himself provoke the man. With either fists or gun, that man could destroy him. Luke knew it, but his body never got the message. He stepped away from the bar, slipped the leather thong off the hammer of his Model 3 and waited. If he listened to the detached part of his brain he would have been scared and run like a scalded dog. Nothing of the sort penetrated the alcoholic fog.

"I've never killed anybody in Preston before. Looks like I've got the chance now—unless you tell me real sincere like how sorry you are."

"Busby, wait. Busby!" A voice from the direction of the door made Luke half turn. It was stupid to do that when he faced a man ready to throw down on him, but he wasn't thinking clearly. Or thinking at all.

Standing with the batwing doors held open, the stagecoach driver looked downright perturbed.

"Busby," he called again. "I need to talk with you."

"In a minute, George. First, this galoot's going to apologize for being such a—"

"Busby!" The driver rushed over and grabbed the man's hand to prevent him from drawing.

Luke recognized this as an opportunity. If he drew and fired, that would end the fight. But nothing made any sense. He was mad but had trouble remembering why. He wiped his beer-soaked hand on his lapel and tried to focus.

The stagecoach driver interposed himself between the two of them. His back was to Luke. Shooting him in the back made no sense. Luke wanted to fight with the big man. Busby he'd been called. By George. The stagecoach driver. Why hadn't he known their names before? He rubbed his eyes to clear them and staggered just enough to fall against the bar. He used it to support himself.

George turned and gripped Luke by the shoulders. A hard shake rattled Luke's senses enough to get him to focus.

"Show him. Show Busby your badge."

"Badge?"

"Your Pinkerton badge. The one you showed me."

"This one?" Luke reached into his coat pocket and found the strip of leather with the tin star on it. He pulled it out and slapped it down hard on the bar.

Busby stood on tiptoe and looked over George's

shoulder at it. Then he stepped back and held out his hands, palms forward.

"I didn't mean nothing, mister. You just keep on drinking." Busby waved off the barkeep and left in a powerful hurry.

Luke tried to figure out why. Nothing fit together right anymore.

"Here. Put this back in your pocket. Busby's a good old boy, but he gets touchy now and again. Don't go after him. He'll let you be."

"Because of this?" Luke picked up the tin star and stared at it. He laughed harshly and tucked it into his pocket. "But I wanted to fight him."

"Busby's a tough customer. He'd have flattened you. Maybe even put a slug in your hide, but he's no killer."

"And I am?"

"Maybe not you, but other Pinks. You got the reputation. If anything had happened to you, there'd be an army of agents descend on Preston. We don't need trouble like that, not with Rhoades and his family already causing trouble for us all."

The mention of the outlaw's name sobered Luke. His hand twitched as it moved toward his six-gun.

"I'm gonna kill him. Him and his partner, Mal Benedict."

"That's what I mean," George said. "You Pinks got a reputation for trouble. You string up that gang or turn them over to the law. You do what you have to, but don't go stirrin' up trouble with the fine folks in these parts. All we want to do is live peaceably and raise our families."

"Raise families," Luke said dully. The flash of sobriety passed. Once more he had trouble staying upright. Using both hands, he supported himself against the mahogany bar.

O'Malley edged down and pointed at Luke. George shook his head.

"You tell him," the barkeep said.

"Tell me what?" Anger flared once more. Luke felt his face flush and his ears turn hot.

"It's time for you to go home. Or to a hotel or stable. Sleep it off. You're gonna have one lightning-struck headache come the morning after purty near finishing an entire keg of beer."

"Why'd you stop me? That fellow was . . . was . . . one of them." Luke tried to remember what he was saying. Thoughts jumbled and caused the world to spin around him.

"One of 'them'? You mean one of Rhoades's gang?" George exchanged a quick look with the barkeep, took Luke by the elbow and moved him toward the door. His voice hardened with the snap of command. "Get out 'fore there's nothin' I can do for you. It's gettin' closer to that sorry state of affairs every time you open that yap of yours."

"You were a soldier, weren't you?"

"I was a sergeant, Fifth Kansas Volunteers out of Fort Scott."

"Fort Scott," Luke muttered. He smiled. "Lane's Brigade. I remember hearing of you."

"Mister Pinkerton, you have to go. *Now.*"

Luke about flew through the air. For a short man, George packed quite a wallop. Maybe it had to do with driving the stage and handling a team of six horses. Luke fluttered about and spun twice in an effort to keep his feet. He almost succeeded. Rather than tumble over, he sat hard enough to click his teeth together. The saloon door slammed and lights inside began to dim. The Drunken Cow closed after throwing him out.

He wasn't going to put up with that indignity. More than that, thirst turned his throat into a raging desert. He got to his feet, but the straight line to the front door took him into the alley alongside the saloon. Luke fell again. With some relief, he pulled his legs up and drifted into a boozy sleep.

CHAPTER THREE

THE DREAM TURNED into a nightmare. Luke and Audrey under the springtime bower, the preacher and fine words and then the invasion! A powerful hand grabbed his shoulder and shook hard. Luke fought back. He flailed about, kicked out and connected with something hard. He groaned as the shock went all the way up his leg to his hip. He had smashed into a wall.

"No, you can't take her. She's mine!"

The shaking stopped, but an instant later he felt a slap that rattled his senses. This brought him awake in time to see a callused hand swinging in the other direction. The second slap left burning fingerprints on his cheek.

"Get up, you wastrel. Get up, I say!"

Before he could understand he had gone from a nightmare to reality, he was jerked to his feet. His legs buckled, but he wasn't allowed to fall. The hand that had left its imprint on his face shoved him back hard against the wall. Wood creaked and a nail popped out beside him. He stupidly looked at it. Every single detail of the nail etched itself into his brain, but he still failed to focus beyond it. Inches. In focus. Feet. Like everything shimmered in a desert mirage.

"I ought to hang you out to dry, but no, the mayor says I have to run all the drunks in. He wants the citizens to feel safe and not have sots like you littering the streets. You're due for a week in the hoosegow."

This time the hands that had punished him grabbed a double handful of lapel and pulled him out into the street.

"Walk or I'll drag you. It's too early to be dealin' with the likes of you."

Luke peered out through bloodshot eyes and squinted. The new sun's rays glinted off a marshal's badge pinned to the man's fancy brocade vest. He started to protest and pull out his own badge, then thought better of it. The lawman wouldn't be impressed with a Pinkerton badge. Or it might make him even more determined to toss his prisoner into jail and throw away the key. Luke knew he hardly represented the best qualities of an agent right now. He still fingered the strip of latigo and the badge as he stumbled along, arguing with himself about whether to show it or take his punishment. Every step grew stronger and more sure until he walked steadily to the jailhouse.

Since beginning his search for Audrey and the Rhoades gang, he had seen jails in dozens of towns. The pride of Preston was no different from any other. If anything, it showed better repair than many. The plank walls had been whitewashed recently, and the front door had been squared properly. The door opened on well-oiled hinges, and the dim interior showed a desk with neat piles of wanted posters to one side and the cell keys resting in the middle.

The marshal scooped up the key ring. As the lawman pushed Luke toward the rear, he managed to snare his Model 3 and do a quick pat-down to be sure he didn't have a hideout gun or knife sheathed at the small of his back.

"Last cell. In." The lawman sent Luke reeling with a hard push that carried him inside. Before Luke recovered his balance, the iron bars clanged shut and the key turned with a depressingly loud click!

"I can pay a fine. Go on and let me out, Marshal."

"I'm tempted, but I got orders. Drunk and disorderly means you go before a judge. I got a complaint about you from a citizen." He tossed his keys onto the desk. They landed in exactly the spot where he had picked them up. The marshal showed how exacting he was in every detail of his life.

Luke eyed the man. Some lawmen were hardly better than the drunks they jailed every Saturday night. This one wore clean, neatly pressed clothing. Not a speck of dust or lint showed on the jet-black broadcloth coat or britches. His black string tie had been precisely tied so the dangling ends perfectly aligned, and the gold chain hanging across his taut belly to a pocket watch gleamed and flashed as he moved. Real gold. Even the lawman's boots were polished to a mirror finish. What sent a cold chill down Luke's spine was the hard leather holster and the .44 Colt in it at the man's right hip. The six-shooter had seen hard use and had been well taken care of. The marshal might not have been a gunman before taking the job, but he was no stranger to using that formidable weapon.

"Who made the complaint?" Luke hung on the bars and strained to look out at the marshal to better take his measure. "It was a man named Busby, wasn't it?"

"It was. From what O'Malley said, I'm surprised you have any recollection of your night of debauchery."

"If I apologize to Mister Busby, can I get out?"

"Important business, eh? Busby's gone on back to his ranch. He's foreman out at the Triple B."

"An upstanding member of the community, then," Luke said. "All the more reason to let me apologize."

"Do it in court. The circuit judge'll be here in a week."

Luke fought against the rising panic.

"I can't be locked up that long!" Rhoades and his self-styled family would be a hundred miles away by then. It had taken him months to get even this small hint about Rhoades. Starting over on his hunt only wore at his strength and determination. Those stolen horses meant they intended to travel far and fast. Again he put his hand in his coat pocket and fingered the badge. Again he decided against using it. The marshal wouldn't give two hoots and a holler about any Pinkerton agent.

Worse, he might ask questions Luke wasn't inclined to answer. The threat of standing in front of a judge and swearing to tell the truth rattled him even more.

"We're not the worst jail in Kansas," the lawman said. "Settle down and enjoy your stay." He left the jailhouse whistling "Camptown Races."

Luke sagged and then stepped back to perch on the

edge of the hard bed. It wasn't anything more than a plank with a blanket thrown over it, but he had slept on worse. But a week!

"You got the look of a man who has to be somewhere soon."

Luke looked up. He hadn't noticed that the next cell over was occupied. The other prisoner had the look of a cowboy about him. Bowed legs, face weathered into dark leather, squinty eyes from too much prairie sun, all he lacked was a horse under him and a herd on the horizon.

"I'm looking for some men."

"That makes you sound like some kind of law. You don't look like a sheriff." The man spat on the cell floor, wiped his lips and fixed his squint on Luke again. "If you was, Marshal Hargrove would never have locked you up."

Luke refrained from flashing his badge. The cowboy's words carried an edge to them telling of dislike for the law. That made sense. He was locked up, too.

"What did the marshal arrest you for?"

The cowboy shook his head sadly.

"Mostly not being liked. Folks here don't take kindly to my kind."

"What's that mean?"

"I'm a half-breed. When I get out of Preston, I'm headin' back to Indian Territory."

"What tribe?"

The man dismissed it with a wave of his gnarled hand. He spat again.

"Who's it you're lookin' for? I run across all kinds of pilgrims out on the trail."

He had nothing to lose by asking after Rollie Rhoades. "And his henchman's named Mal Benedict. You know either of them?"

He caught his breath when the cowboy nodded that he knew the outlaw and kept adding details that proved it.

Luke watched closely. The man's eyes tightened up even more.

"Fact is, I do know the ones you're talkin' about. Crazy Water's what they call that Benedict fellow. Puts weeds into his whiskey to get even ornerier than he usually is. I never seen him drunk and all toked up on locoweed, but I can imagine." The cowboy laughed harshly. "I seen how he is in what passes for sober with him. He'd wrestle the devil and win by cheating. That's the sort of man he is, that Crazy Water Benedict."

"Where? In Preston? Somewhere nearby?" Luke shot to his feet and went to the bars. "You've got to tell me."

The cowboy stepped away. He rightly saw that Luke would reach through the bars and grab him by the throat to squeeze information from him.

Luke had no intention of doing that, but he couldn't hold back his eagerness. This was as close to finding out where the gang was as anything he'd come across in a month. Longer. He forced himself to settle down. When he spoke, he was hardly calm and collected, but the wildness had died down. A little.

"What do you know about the gang?"

"Well," the cowboy said, sitting on the bunk after making sure Luke couldn't reach him, "it's like this. I was in the saloon and these two hard cases came in. The place went quiet while they looked us all over. I didn't feel anything, no fear because I've faced down a stampede of longhorns. There's nothing that'll make a man feel real jimjams like facing tons of charging beeves."

"Rhoades. Benedict! What about them?" Luke tried to bend the bars to get to the cowboy. There had to be something in what the talkative cowboy said. There had to be. If only he'd get to it!

"As I was sayin', it didn't take no genius to see these were killers. They stood there lookin' round, wantin' to find somebody to gun down. Nobody was loco enough to draw their attention. That would have meant lead flyin' and the whole lot of us ventilated."

The cowboy looked smug. Luke forced himself to silence. The man would get to real information soon enough. The price Luke had to pay was listening. It was the hardest thing he had ever done, short of watching Crazy Water Benedict dragging Audrey away. He touched the spot where the shrapnel had saved his life from what should have been a killing shot. The buried metal felt hot to the touch.

"Not seein' any impediment to their drinkin', they went to the bar and ordered. Don't rightly remember what they ordered."

"Whiskey. Crazy Water drinks whiskey."

"You surely do know your quarry. You're right about that. The ugly one ordered whiskey. The other was a pretty boy. Almost cute with that baby face of his, but I read cruelty in the eyes. You can always tell. But the one you call Crazy Water ordered whiskey and put in a few drops of something from a bottle he took from his vest."

Until now Luke had worried the cowboy was just

joshing him to pass the time. This meant he had seen Benedict in the saloon. That wasn't something any range-riding wrangler would think up on his own.

"I was next to the baby-faced yahoo and heard him as easy as I'm hearin' you suckin' air right now. They were drawin' maps in spilt beer on the barm, and it sounded like they intended to rob a bank."

"A bank?"

"I wondered about that. The bank here in Preston is nothing more 'n a sitting duck for outlaws like them."

"You heard their names? You told the marshal about what you heard?"

"Do I look like I just fell off the turnip wagon last night? Of course I didn't say a word to Marshal Hargrove. He'd get it all confused in his head and think I had throwed in with them. I'm not an outlaw. All I want to do is wrangle beeves, even if I get stuck ridin' night herd now and again. I hate that. There's always a fool calf that wanders off and—"

"A bank? If not in Preston, where?"

"I might have been wrong about that since they was talkin' so low. I wasn't about to ask them to repeat what they'd done said." He sat straighter. "Truth was, even if I'd been that stupid, it wouldn't do any good since two more outlaws came swaggering in."

"How do you know they were outlaws?"

"They was all puffed up and pushin' everyone out of the way until they spotted Crazy Water and his partner at the bar. Never seen anything like it. It was like they deflated. Whoosh! One minute all cock of the walk, the next they was bowin' 'n scrapin' like menials."

Luke wished he had his saddlebags. More than one wanted poster followed the owlhoots in Rhoades's gang.

Over the months he had accumulated a big stack with their criminal likenesses. He hardly needed to know the identities of the two men talking with Rhoades but it would be nice to be sure they rode with him.

"What did they talk about?"

"Well, now, they got back to how the baby-faced one needed to steal dynamite. That seemed real important for them. The only place around here they could get even a stick is—"

The cowboy shut up abruptly and got to his feet. He pressed against the iron bars as Marshal Hargrove came up, the cell key dangling from his finger. The lawman spun it around and then gripped it hard.

"You're out of here, Little Raven. Your boss vouched for you."

"So he figgered out he needed someone to ride night herd? It's 'bout time."

"Wait, tell me more!" Luke rattled the bars but the cowboy never looked back as he rushed from the jail. Luke heard two men talking just out of his sight. The foreman had sprung his wrangler. Luke dropped back to the bunk and tried to remember every detail of what the other prisoner had said about his brief meeting with Rhoades and Benedict.

A bank. Rhoades wanted dynamite. That was too slim a lead to go on.

Luke got to his feet and shouted to the marshal, "Let me out, too. I'll ride with . . . with Little Raven." He had hardly believed the man was part Indian but that must be the case with a name like that. From what the cowboy had said, he wouldn't be herding cattle long. He'd head south into Indian Territory and vanish for good.

"A week, I said. You're in jail until the judge shows up."

"I'll pay a fine. How much?"

"Don't go trying to bribe an officer of the law. If I hinted that you'd tried, Judge Benbow'd send you to prison for a year."

"I'll pay the judge, too!" Luke knew how desperate that sounded. Worse yet, it fell on the ears of an honest marshal.

Pacing the cell like a caged animal, he hunted for any weak spot. The Preston mayor had himself an honest lawman, and worse, a secure jailhouse. Luke failed to find even a speck of rust hinting at weakened bars. The window was securely set in the wall. For a plank jail, it had been built to keep outlaws in until the circuit judge passed sentence on them.

He stretched out and put his arm over his eyes. He hadn't intended to sleep but exhaustion set in. He drifted to sleep, only to come awake a few hours later when he overheard the marshal talking with a woman. The words that brought him bolt upright were ". . . let him go."

"I'm in here. You going to spring me?" He had no idea who might be talking to the marshal about him since he knew no one in Preston other than the stagecoach driver. And the soft voice hardly belonged to George. "Let me out!"

More hushed discussion went on. Luke's heart sank when he heard the outer door slam shut. He pressed his forehead against the cool bars in defeat, then looked up when the marshal stopped in front of the locked door. He spun the key around and around his finger as he had before letting Little Raven out.

"You can go." A quick key twist caused tumblers to fall into place. The door swung open silently.

Luke started to ask what had changed the lawman's mind, then thought better of it. The unseen woman had to be the reason. Curiosity itching at him, he held his tongue out of fear that the marshal would change his mind.

He pushed to the desk. The marshal handed him his six-shooter.

"You know what I'm going to say. Get out of town. Keep riding until Preston is only a memory and never let me see hide nor hair of you again."

Luke shoved the Model 3 Schofield into his holster. As he looked down he saw a map stretched across the marshal's desk. Preston was underlined. He followed the road back to where a red circle with a huge X through it marked the stagecoach way station that had been burned to the ground. Black dots crisscrossed the map. More than one red circle had been added. Luke tried to memorize it all but found it confusing.

"Let me check my iron," he said to the marshal. "Just to be sure you're giving me everything you took." He broke open the action and spun the cylinder. All the chambers carried a load. Luke took his time snapping the gun back and replacing it so he could shuffle to one side for a better look at the map.

"I don't have any reason to steal a few .45 bullets. I pack a .44." Marshal Hargrove slapped his holster and the Colt sheathed there. "You heard the conditions of your release."

"Out of town, don't come back." Luke sneaked a longer look at the map when he brushed against the desk and swept a stack of wanted posters to the floor. He caught his breath. Written in a precise, small script across the top of the map was the single name RHOADES.

The marshal grabbed for the fluttering posters and caught one. The rest scattered. Luke made no effort to help the lawman pick them up. He was too busy studying the map with its enigmatic markings. The black dots had to be trails and the question marks possible hideouts. The lack of marking on Preston made him think the Rhoades gang intended a robbery somewhere else. Or at least Marshal Hargrove thought so.

The lawman dropped the posters across the map, hiding it from sight. He clenched his jaw as he leaned forward, both hands pressed onto the desktop. No one could misread his expression. Luke had no desire to get locked up again when someone had gone to a great deal of trouble to free him.

"Good luck, Marshal," he said as he hurried into the afternoon sun.

For a moment he basked in the warmth, then looked around. He expected to see his mysterious benefactor waiting for him, but the only women in sight were across the street, going into a yard-goods store. They pressed together, chatting, and never so much as glanced in his direction.

He set off for the livery stable. The marshal wanted him out of Preston, and he was willing to abide by that order. He needed to get a map of the countryside first, then figure out where the question mark and red circles were to help with finding the Rhoades gang.

That had to lead to Rhoades's right-hand man, wife-stealing Crazy Water Benedict. And Audrey.

CHAPTER FOUR

"DON'T KNOW IF I can let you have the map," the land clerk said. "It's the only one I have because there's not much call for exploring that part of the prairie. Usually, surveyors ask for an existing map so they can make changes, but we haven't had a gummint surveyor out in, oh, close to five years. All the land's pretty much staked out thanks to the Homestead Act, and farmers and ranchers are happy. So, ain't got a copy other than this one." The weedy-looking man smiled weakly and stared at Luke through his thick-lensed spectacles.

Luke Hadley barely heard the excuse. All the clerk wanted was a few greenbacks to look the other way while Luke stole the map. The surveying was paid for by tax money since Preston was smack in the middle of the map. There weren't railroad tracks anywhere near because so much of the range was open for grazing.

The law said this was fence-out country. If a farmer wanted to keep beeves from his fields, he had to put up fencing to keep them out. The rancher had no responsibility to fence in his herd.

"What's this area?" Luke stabbed down with his finger. "It's marked as being mountainous."

"That's the Flint Hills. Not a mountain like you'd see over in Denver, say, but it's the best we can muster here in Kansas."

"So the circles show elevation?"

"The closer the circles are on the map, the steeper the hills. You never read a topographical map before, you say?"

Luke shook his head. He'd never had reason to even see such a map. The farmland he had sold was as flat as a pancake. He tried to remember the black dotted lines Marshal Hargrove had put on his map. Luke turned the map around so that he looked at it upside down. The physical features scattered across the countryside looked more familiar now. He found the way station, saw how the dotted lines marched off into the Flint Hills, which gave him some confidence that he knew where Rhoades had gone. Rhoades and Benedict and Audrey.

"I can make you a copy of the map, but it'll take a week or two."

"How?"

The clerk picked up the map on its flimsy paper and held it against the window to his right. He pressed a blank sheet against it and mimicked tracing the map.

"A week?" Luke shook his head. He was dodging the marshal until he learned all he could about why Rhoades had stolen the horses and killed the folks at the way station. Bit by bit, everything came together in a picture that made sense to him. Whether any of it matched Rhoades's real motives was something else. At least Marshal Hargrove entertained the same idea he had about the gang. They were up to something in the area. The marshal wanted only to protect Preston, and maybe muster a posse to bring the Tomlinsons' killers to heel. Luke wished he had been able to riffle through the wanted posters and see if any of them showed the ugly faces of Rhoades and his gang. That'd mean the marshal knew who he hunted.

One clue told him the marshal knew exactly who he hunted. The tiny inscription on the map about clinched it for Luke. The law in Preston was on alert, but Hargrove would shoot first and talk later. Luke had to find Audrey before then to keep her safe from both the crooks and the law.

"Maybe faster, if I had incentive." The clerk peered over the top of his glasses. His rheumy eyes sparkled at the notion of getting a few extra dollars for doing his job.

Luke took a final look at the map and thought he had memorized the parts that mattered most. Silently, he touched the brim of his hat and left. The clerk folded the map as he grumbled. He had tried to extort extra money from a customer and had failed. Luke didn't doubt the farmers who relied heavily on surveys to mark off their land paid the clerk a king's ransom for his work, so he couldn't feel too sorry.

The early evening wind whipped down Preston's main street and kicked up small dust devils. He grabbed the brim of his hat to keep it from flying away. The sudden stinging sandblast against his face caused him to turn away. Once more luck favored him. The marshal came swinging around the corner of the land office, the dust blinding him, too. Without even glancing in Luke's direction, he crossed the street on his way to stare at a dead animal in the street. Part of any marshal's job included removing dead critters from public thoroughfares. This one looked to be a dog. Moving a dead horse would have required a wagon or another horse to drag off the carcass.

Luke slipped around the corner, going in the direction from which the marshal had come. Directly ahead the bank rose like a cathedral, its brick walls a rosy color in the late-day sunshine. A well-dressed man stood on the boardwalk in the front, thumbs hooked into the armholes of his green paisley vest. His belly poked out as he rocked back on his heels to take a deep breath. He sneezed from the dust, wiped his nose with a white handkerchief, then started back into the bank. Luke saw that the doors would be locked in a few minutes. The banker had only stepped out to be sure customers weren't on the way in.

With a lithe motion, Luke snaked around the closing door. The banker's bushy eyebrows rose and wiggled around like irritated caterpillars. Both carried a hint of gray that had yet to show up in the hair plastered down with bear grease on the man's bulbous head.

"I was just closing up, sir," the banker said. "Is there something I can do for you?"

Luke heard the unstated "In the few minutes before we close and I toss you out on your ear."

He looked around the small lobby. Two teller's cages rose directly ahead. To his left were a pair of desks. One carried a sign proclaiming Eustace C.

Monroe to be the bank president. The other desk had a thin layer of dust over it. Eustace C. Monroe didn't have enough business to hire an accountant or vice president or whatever other officer would occupy that desk.

Beyond the president's desk gaped a bank vault. It was hardly more than an overgrown safe. The door could be peeled off using a crowbar. Rollie Rhoades and his dynamite wouldn't be necessary. If anything, blowing the safe would destroy anything inside. And all Luke saw in the safe were stacks of greenbacks. A small fire burned the bills. If there had been sacks of gold coins or bullion bars, the force of the explosion wouldn't matter. But scrip?

Luke saw both tellers eyeing him. One had reached under the counter and had frozen in what had to be an uncomfortable posture. The other teller was more obvious. He rested a six-gun on the counter, where he could grab it in a flash.

"I won't bother you right now. I can see you all want to get home to the family for a good dinner." Luke tried to smile disarmingly. The glare from Eustace Monroe was anything but friendly.

Trying not to look too suspicious, Luke walked off, turned a corner, then hurried to a spot where he saw the banker waving down the marshal. Luke cursed under his breath. Hargrove was no one's fool and would be on the lookout for the man he'd just released. Casing a bank trumped whatever the woman had told the marshal about his prisoner.

Knowing his time was running out, Luke made his way to the stage depot and checked the schedule. His only friend—acquaintance—in town and a source for gossip was due to arrive in a few minutes. Luke settled down to wait impatiently for George to drive up. The rattle and clank of an approaching stagecoach warned him of an impending departure from the depot. A quick check of his pocket watch showed the driver was on time.

Dropping to the ground, George grunted from the impact on his bent knees, brushed off trail dust and then opened the compartment door for his three passengers. Luke smiled just a little when he saw how much attention George lavished on a young woman. She wasn't particularly pretty, but she didn't have to be. All she needed to do was flash a come-hither look and the driver was hooked as surely as any lake bass.

"Are you in a rush?" Luke stood close to the stage to cut down the chance of the marshal seeing him from down the street. He inclined his head in the woman's direction.

"Naw, that's Miz Jimenez. Her husband's an old friend of mine. He rode shotgun messenger for me last year until he busted up his arm tangling with an unbroke stallion. He rides in a posse now and again when the marshal hires on a temporary deputy."

Luke wondered if there was more to it than that, but his questions ranged further afield than Preston or the stagecoach driver's affairs.

"The bank's not got enough money in it for Rhoades to bother. Is there a big gold shipment due anytime soon?"

"Not on my stage, there isn't." George scratched himself. "You're the Pink. Have your office do some askin' around. If there is one, you can hire on to protect it. That's what you fellas do, ain't it?"

"There's not time for me to contact the home office." Luke caught his breath. The marshal went to Mrs. Jimenez and spoke quietly with her. Trying not to be too obvious, Luke circled the stage and held the harness on the lead horse.

"You're spookin' her," complained George. "Just let her be. That there mare's the best horse I ever had in team, but she don't take kindly to anyone tugging on her like that."

Luke released the horse and kept walking until the full team and coach blocked the marshal's view. He had to get what he needed fast.

"You're not carrying anything worth the time of road agents. Where would Rhoades look for a bigger score?"

"Well, now, that's a poser." George rubbed his stubbled chin, pursed his lips and squinted a bit more. "There's a big stock auction over at Crossroads. Don't recollect when exactly, but soon. Might even have happened by now. I don't pay no attention to the doin's of them fancy-ass ranchers. There's more money flowin' through that town than there's water in the Missouri River."

Luke hurriedly duplicated the map he had seen in the marshal's office. "This is Preston. Would Crossroads be about here?" He pointed toward the northwest.

"Pretty much. I got to get the horses to the stables. You lookin' for a drinkin' partner tonight? I don't have to pull out until noon tomorrow. You prob'ly owe me a drink for all the trouble you put me through."

"Another time," Luke said. He shook the driver's heavily callused hand. Chances were good there would never be another time. He had taken a liking to the man, though he wondered what George would think if he told him about—

"Hey, Marshal, you makin' progress on catchin' the owlhoots what killed the Tomlinsons?" George waved to the lawman and turned to include Luke. But seeing the marshal coming, Luke had already stepped away and ducked into the stage depot.

He caught sight of the driver shaking hands with the lawman. He had avoided a confrontation by seconds. Luke rested his hand on his six-shooter. Facing down a town marshal wasn't a good idea, especially one who had the look of a gunman. A quick look around the depot lobby showed the way out through the back. He pushed past the clerk and popped into the alley running behind the depot. Not ten feet away another building beckoned with an open door. He ducked in, blinked at racks of dresses and looked straight ahead as he left the dress store. The owner and a customer sputtered and derided him as being a reprehensible scoundrel. Luke had no argument.

If they summoned the marshal to come after their peeping Tom, his chance of finding the outlaws was cut to zero. Coldness settled inside. Find Rhoades, find Benedict . . . and find Audrey.

Stride lengthening, he went directly to the livery. The young boy mucking the stalls gratefully tossed aside his shovel and came to settle the bill.

"You've done a good job with my horse," Luke said. He counted out the coins into the boy's filthy palm. Then added a dime. "For you. Don't tell the owner."

The boy's face lit up.

"I'll get your horse saddled for you, mister. You be back later on tonight? It's not usual for folks to leave town this close to dark. There's nowhere much to go within a short ride."

"Business calls," Luke said. He started to ask the boy how long a ride it was to Crossroads and then stopped himself. The marshal would eventually come by to be certain his onetime prisoner had left. Luke had no reason to give the lawman any hint as to where he rode. The telegraph wires hummed with important warnings about such things. Getting to Crossroads without having the law giving him the evil eye when he arrived there made it easier tracking Rhoades.

"You come on back here whenever you need to stable your horse. That's a real purty mare, mister. Billy Simon's always willing to serve you." The boy stuck his thumbs under his suspenders and thrust out his chest. "Billy Simon, that's me. One day I'm gonna own this livery stable."

Luke nodded in the boy's direction as he led the horse from the stable. He swung up into the saddle, got his bearings and headed north out of town toward Crossroads. As he passed the hotel, curtains fluttering at a second-story window caught his attention.

He almost drew rein and went to investigate. At the window stood a woman who showed way too much interest in a solitary rider. Was she looking for someone coming into Preston or did only men leaving town interest her? Or was the interest because she had freed him from jail and wanted to be sure he followed the marshal's orders?

Luke shrugged it off. He had quite a few miles ahead of him. Miles and hunting and killing to get his wife back.

CHAPTER FIVE

CROSSROADS WAS EVERYTHING Preston wasn't. The roads were filled with freight wagons creaking under their loads. People rushed everywhere. The stores along the main street burst with customers. Luke had never seen a barbershop with a long line waiting to get in before. Everywhere he had traveled, the barber took care of customers, usually at two or three an hour. Some of the Crossroads citizens waited for hot water to take a bath. Others sat and jawed, swapping gossip and holding forth on politics. But this barber with his striped pole outside the door had men waiting.

Luke had to stop by the shop. He called out to the last man in line.

"You getting ready for a big celebration?" That explained a great deal. Men wanted to look good for a parade or big church social or even a barn dance.

"What celebration's that? I ain't heard of anything happening." The man scratched himself and looked around, as if he had missed something. He turned back to Luke to study the ignorant newcomer to town.

"Anything at all happening? Is somebody important coming to town?"

"I don't know what you're gettin' at, mister. This is the way it's been since the other barber upped and died a couple months back. Jake was about the best there was, but he was turnin' blind. Wasn't any surprise when he woke up dead one morning. The doc said it was his ticker."

"Jake died in his sleep?"

"Old man Schulmann gave a real purty elegy at Jake's funeral. That wasn't such a big deal, though, not like a celebration or anything. Mister Schulmann gave the pallbearers a free haircut for their service. We were all sorry to see the last of Jake."

"Even Schulmann?"

"They carried on a fierce rivalry during the day, then bought each other drinks after work and bragged on how many beards they trimmed and miles of hair they cut off." The man moved a few feet along in the line when a satisfied customer came from the barbershop. "One month they even saved all the hair they clipped off and had a contest weighin' it." The man scratched himself again and looked thoughtful. "You know, I don't recollect who won. Me, I always went to Jake. Him and my brother-in-law were partners in a saloon 'fore Jake's wife got bit by the prohibition bug."

Luke wondered if either barber had cut the hair of Rollie Rhoades or Mal Benedict. If they had, they didn't know how close they'd come to doing society a favor. A quick slip of the straight razor across a throat and the world improved.

Only Luke would never find out where Audrey had been taken. He shook his head. Such daydreaming served no purpose. He had to concentrate and outsmart the crooks.

"Enjoy your haircut," he said, bidding the garrulous customer farewell. The man wanted to spin more tales of barbering in Crossroads but Luke had business to conduct.

He rode slowly down the main street until he reached the far side of town. Cattle pens held several hundred beeves. Some carried brands on their rumps. Others were corralled in marked enclosures. The crowd of men here matched that going into the barbershop. Luke rode past a wall covered with wanted posters—only these hunted for cowboys willing to work. A half-dozen ranches needed wranglers.

Crossroads showed the kind of prosperity that piled up a mountain of gold ripe for the pickings. Rhoades always had a yen to be notorious. Robbing the Crossroads bank would get his name known and make him a rich man—if that was what he planned.

Luke stepped down and tethered his horse at a watering trough across the street from the bank. The one in Preston had looked out of place, being a showy brick building set among lesser structures. The Crossroads State Bank was as ornate and sported a second story with windows, but it fit right in. The town's prosperity outstripped even a rich rancher's need for a fancy bank.

A gaunt man outside the bank's carved wood double doors built himself a cigarette. A practiced move striking a lucifer across the seat of his britches caused a momentary flare that lit the cigarette with no fuss or bother or wasted motion. Luke saw a rifle leaning against the wall beside the man. A guard. If there was one outside, there must be more in the lobby.

Luke walked back and forth, getting the lay of the bank. He went down a cross street and came up behind the bank. An open field littered with trash butted up against the building. He paced slowly back and forth, hunting for any sign that robbers planned to tunnel in. Seeing nothing out of the ordinary, he went to the far side of the field. Two tumbledown shacks looked to be perfect for thieves to use to start working across the open stretch and up into the bank itself.

He kicked open the door of the first shack. The hinges protested. Nails pulled free and the door crashed to the ground. A quick look inside showed a dirt floor packed so hard it'd take dynamite to start a hole. That thought made him hunt for any explosive Rhoades thought to use for such an excavation. All he did was cover himself with dust and cobwebs. Sputtering and brushing the dirt off, he left to scout further.

As he went to check out the other shack, the hairs on the back of his neck began rising. He slid the leather thong off his six-gun's hammer. He reached out with his left hand for the dilapidated door, then spun, went into a crouch and had his Model 3 out in a smooth motion. He froze. He stared down the twin barrels of a shotgun pointed directly at his head.

Shrapnel in his chest might deflect a .45 slug. Nothing would keep him from getting his head blown off from a storm of 00 buckshot.

"Relax," came the cold command. The man with the shotgun never wavered. His grip was steady and his pale eyes looked like chips of ice. If Luke had ever seen a killer, this was it.

"I'm holstering my six-gun," Luke said. With exaggerated moves, he lowered the hammer and slowly came out of his crouch. All the while, until he finally dropped his pistol back into his holster, the shotgun remained unwaveringly trained on his head. "Your turn to lower the scatter-gun."

"Seeing as how you've given up, why don't you unbuckle your gun belt and let your hardware drop to the ground?"

"I didn't give up. I decided to palaver rather than spray lead everywhere."

"A good idea. Now drop the belt." The man didn't move a muscle, but Luke felt the danger rise.

"Are you the law?"

The man silently pulled back his coat. A shiny badge pinned to his vest caught the light just right and blinded Luke. He threw up his arm to shield his eyes. The marshal moved like lightning. Two quick steps forward and a short swing landed the shotgun stock alongside Luke's head. He crashed to the ground, stunned.

"I wasn't resisting. The reflection off the badge blinded me." He started to put his hands up but froze. The lawman still had the shotgun trained on him. After a few more seconds of the impasse, Luke said, "Either pull the triggers or let me up."

"I'm thinking on the matter."

"In my coat pocket's something that can solve this." Luke reached down and fumbled out the strip of leather with the tin star fixed to it. He took a real risk showing it to the marshal, but other ways out of his dilemma didn't look too good.

He held up the latigo strip and let the badge swing slightly. The shotgun never followed the badge's motion. The marshal had seen such distractions in the past and had learned from them. Keep the prisoner covered. Everything else took care of itself.

"What's it say?"

Luke felt a thaw in the man's icy demeanor. He stretched to hold it up where the badge could be seen better.

"It says Pinkerton. You're a Pink agent?" The lawman took a half step back. The barrels began to look less menacing to Luke, but he was still a goner if the marshal so much as twitched.

"On the trail of the notorious Rhoades gang. Your bank looks like easy pickings for killers like them."

"It's not. Charles spotted you right away and signaled me to come running."

"Charles? Is that the guard outside the bank? The match was a signal that the bank's being robbed?"

"That some yahoo was watching a bit too close for comfort. When you went around to the back and started poking at the ground like you wanted to tunnel in, I decided to have words with you."

"I'm protecting the bank, not sizing it up to rob it."

"The Rhoades gang. You said that." The marshal stepped back two more paces and lowered the shotgun so it lay across his left arm. He kept his trigger finger at the ready. The man trusted no one. Luke appreciated that. The marshal hadn't asked who Rhoades was. Either he didn't care or he already knew.

"So there's no way for them to tunnel into the bank and attack the vault from below?"

The marshal snorted in contempt. He motioned for Luke to walk with him back across the open field.

"The ground here's baked harder 'n stone. It'd take a real frog strangler to turn it to mud, and if anybody had worked to dig a tunnel, it'd collapse on their heads. But there's another reason why no self-respecting outlaw would try tunneling into the bank."

"What's that?"

"You," the marshal said, leering, "are one of them exalted, highfalutin Pinkerton agents and you don't know the reason? It's simple as pie. Think how much work it'd take. It's easier to just walk in, shoot up the place, steal the money and leave. I never saw a robber willing to do much more work than that. From rumors about this here Rhoades gang, they're even worse. They'd consider it a waste of time if they took more 'n five minutes in and out for a robbery."

"You've got the bank guarded well enough that any robbery like that would fail?" Luke kicked himself for not thinking of that. For the life of him, he couldn't picture Rhoades burrowing underground like a gopher. And that went double for Benedict. That owlhoot had a positive aversion to any kind of real work. Their kind destroyed. And he knew riding into a town, shooting it up and laughing at the death and destruction appealed more than being all sneaky. Tunneling in on a Friday night gave them two entire days to make an escape, but gunplay excited them.

"Come on in and look it over." The marshal hesitated, then asked to see the badge again. Reluctantly, Luke handed it over. He held his breath as the lawman made out the letters stamped into the tin. "Nothing's like it seems these days." He tossed the badge back. Luke snared it and looked at the ragged edges and crude lettering.

"What makes you say that?"

"An outfit as rich and powerful as the Pinkertons send their agents out with crappy badges like that." He shook his head. "And I thought the Crossroads mayor and city aldermen were stingy pinchpennies. At least they let me hire deputies and give them decent badges. If I was you, I'd be plum embarrassed to carry a badge like that."

Luke held his tongue and walked along, taking in every detail of the bank construction. It was sturdier than he first thought. That meant Rhoades intended to do what the marshal claimed wasn't possible. The gang would go in, guns blazing, steal the money and hightail it.

"The horses," he said, all the pieces coming together.

"What horses you going on about?"

Luke hesitated to mention the stage depot murders and the horses stolen but did. He sketched out what he thought, though it meant the marshal had an improved chance of catching Benedict because of it. Once Crazy Water Benedict was locked up, there was no way to make him tell what had happened to Audrey.

Where they were keeping her, Luke mentally corrected. He had a gut feeling that she was still alive.

"I heard of other outlaws trying that trick with the horses. Chances are Rhoades, if it was him who stole the stage line's horses, sold them before the week was out. Easy money. That's all his type wants. I've got wanted posters on his entire gang. Too bad we can't claim any of the reward. We'd be a couple thousand dollars richer."

Luke made a noncommittal grunt.

"You Pinks can't claim a reward, can you, not if you're hired to bring in the outlaws?"

"I wouldn't want the reward. Catching them's enough reward for me, if they swing for their crimes."

"That's about the way I feel, too," the marshal said, "but that much money's a real carrot to hang in front of a man's nose. If it was Rhoades and his bunch out there like you say, the countryside would be filthy with bounty hunters buzzing around for the reward money."

"You caught him, Marshal?" The sentry stood at attention as if he were a soldier guarding an Army fort.

"Good job spotting me. You deserve a bonus for being so alert, Charles," Luke said. Using the guard's name caused him to react. Right now, Luke wanted nothing more than to put someone else at the center of attention.

"Calm down, man," the marshal said to the guard. "He's on our side. This here gent's a Pinkerton agent hired to watch the bank."

Luke started to correct that, then faced a small man wearing a pin-striped coat, a flowing red silk cravat held down by a headlight diamond and a white shirt starched so hard it would hold him upright even if he died then and there. His pants had been creased so firmly he could use the edges as knives and his shined shoes caught every ray of light and seemed to glow. The watch chain dangling across his belly sported a Masonic emblem. Luke wished he had joined the local

Masonic temple back home, but marriage plans had gotten in the way.

If he knew secret signs or handshakes, he could have cemented his place with the bank president.

"You two are mighty chummy, Marshal. What do you have to tell me about . . . him." The banker looked Luke over from head to toe and back. He looked as if he had bitten into an unripe persimmon. He expected sweet and got bitter.

The marshal explained all over again what had happened. Luke hesitated to flash the badge once more. A quick look into the bank lobby showed three armed guards in separate corners. From the eagle-eye tellers, one or more of them probably had a six-shooter under the counter and longed for a chance to show their bravery by blasting away a robber or two. For all he knew, the bank had offered a bounty for any thief gunned down trying to rob the vault. That'd make a hero out of any underpaid teller.

"I wasn't aware that Allan Pinkerton sent an agent to guard my bank. I am certainly not paying your agency a penny for something I never asked for. As you can see, I already have a small army to protect the vault. And the marshal, of course, is a stalwart." The banker's smile came across as insincere. Luke guessed the banker had little confidence in the marshal—or not enough confidence to matter. Otherwise, why hire so many gunslingers for his own vigilance committee?

Luke held his tongue, not pointing out how these guards might take it into their heads to help themselves to the contents hidden away in the vault. They were armed to the teeth and could bide their time, waiting for the most opportune moment to commit the robbery. Some Latin words he'd heard once popped to mind. *Quis custodiet ipsos custodes?*

"I can tell that," Luke said with equal insincerity. "Give me a quick tour to look over your security, let me report back to the home office that there's no need for our services, and I'll be on my way. My primary job is to capture the Rhoades gang."

"Cutthroats," muttered the banker. From the way he looked at Luke, he included Pinkerton agents along with bank robbers. "Marshal Wilkes has warned me about them. They won't dare show their ugly faces anywhere in Crossroads, mark my words!"

"They wouldn't," Luke said. "They'd be wearing masks during a holdup."

Marshal Wilkes smiled crookedly, and the banker's expression turned even sourer.

The banker led the way. Wilkes and Luke trailed behind him, going behind the low railing at the rear of the lobby. Luke saw right away that Crossroads intended to hang on to its money with far more fervor than Preston. The Preston bank had a safe. Crossroads' vault had been built into a solid brick wall. The thick steel door stood man-high. Locking rods were retracted since the door stood ajar. Once those were spun into place by the locking mechanism, the door presented a challenge even Rollie Rhoades could not surmount.

"Go on, look in. Just a peek," the banker urged. His sour mood had evaporated. Ebullience at being so important because of the vault contents made him smile broadly.

Luke poked his head around the door and let out a

whistle of surprise. Shelves were piled high with neatly wrapped packs of greenbacks. He was no expert but there had to be thousands of dollars in scrip. Even more startling were the heavy canvas bags marked COINS stacked waist-high on the floor.

"Ten- and twenty-dollar gold pieces," came the answer to his unspoken question. "We have a few bars of gold, too, but the ranchers prefer coins. Paper money is good, coins are golden." The banker laughed at his small joke.

"And we always give the ranchers and their hands what they ask for," the marshal said proudly. "Without them, this place would be nothing more than two dirt roads crossing over a prairie-dog hole."

"Like Preston," Luke said. Both men laughed, and the banker slapped him on the back.

"You are more perceptive than I thought. Unlike Preston, we're a growing town. Now, I must return to business. Rest assured, Agent, that we are prepared for any robbery attempt. Any!"

"Yes, sir, you seem to be." Luke looked up and saw a pair of perches nailed onto the walls. Two more guards crouched there. If the floor guards were taken out, these men could back-shoot any robber facing the tellers' booths. It was a good thing the floor was marble. If blood was shed here, it'd be measured in buckets, and stone was easier to clean than wood floors.

Luke let the marshal herd him from the lobby into the street.

"When you're done with your business, you'll be moving on, won't you?" The intent of Marshal Wilkes's question wasn't lost on him. He was an annoyance in an otherwise peaceable town.

"I won't waste any more of your time, Marshal. Thanks for the hospitality." He held out his hand to shake. Wilkes hesitated, then shook it as if afraid he'd get fleas from the brief contact. When he released Luke's hand, he gave a little push to get the unwanted visitor on his way. He spun and sauntered off, head high, shoulders back and looking like the cock of the walk.

Luke vowed to avoid the lawman. With any luck, there'd be no reason to stay in Crossroads much longer. His trail ended when he found Benedict and his boss. A quick swipe of his bandanna dispatched sweat and dust from his eyes. He went off in the opposite direction from the marshal. Again he was struck by the frantic activity pulsing all around him. He had never been to Chicago or St. Louis or even Kansas City but imagined the citizens there were like those of Crossroads. Busy, intent and prosperous. Everyone had a place to go and lucrative business to transact.

He jumped back when a rider galloped past so close he felt the sting of the reins. The rider whipped his horse furiously for no reason Luke could see. A quick brush cleaned off dust from the encounter. He looked after the rider, but the man had skidded to a halt, raising an even bigger cloud. With a loud shout, the man went into a saloon.

For a moment Luke thought the grit in his eyes blurred his vision. Or maybe locoweed had mixed with the dust, and he was seeing things. His hand went to his six-gun, but he paused. Should he alert the marshal? Even if he wasn't for certain who he had seen?

He drew his Model 3, broke it open and checked to be sure he carried six rounds, then snapped it shut and ran for the saloon. If that wasn't Crazy Water Benedict who had almost run him down, it was someone who could be his twin.

The saloon was crowded with men spilling out almost as fast as others went in. Luke pushed his way through and stood by the faro case box, where a bored dealer in a frilly scoop-neck dress went through the motions of flopping out cards and taking drunk patrons' money. Luke stood on tiptoe to get a better look at everyone in the jammed room. Faro bettors intent on bucking the tiger kept jostling him. He pushed one back, then jumped onto the faro table, creating quite a commotion. It might have been the most interested the dealer had been all day.

"You get on down from there, honey. Unless you're putting yourself up to bet. You're about the handsomest chip I ever did see." This caused a ripple of laughter and saved Luke from being dragged off by irate gamblers all trying to catch a glimpse down the dealer's décolletage as she leaned forward.

He whirled around. His heart almost stopped when he saw Crazy Water Benedict at the rear of the bar, talking with two others. In spite of studying the wanted posters and etching likenesses of the gang into his head, Luke didn't recognize either of the men Crazy Water harangued. He threw caution to the winds and jumped from the faro table to the top of the Brunswick bar. Men along the entire length grabbed their drinks to keep him from kicking them over.

Luke had made it halfway to Benedict when the bartender wrapped strong arms around his legs and tackled him. Crashing forward onto the bar knocked the wind from his lungs. Gasping for air prevented him from effectively fighting. The barkeep grabbed him by the coat collar and heaved him out onto the sawdust-covered floor. Luke overturned a cuspidor when he hit hard. He recoiled from the sticky, brown, smelly gunk and clambered to his knees. The men at the bar crowded him and made no effort to help him stand.

"You loco drunk!" the barkeep raged at him, shaking a fist. "You don't walk on *my* bar. I paid good money for it to be sent all the way from Philadelphia!"

Luke clawed his way to his feet. His gun hand was sticky with sludge from the cuspidor. He wiped his hand on his pant leg. Then he pulled his six-gun. This got everyone's attention. The barkeep yelled for his bouncers and a fistfight broke out between two nearby patrons as he made his way toward the back of the gin mill.

The bouncers ignored him in favor of breaking up the fight. This created even more chaos, like dominoes falling over. Luke twisted and turned and kicked his way free into an oasis of calm not ten feet from Benedict.

Their eyes met. For a moment, Benedict looked puzzled. Then he let out a yelp of pure anger and went for his six-shooter. Luke had his out already and fired. Just as he squeezed the trigger a drunk crashed into him. The shot went high and shattered the huge mirror behind the bar. Luke cursed his bad luck, but it also saved him. Benedict opened fire, spraying lead everywhere. If Luke had remained where he was, he would have been a dead duck. One bullet cut through the brim of his hat and another creased his cheek.

He regained his balance. The world seemed to have been dipped in molasses. Everything moved slowly, deliberately, with every detail sharp-edged and vivid. Luke raised his six-gun as if fighting against heavy weights on his arm. His thumb drew back the hammer. Hair by hair his trigger finger tightened. Fear blossomed in Crazy Water Benedict's face. That was almost as good as killing the man.

Almost.

The trigger finally came back all the way. The hammer fell with a dull click on a dud round.

Two bouncers grabbed Luke and lifted him high. He twisted around to see Benedict kick open a door at the end of the bar and vanish through it. Then he was fighting both men intent on whaling the tar out of him.

CHAPTER SIX

A SOLID PUNCH TO the breadbasket drove Luke Hadley to his knees. He gasped for air and tried not to bend forward too far because he knew what was coming next. A rising knee barely missed his chin. If it had connected, he would have been out like a light. With a twist that took him away from the bouncer so intent on turning him into a battered side of beef, he staggered into a trio of men fighting one another. Luke was too confused to figure how that fight went. He threw his arms around the closest cowboy and bull-dogged him to the floor. A tiny tornado of sawdust kicked up, giving him the chance to roll until he fetched up hard against the back wall.

Fighting to get his breath back, he watched the ebb and flow of the donnybrook. In a way it mesmerized him. He had always enjoyed watching waves go down the Mississippi. They'd rise up and move swiftly out of sight, but another always followed and another and another, marching off with precise spacing like soldiers on parade. Washing against a shore caused them to break apart. The bar fight was like that. As the tide came back, men broke off in pairs and the fight went out of them. A few righted tables and gathered scattered cards from poker games interrupted by the fight. The faro dealer was no novice. She had scooped up all the bets on her table and clutched them to her ample bosom until the fight ended and the gambling started back up.

As his senses returned, he realized this was *his* fight. Luke had started it by running along the bar. He had a chance to stop Benedict and had failed. Lifting his six-shooter, he broke it open, knocked the brass out and reloaded all the cartridges to be sure he got rid of the dud round. The outlaw had hightailed it out the back door. He couldn't have gone far.

Standing on wobbly legs, Luke realized he had let his anger get the better of him. If he'd killed Mal Benedict, he might never find where Audrey had been taken.

He thrust his six-shooter back into the holster and edged along the wall, avoiding the increasingly sporadic fighting the best he could. When he got to the back door, a heavy hand landed on his shoulder and whirled him around. He thought a bouncer had caught up with him, but it was one of the men Benedict had been arguing with.

"You're stayin' put," the man said. He lisped a little because of a harelip. "Crazy Water, he tol' me to give him a big head start."

Luke feinted with his left and landed a right on the man's cheek. His head snapped back and he stumbled.

Before Luke could get out the door, the man pulled himself upright using the bar and went for his gun. The discharge filled the room with gun smoke and an echo that sent some of the men diving for cover. The more determined kept fighting.

The slug intended for Luke's head took another chunk out of his hat brim. If it started raining, that hat would be like a rain gutter funneling water onto his face. A quick twitch brought his Model 3 into his fist. He fanned off two fast rounds. Both missed. One tore splinters from the bar and another broke a beer mug.

Benedict's partner got off another round, but he wasn't aiming. The bullet went wild and brought down plaster from the ceiling. Luke knew this gunfight had to end fast or some bystander would get ventilated. He took more time aiming and squeezed off a third round. Again he missed. Going back to his original tactic, he fanned the remaining three rounds in the outlaw's direction. By now the man had rolled a table around and crouched behind it. He peered out and took a couple shots at Luke.

"I don't want you," Luke shouted. "I want Benedict."

"He'd skin me alive if I let you go after him. Knowing Crazy Water, that might be the kindest thing he'd do."

"The woman he kidnapped. She's what I want. I . . . I'll let Benedict go if I get my wife back unharmed."

"She's Benedict's now. And I know who you must be, in spite of him filling you full of lead back then. He told me all about how he took her from your wedding."

Luke saw red. The man's taunts ripped away any remaining good sense he had. He rushed forward and smashed into the table. He turned it over and pinned the man under it. One hand holding a six-gun flopped around. The man's finger tightened and a round went sailing off to hit a gambler who had refused to leave his table. The gambler screeched like a banshee and produced a derringer from some lever-and-rod attachment fastened to his left forearm. He fired, and he didn't care if he hit Luke or the outlaw under the table.

A splinter from the derringer round kicked up into Luke's face. He winced, giving the outlaw a chance to heave out from under the table.

The entire saloon was in pandemonium. Men still fought, not caring who they punched, but the real danger came from the few who added their six-shooters to the fray. Lead flew everywhere. Luke plucked at the splinter in his cheek. His fingers came away red with his own blood. Not only had a sliver of wood embedded itself in his face but at least two rounds had creased him. The blood oozed from the shallow wounds. When he saw it, his fury rose to Olympian heights.

He roared and dived for the retreating outlaw. His arms circled the man's waist and pulled him down. He was rewarded with a kick to the groin. For a split second, he loosened his hold. The outlaw kicked again. A new bloody groove appeared on Luke's face as a spur raked his cheek.

Arms windmilling, he threw punches at anything that moved. Some of the blows landed where they did the most good. One hit the barkeep as he came around to break up the fight.

"Quit it, you two. I'm throwing you out. Where are the bouncers! Get over here and help me!"

Luke tried to use his six-gun again, but strong fingers closed around his wrist and forced him to aim at the ceiling. One round fired. With a heave, Luke got the barkeep off him and leveled his six-gun at the outlaw. His finger came back on the trigger, then his arms were pinned to his sides. A lariat tightened. A second rope caught his foot. With a jerk on the ropes, he crashed to the ground. He had seen calves hog-tied for branding. Whoever used the ropes duplicated the technique way too well.

"Quit struggling. Don't make me drop a noose around your neck." The circle of rope around his upper arms tightened.

He tried to kick free of the loop about his foot and only fell heavily. Panting harshly, he looked up and saw the marshal holding the lariat pinning his arms down. A deputy tugged on the other rope to keep him stretched out helplessly.

"Arrest that one, Marshal Wilkes. He's one of the Rhoades gang!" Luke saw how little effect his demand had on the lawman or his deputy. He watched in fury as he lost his chance to catch Rhoades's henchman.

The owlhoot Benedict had been speaking to blasted free of the saloon and into the night. Luke raged. He tried to slip free from the ropes, only to find they tightened no matter how he moved. If the marshal came up with a branding iron, the scene from a roundup would be complete.

"He won't get far." Marshal Wilkes yanked on the rope and brought Luke to a sitting position. The deputy released the rope around his foot so Luke lurched to his feet. "You calm enough?" The lawman yanked on the rope and pulled it so tight it cut off Luke's air.

The lasso had another purpose. Circulation to his arms was cut off, forcing him to drop his six-gun. The marshal picked up the pistol and tucked it into his belt. He yanked hard and sent Luke staggering.

"Let's go. Your barroom brawling is over for the night."

"It's over for all time!" the barkeep yelled, and waved his fist in the air. "He's banned for life! If he sticks his nose in here again, I'll shoot it off! I'll have the bouncers cut it off! And feed it to him!"

"Cool down a mite," the marshal said. "Tally up a bill for the damage. I'll see that it gets paid."

This mollified the bartender a little. He went to the back of the bar and picked up a rag to begin the cleanup. The last thing Luke heard as he was dragged outside was a customer saying to the barkeep, "Stand us all to a drink and put it on your repair list. You owe us!"

The response became too muffled to understand. But the real drama unfolded in the street. The outlaw had been roped by three deputies, and they held him spread-eagled in the dirt. Only one arm thrashed about. The other was pinned to his side and each of the remaining deputies had lassoed a leg.

"He's one of Rhoades's gang. He was getting orders from Crazy Water Benedict!"

"I told you to quiet down," the marshal said. "Ask anyone in town about me, Benson Wilkes, and they'll tell you I am not prone to get upset. That said, my patience is at the end of its rope. If you push me, I'll see that you're at the end of your rope, only it'll be a noose around your filthy neck."

As if Luke were nothing more than a dog on a leash, the marshal pulled him along. As they passed the outlaw flopping around in the street, Luke tried to kick him. This got him an especially hard tug on his rope.

"I got you for disturbing the peace, shooting up the best saloon in town—and that's saying something special since Crossroads has a dozen—and now I got you for assault and battery on a helpless man."

"He's an outlaw!"

"So you say. I don't remember seeing his aspect on any wanted poster, and I keep a close lookout."

"But Benedict! He—"

"Inside. Now." The marshal released the rope with a deft flip. He added a boot to the rear to get Luke moving in the right direction.

Luke fumbled in his coat pocket and pulled out the tin star.

"Look, Marshal, I'm sorry this happened but—"

"I don't give two hoots and a holler if you're Allan Pinkerton himself. In there. Second cell."

"But—"

Benson Wilkes held up a cautioning finger. There wasn't anything that would change his mind. Luke put the badge away. It wasn't going to keep him from being jailed. The best he could hope for was being run out of Crossroads as he had been from Preston. That wasn't going to make finding the gang any easier.

As he perched on the edge of the bed, a thought gave him a rueful smile. He was spending more time in the lockup than either Rhoades or Benedict. It was as if everything in his life had been turned upside down. Bitterness accomplished nothing. He had to use his head to get out of this predicament.

A commotion outside the jailhouse brought him to his feet. For a moment he hoped the marshal would put the other man in the same cell. Beating the location of Rhoades's hideout from him would vent some of the steam Luke felt building inside. Without some release, he'd have no option but to explode.

"In the first cell," the marshal said. He shoved the outlaw hard enough to make him trip. Before the man recovered, the marshal slammed and locked the cell door. "I got additional charges to file against you." He motioned. A deputy came in holding his nose. "Assaulting a peace officer's good for a week in jail. After that sentence is served, we'll talk about that ruckus in the saloon."

"It was all *his* fault." The prisoner fixed sullen eyes on Luke. "He tried to do a cancan on the bar, then he went crazy."

"It'll all get straightened out eventually." The marshal opened a cabinet and put his prisoners' six-guns in a drawer. Luke watched carefully. The cabinet was locked and the key vanished into the lawman's vest pocket, next to his pocket watch. It would be easier to rip off the cell door than to steal the key without Benson Wilkes realizing it.

Luke sank back to the bed. Crossroads was more prosperous and had an actual bed in the cells, unlike Preston. That did nothing to make being locked up set better with him.

"When's your judge supposed to get to town?" Luke tried to figure out if the one promised for Preston was likely to arrive before or after Crossroads. He wanted the trial to be over and done.

"No set time. He leaves sentencing up to me, mostly." The marshal sank into his chair and hiked his boots up to the desktop. With a practiced nod, he brought the brim of his hat down over his eyes. In less than a minute snores filled the small jailhouse.

Luke went to the bars between his cell and the outlaw's. He tried staring the man down but didn't get too far.

"I'm not sayin' a word, not to the law and not to you." The outlaw stretched out on his bed and laced his fingers under his head. "The deputy said you was a Pinkerton man. The Pinks got no call comin' for me."

"What'd Crazy Water Benedict tell you? The pair of you were having a real good talk."

"Who's that? Crazy Water? Never heard of a gent named Crazy Water."

"Mal, then. Mal Benedict. But you know him. He made a beeline for you when he got to the saloon. You were waiting for him. Was he giving you orders or finding out something you'd learned about the bank?" Luke was pleased to see the man's reaction. He tried to hide it, but he stiffened in shock.

"I don't know what you're talkin' about, Mister Pinkerton agent man." With that sarcastic gibe he rolled over to face the wall, but Luke saw he wasn't asleep. He just refused to talk anymore.

Luke began pacing the small cell. His quick eyes hunted for a way out. If anything, this cell was tighter than the one he'd been locked up in back in Preston. For a bunch of farmers and ranchers, they spent the money to securely incarcerate the town's prisoners. He jumped up onto the bed and peered out the barred window. He was downwind from the livery stable. He inhaled deeply, as if this had the ability to transport him to his horse. All he got out of it was a frustration at being locked up.

He leaned back against the wall and let his chin drop to his chest. Sleep never quite arrived, but he heard sounds in the town that weren't part of any dream. Horses and boisterous music from the dance halls and the joyful cries of cowboys come to town to whoop it up. Somewhere mixed into that stew pot of humanity floated Crazy Water Benedict. The bank robbery was going to happen, as sure as the sun came up every morning. But when? And what did the other prisoner have to tell Benedict?

Almost asleep, Luke heard a scratching sound outside the barred window. He looked over to see the marshal still snoring at his desk. The other prisoner had also drifted off to sleep. Climbing up to look out again, he hunted the shadows for whatever caused the curious, rhythmic sound. Craning his neck, he managed to look straight down the outer wall. A floppy-brimmed hat hid the face of whoever used a rock to scratch at the wall.

"You can't dig through that way. The wall's too thick," he said.

"Shut up. You got yourself into a real pickle this time." The shadowy figure dropped the rock.

Luke's heart skipped a beat. A woman! This had to be the woman back in Preston who had gotten him out of jail.

"I need help. The marshal wants to hold me for a week."

"What's so bad about getting fed three times a day and having a roof over your head?"

"The Rhoades gang!" The words exploded from a reservoir of hatred deep inside him. Trying to hold back his emotions wasn't possible. "They're planning a robbery, but you don't care about that. Get me out of here!"

"You're going to stop them? All by yourself?" The woman laughed. This further irritated him.

"You sprung me before. Do it again. I'll owe you."

"Tell me everything about the man in the next cell. Everything."

"He was talking to Benedict. Crazy Water Benedict. He's—"

"Never mind that. Tell me what you know." Her testy voice made Luke want to snap at her, but she was outside the jail and he was locked in the cell.

"I think he was telling Benedict something about the bank. He doesn't have a wanted poster on him. The marshal would have recognized him if he rode with the gang. From a few things he said, he might be a local who's joined up."

"Is that something you believe?"

Luke thought a moment. He shifted around hoping to get a better look at her. The broad-brimmed hat prevented him from seeing any part of her face.

"I don't know. Rhoades is mighty picky about who he lets ride with him. Ever since the war, he's never had a big gang. But they're crazy fanatical following him." He paused a moment and thought a little harder. "He buys information about train schedules and the best spot to hold up a stage. The guy I had the dustup with in the saloon doesn't dress like a cowboy. More likely he works somewhere around town."

"At the bank?"

"I didn't see him when the marshal introduced me to the bank president." Luke waited for a reaction. He got none. The woman either cared nothing about that or she already knew about his sightseeing tour of the vault.

"He doesn't have the look of a teller, either," Luke went on. "Rough-and-tumble. Maybe a clerk at a store near the bank. He could be a lookout. Yeah, that's possible." He thought out loud now. "Rhoades will use him to warn them when to rob the bank or if the law gets too close."

"There's a mining supply store at the edge of town. He doesn't have to be a full member of the gang. If what you say is true, Benedict is only paying him off for whatever he finds out about the gold shipment schedules and anything else affecting the timing for the robbery."

"If he worked there, how'd he pass along anything about the bank to the robbers without somebody getting suspicious? The wanted posters have been sent to every lawman in the entire state."

"You've blundered into some good information, Mister Hadley."

"You know my name. What do I call you? I suppose you got me free from the Preston jail by sweet-talking Marshal Hargrove. How can I properly thank you?"

"Consider us even stephen."

"Wait!" He strained even more to look out. All he saw was the woman's shadow-cloaked shape melt into deeper shadows. She was gone.

Luke spun around and sat on the bed. It wouldn't be long before she got him out just like she'd done before. He was still impatient and almost jumped out of his skin when the outer jail door opened.

The marshal came awake in a flash, his hand going to his six-gun. He saw whoever was outside but Luke couldn't. But it had to be the mystery woman. His benefactor had come to help him out of another jam.

"Ma'am, this is real unusual," the marshal said, looking over his shoulder into the cells. "I don't usually conduct business this late at night."

"Please, Marshal, make an exception."

Luke's heart pounded. It was her! Finally!

"I do so want to help out my friend. Letting him spend the night in a jail cell, even one as clean and pleasant as yours, will put him in such a bad mood."

"I can believe that. The fine's likely to be steep."

"Would a hundred dollars cover it?"

"Purty near. At least for his share of the destruction. They busted up the saloon good and proper."

Luke caught his breath. A gloved hand stretched out into the jail just far enough for him to see five twenty-dollar gold pieces resting in the woman's palm. The marshal took it, bit down on one coin to be sure it was gold, then tucked the money into his vest pocket.

"He's a lucky man to have a friend like you, ma'am."

Luke bounced with energy now. The marshal was right. And Luke didn't even know the woman's name or why she was championing him. He intended to find out before he hit the trail to rescue his wife.

He stepped back from the door so the marshal could open it. He let out a cry of outrage when the lawman opened the other man's cell.

"You're free to go."

"Wha . . . ? What's that?"

"Clear out. You've been bailed out." The other cell door swung wide. The man shot out, waited impatiently for the marshal to return his six-shooter, then ran into the night.

"She was bailing me out! You let the wrong man go!"

"No sir, that's not true. The little lady was quite specific about which of you to let go."

"So how do I get out?"

"Might be paying for all the destruction you caused would smooth ruffled feathers."

"I have money!" Luke had a wad of greenbacks as well as a few coins. The profit he'd made from selling his farm to the railroad for right-of-way had been paid out in gold dust. He had sewn it into the hems of his coat for safekeeping, letting a few grains free every now and then when he needed spending money. The coat still weighed him down, so he had a young fortune left, in addition to the coins and scrip. The princely sum had financed his hunt for Benedict without need of taking a job just to eat.

"I'll see what the tally is in the morning."

"Morning! Now. I want out now!"

"The saloon owner's in bed by now. He don't like to be disturbed. Besides, there's no reason for you to be in a hurry. You just curl up and get some shut-eye. I'll find out what the damage'll cost you, and you can be out of here before I have to feed you lunch."

"Lunch!"

"If you don't quiet down, you might be spending more time 'n that, compliments of Crossroads."

Luke sank to the bed, stunned. He felt betrayed. Worse, the trail was getting colder every minute he was stuck in the cell. Lady Luck had to deliver a powerful amount of good tidings for him to find the other man.

If he ever found who the woman was, he'd make her pay for this betrayal.

CHAPTER SEVEN

LUKE HADLEY SPENT the night in the cell, getting madder and madder. By the time the marshal acknowledged him around noon the next day, he was ready to chew nails and spit tacks. The woman had paid the fine—bribe!—and let the outlaw go free. Luke felt his chances of finding Rhoades and Benedict and the other cutthroats in that "family" slipping away with every second he spent in the cell.

"Come on with me. You said you got money?" The marshal stood back a pace from the cell door and fixed a cold gaze on his prisoner.

"I do. You want it?"

"I'm not that kind of lawman."

"Then why'd you let one of Rhoades's men go free last night?"

"He wasn't any kind of outlaw. Whatever gave you

that idea?" Wilkes looked as if he wanted to spit. Luke felt the same, but for an entirely different reason.

"You know him?" A cold lump formed in Luke's belly. The notion that the marshal was in cahoots with Rhoades had never crossed his mind. Crossroads looked peaceable enough and Wilkes had been friendly enough with the banker. The tension there came from a small army outside the marshal's control guarding the bank.

"I know Nelson well enough. He's a drifter and came into town a couple months back. He's worked pretty steadily and kept his nose clean until you bloodied it."

Luke wanted to rage but knew it'd do him no good.

"Who was the woman who bailed him out?"

The lawman shook his head.

"I don't have any idea, but she convinced me you were the dangerous one. Now, are you living up to your promise to pay for the damage or do I keep you in that cell until I can figure how to make you work it off? From the look of the wreckage, you'd be scrubbing floors and mucking stables for a month of Sundays. Then again, I'm sure the mayor would go along with punishment worse than that."

"You'd put me on a chain gang?" The very notion of being shackled and forced to break rocks or swing a pick for a month or two infuriated him. He was no stranger to hard work and had cleared more than one field of stone and stump by himself, but by the time he got free, Rhoades and his gang would be long gone. It had been hard enough finding the general terrain where they roamed. As bad as it was for the Tomlinsons and the Willum girl, Rhoades had tipped his hand burning down the way station.

Or by blowing it up. Luke's thoughts drifted for a moment. The road agents had horses. Rhoades had to feed his peculiar desire to use dynamite wherever possible by buying—or stealing—the explosive.

"You still with us? You got a far-off look in your eye that's not going to be satisfied unless you pay up. The notion of locking you onto a chain gang isn't something we do around here. Besides, you're the only prisoner. That's not much of a gang."

Luke snapped back to the here and now. Buying his way out of jail was the first step. Tracking down any place Rhoades might steal dynamite was next.

"I'll pay whatever is fair." Luke knew his willingness to pay for the damage went beyond that. He'd pay whatever got him off the hook and out of this jail cell.

"That's what I wanted to hear. Come along now, and don't do anything stupid. You've already done enough of that for a lifetime."

Luke walked ahead of the marshal to the saloon. Every step he worried the lawman had a pistol trained on him. Any stumble and a .45 slug would shatter his spine or blow the back of his head off. Reasons for Wilkes's precaution became apparent when he pushed through the batwing doors and stared at the saloon interior. He hadn't any good notion of how badly busted up the place was. The light of day caused his heart to sink. He had a pocketful of greenbacks but paying for the destruction would take most of it. But that was all right if he walked free.

"Mister Underwood there, he's the barkeep and part owner. You got a bill done up, Billy?"

Underwood glared and muttered under his breath. He reached under the bar and pulled out two sheets of foolscap. Luke winced at the sight of the tiny rows of numbers marching from top to bottom of both sheets. Beside each number rode an explanation of what had been destroyed in the melee.

"I didn't cause all the damage," Luke protested. "That table! The one with the bullet holes in it. I saw a gambler fire his derringer and . . ." His voice trailed off. His protest fell on deaf ears. The way the marshal tapped his fingers on the butt of his now holstered Colt reminded Luke of his real purpose. Saving a few dollars meant less than getting free.

He grabbed the sheets and ran down the list. More than three hundred dollars seemed excessive in a place that got busted up on a regular basis. For all he knew, more damage was done to the saloon every Saturday night than he'd caused. Grumbling but making sure neither the barkeep nor the marshal heard his cursing, he pulled out the sweat-stained wad of greenbacks and started counting them out on the bar.

"There's your blood money." Luke saw how Underwood bristled at that and immediately regretted the gibe. He mumbled an apology.

"You satisfied, Billy?" The marshal leaned over and put his elbows on the bar.

"I am, Marshal Wilkes."

"Then serve me a shot of your best rye whiskey, and I'll be on my way. Mister Hadley will pay for it. Pour one for yourself, if you've a mind. He's feeling right generous about now."

"Make it three shots," Luke said. He fumbled in his vest pocket and found two bits in silver. He dropped the coin on the bar. It spun around twice, its silver melody mocking him.

"Two. I ain't drinkin' with the likes of you." Underwood slapped it flat with his hand, poured two shots and stalked off, counting the stack of greenbacks again to be sure Luke didn't cheat him.

"Make this your last drink here," the marshal said. "Not banning you officially or anything like that. That'd be up to a judge, and he won't come this way for a spell. Just offering up a bit of common sense. I don't think Mister Underwood there has taken a shine to you. No, sir, not at all."

"Or the galoot I was fighting with."

"Nelson might not have the sense God gave a goose, but he's not dumb enough to come in here again. We got plenty of other drinking emporiums in Crossroads. You keep your nose clean, hear?" The marshal lavished one long last cold stare in Luke's direction, then left.

The barkeep came back, his expression stormy. "You follow him out. I don't want you in here." The bartender laid a six-gun on the bar, his intent plain. If Luke hightailed it, nobody got shot up.

Luke touched the empty holster at his side. He had to retrieve his sidearm from the marshal, not that he wanted a shootout with the barkeep. He needed information and swapping lead wasn't the way to get it.

"Yup," Luke said, "me and Nelson tore up this place good." He saluted Underwood with the full shot glass and downed the last of his whiskey. It burned all the way to his empty belly. It had been a while since he'd had a decent meal, and he hadn't been fed in the jailhouse. In that regard, Preston came out ahead in the race for best Kansas jail. He wiped the stray drop off his lip and carefully put the glass on the bar. "I should go patch things up between us."

"The way he's so reckless, he'll blow himself up before you get the chance. Good riddance to him. And to you. But you go on, find him. Let him blow you both to kingdom come." Underwood rested his hand on the gun. If Luke thought the marshal's glare was cold, he felt polar shivers from the barkeep.

He didn't quite dance on his way out, but he felt more optimistic than he had in weeks. He had learned the name of the man who'd talked with Benedict. Even better, he had a good idea what was being bandied about. Rollie Rhoades enjoyed blowing up buildings and bridges—and stagecoach depots with people still inside. It sounded as if Nelson could supply him with explosives. There couldn't be too many places, even in a prosperous and growing town like Crossroads, where farmers went to buy up dynamite to blast stumps or builders got their explosives to crush rocks in the roadways.

In spite of his eagerness to find Nelson, he went back to the jail. The marshal had broken down his six-shooter to clean it. The smell of gun oil made Luke's nose wrinkle. Soon enough, he'd have to clean his own Model 3 because it had been fired to send a bullet smack-dab through Benedict's vile heart. He could put off oiling the six-shooter until after that deadly reunion.

"I wondered if you were leaving this behind." The lawman opened a drawer and took out Luke's gun. He slid it across the desk. "Don't get too antsy about using it, not in my town. I try to keep things peaceable. That commotion last night is as grievous as I ever want to see in Crossroads. You understand me?"

"Thanks, Marshal." Luke broke open the action and checked to be sure a fresh cartridge rode in each cylinder. He had no reason to think he would use the gun anytime soon, but he wanted to be ready. If his path crossed Rhoades's, there'd be lead flying. What he would do when he found Benedict depended on what it took to find Audrey.

"Don't make me run you out of town—or worse."

"Worse? What? You said you didn't cotton to chain gangs. You'd tar and feather me?" Luke laughed at that. The marshal kept a serious expression.

"I don't want to take you out of town in a pine box. Our cemetery's getting mighty full. Get along, now." Wilkes grumbled to himself as he carefully oiled his pistol. Luke saw the weapon had been used hard and cared for so it wouldn't fail when needed.

Seeing the well-used six-shooter provided better advice than what the marshal put into words.

Iron riding at his hip once more, he felt ready to take on his weight in wildcats. The first place he went was the general store. The clerk looked up when he came in and turned white.

"Wh-what do you want?"

"I'd like to buy a few sticks of dynamite." He didn't get an immediate reply. "Why're you so skittish?"

The clerk looked ready to bolt through the door and go screaming down the main street.

"I heard what you done last night. Mister Underwood's tellin' everyone who'll listen how you almost killed him."

"Stories grow the more they're told. It's like some people's noses." A quick look around the store showed a little bit of everything for sale, but a small keg of gunpowder was as close to explosives as anything. There wasn't even a keg of Giant Powder.

"And Geoff Nelson. You tried to plug him with that six-shooter of yours. Don't go sayin' that's not true!"

"I settled accounts at the saloon and want to buy Nelson—Geoff—a drink. Bury the hatchet. Make things right."

"Then let him get you the dynamite. We don't carry anything like that. Mister Bellamy'd never permit it. He's the owner. We don't even sell pistol or rifle cartridges. For them you'd have to go across the street to the gunsmith."

"Does the gunsmith sell kegs of powder?"

"Not that I know. What he's got is for reloading. From what I hear, he's the best there is within a fifty-mile radius of Crossroads. But you want a case of dynamite, he won't have it to sell."

"Now, why would I want to let Nelson get me dynamite?"

"That's what he does. He peddles it from a shed at the edge of town. The mayor run him out of town trying to set up shop along the main street. If Nelson gets soused and decides to smoke, the mayor didn't want the whole danged town to blow up. His shed's far enough out, so that's not a concern." The clerk pointed north.

"Much obliged." Luke heard the clerk's gusty sigh of relief at not getting killed. He let out one of his own. Benedict had put in an order for dynamite with Geoff Nelson when they met in the saloon last night. Who else would want it but Rollie Rhoades?

Luke considered going directly to the store, then considered another mystery to solve first. Once he tracked down Nelson, there'd be no turning back. Walking slowly, he kept a sharp eye out for a woman wearing a floppy-brimmed hat. Most of the ladies wore hats, but nothing like the one he had seen through the jailhouse window the night before. After twenty minutes he had yet to spot anyone who might have been responsible for pumping him for information about Nelson, then freeing the dynamite salesman.

He realized the dark had masked more than the woman's face. He wasn't even sure what color the hat had been. Black? A dark blue? Something else? The closest he came was a woman wearing a bright red hat whose brim flapped about in the rising wind whipping down the street.

He counted four hotels in Crossroads but saw no way to get information from the clerks in any of them about their customers. Bribery might work, but without a better description of the woman, who did he ask to find? Forking over a lot of money to find a solitary woman wasn't a plan designed to work. If anything, the hotel clerks would take his money and then lie before summoning the marshal.

The best hotel in town struck him as the place the woman would stay. He had nothing to base this gut feeling on other than how quickly she'd forked over a hundred dollars to spring Nelson, and if he found her, luck had to be a big part of the search. Settling in a chair on the boardwalk across the street from the Mercator Hotel, he tried to think through everything he knew. The woman had helped him back in Preston but now shifted her allegiance to men working for Rhoades. That meant she was either one of the gang or had dealings with them. That struck him as wrong. A better explanation was that she worked for her own best interest and nothing else.

"A bounty hunter?" Luke wondered aloud if the mystery woman sought Rhoades to turn him in for the reward. How she intended to capture the outlaw was a poser. Luke walked a dangerous trail, but his goal was more limited. He wanted his wife back. And because Benedict or Rhoades had stolen her away, he'd bring them to justice at the end of his barrel.

He forced himself to relax. Thinking about what he would do to the outlaws caused him to tightly clench his fists. Audrey had to be alive. What would he do if—when—he rescued her? Turning the gang over to the law was one choice. But pulling the trigger, especially on the man who had gunned him down at his own wedding, felt like justice.

His trail was clear and straight. What path did the woman take?

Luke heaved to his feet. Waiting for a woman he couldn't identify to show up at one of four Crossroads hotels got him nowhere. Turning northward, he walked quickly to the edge of town. Where stores were jammed wall to wall with an occasional alley between them in the center of town, stores were now scattered among boardinghouses and even a few private homes. Since this was the major road out of Crossroads, he doubted he would miss Nelson's store.

Less than a quarter mile farther, he spotted the man before he came to the shack with the "Dynamite for Sale" sign dangling from a tree limb. Nelson put his back to a buckboard that had slid off the road into a ditch. Luke watched the man struggle, taking some pleasure in how increasingly futile his efforts were. The more Nelson tried to keep the buckboard from slipping deeper into the muddy ditch, the deeper the wheels sank.

Whatever he hauled was covered by a tarpaulin in the back of the buckboard. Giving up, Nelson stepped away and kicked at the wheel. He kicked a second time, then unhitched his horse and led it to the ramshackle one-room building just beyond the sign. Luke let him get almost to the shed before going to the buckboard. His boots sank deep in the sticky mud as he edged over to see what freight Nelson carried. Leaning over, he caught the edge of the tarp and tugged enough to show a wood crate.

Luke recoiled, then calmed down. A box of dynamite was safe enough to carry. He had used a stick or two when he proved his farm. Stumps were stubborn to remove without enough explosive. But this much—four crates—was enough for a miner to blast into a mountainside. Only there wasn't any mining going on in the vicinity that Luke knew of. This much explosive could clear a couple sections of land.

He edged his way out of the ditch and scraped off as much mud from his boots as he could. As he turned toward Nelson's store, a slug sailed past his head. As if he had been shot, he dropped straight down. He hit the road and rolled away from the buckboard. He flopped into the ditch on the far side of road. It was only a little less muddy.

Poking his head up, he got his hat shot off. Nelson ran toward him, six-gun blazing.

Luke rolled to one side, dragged out his own smoke wagon, then settled down on his belly. Supporting his gun hand against a rock, he returned fire. Nelson had been lucky. Luke was accurate. His first round hit Nelson in the leg and sent him tumbling.

"All I want is to know where he is!" Luke rose

enough to see that Nelson wiggled like a snake for cover. "I'll let you go if you tell me."

"Who are you talking about? You're trying to rob me! It wasn't enough to get me locked up last night. You want to kill me!"

There was something in what Nelson claimed. Luke wanted to get to his feet and rush forward. But that was a good way to get killed. Nelson's original attack had been blunted by buck fever, but now he calmed down and became increasingly dangerous since he was wounded. A trapped rat, a trapped, wounded animal with a six-shooter. Patience won this fight, as hard as that was for Luke to accept.

The Schofield's hammer came back in full cock. Luke pulled just a little on the trigger to take up the play. The next shot would come almost instantly if Nelson showed his ugly face.

"Is Benedict coming around to pick up the dynamite? Or were you going to deliver it to him?"

"I don't know what you're talking about. Go away or I'll fetch the marshal and he'll lock you up and throw away the key."

"Who bailed you out last night? What's her name?" Luke shifted, knowing Nelson was also on the move to get a better angle of fire.

"Whoever you are, you're crazy. Go on, get outta here. Leave!"

Luke heard the change in Nelson's voice and was ready when the man popped up like a prairie dog. In spite of knowing this would happen and preparing for it, Luke jerked at the trigger instead of squeezing it. His shot went wide. Nelson moved a little closer on the far side of the road. It took only a second for Luke to realize Nelson wanted to get to the buckboard and its explosive load. From his own position in the other ditch, he couldn't stop him by making a frontal attack.

Nelson would cut him down if he did that.

The crown of Nelson's hat slowly rose above the edge of the opposite ditch. Luke started to fire, then relaxed. Nelson tried to get him to waste ammo. A bullet through the hat would hit a stick and not the man's forehead. Luke kept moving, slipping and sliding in the gooey mud. Jockeying for better position got him nowhere.

"Are you delivering the dynamite to Rhoades? What's he going to do with it? Four crates is enough to . . . blow up a bank." That realization caused him to freeze in place. Rhoades was loco enough use that much to reduce the bank to rubble and destroy the vault. The greenbacks might turn to ash but the waist-high stacks of gold would survive. The scrip meant nothing to the outlaw if it was issued on the local bank. Even if those were federal notes, Rhoades likely shared most westerners' disdain for any money that didn't give a metal clink when dropped on a bar.

"I don't know who you're talking about." Nelson moved his hat toward the shed. Luke was ready when the man popped up in the opposite direction, finally leaving the protection afforded by the ditch bank. He fired. The bullet skimmed along the roadbed. He got dirt in Nelson's face but didn't touch him with the bullet.

"The marshal will be along to see what all the gunfire's about," Nelson called. "I'm local. You're not. He'll believe me when I say you tried to ambush and rob me."

"You've only been in town a couple months. And

you're no stranger to that jail cell. Unless I miss my guess, you're the one who'll be waiting for the circuit judge."

Luke cautioned himself to patience. Nelson would make a mistake and he'd have him, but how hard would it be getting him to spill his guts about Benedict? And about the woman who had bailed him out the night before. The gang and the woman must be connected in some way.

Nelson reversed course and bolted for the buckboard. Luke rose to his knees and started firing. Every shot missed. Nelson flopped into the mud by the buckboard, daring Luke to come for him.

"Patience," Luke whispered. He broke open the six-shooter and reloaded. He'd had a chance and muffed it. Then a different tidbit of wisdom came to him. He started toward the shed. If he got inside, he might swap Nelson's livelihood for the information he required to find Audrey.

"You can't go there. You can't!" Nelson shouted in rage when he realized Luke's strategy.

"I'll burn it to the ground and everything in it. Tell me what I want to know and I'll leave you alone."

"I can't trust you."

"You can trust me to destroy everything you've worked for." Luke realized he had struck the mother lode. Nelson had been on the run most of his life and had settled down in Crossroads. This shack contained all his hope for the future. "Tell me!"

"All right, all right, don't shoot." Nelson stood, using the buckboard as a shield. He held up his hand. His six-gun pointed toward the sky. From the way his shoulders slumped, he was defeated.

Luke climbed to his feet, dripping mud.

"I want to know where Rhoades and his gang are holed up. The dynamite's for Rhoades, isn't it?"

"Yeah, he paid me a pretty penny, too. Or his partner Benedict did. I ain't never seen Rhoades, but Benedict talks about him all the time like he's some kind of genius." Nelson sagged even more. "You won't let me deliver to him now, will you? I need to get paid the rest of what he owes me. There's nobody else around here who'd take this much explosive off my hands."

Luke played it by ear.

"I'll let you deliver the load and get paid. Then we'll ride in different directions."

"I—" Nelson cut off his sentence and looked over his shoulder. Thundering down the road from town came a rider bent low so his head and his mount's were side by side.

Luke shifted his attention to the rider. Recognition hit him like a sledgehammer.

"Benedict!"

The outlaw began firing, but not at Luke or Nelson. Every round tore up a bit of the buckboard. Then he hit the jackpot. A bullet slammed into a crate of dynamite and detonated it. The shock wave lifted Luke off his feet and threw him into the ditch. A second explosion rolled above him, but he was deaf and stunned and could not appreciate how powerful the blast was.

After a few seconds, he shook himself and got to his feet. His knees almost buckled. He lifted his gun and tried to find Benedict, but the outlaw was long gone. The only evidence of his handiwork lay in the deep blast crater. Nelson, or what remained of him, would never betray the Rhoades gang now.

His ears began to ring. He regained his hearing slowly and when he did, he heard a horse neigh. Luke homed in on the sound. It took a few more seconds for understanding to penetrate the shock.

"Benedict!" He stumbled a few steps before regaining his strength. He ran for Nelson's shed. A saddled horse stood off to one side. When Benedict came from the shack carrying a gunnysack, Luke began firing. The distance was too great, but he wanted to slow the outlaw down.

Crazy Water Benedict was too cagey for that. He slung the gunnysack over his horse's rump and vaulted into the saddle. Spurring the animal, he rocketed away. Luke barely got halfway to the shack when it erupted in an explosion that shoved him flat on his back again. He stared up at the sky, deafened once more. Bits and pieces of fiery debris floated through the air.

All he could think of was that he watched the destruction of his chance to find his lost love. Then the ash and soot and burning rubble began raining down on him.

CHAPTER EIGHT

"DON'T YOU GO bleeding on my floor. I just washed it."

Luke Hadley stirred. The slightest movement sent waves of white pain lancing through him. To make matters worse, the town doctor had stitched up some deep cuts. Going to the town seamstress would have given him better results. He flexed his arm, then balled his fingers into a fist. The stitches pulled and tore at his flesh, but he wasn't bleeding around any of the unbandaged sutures. The doctor began wrapping them up with white cotton strips. He sewed better than he wrapped.

"You still got 'em all, no thanks to being so close to that explosion. What were you doing playing with fireworks? Not even the young 'uns in these parts are so careless, and that's saying a mouthful. There's one last cut to suture. This'll hurt a mite." The doctor dropped his needle onto a metal tray with a dull clank. With a practiced move, he swung Luke around on the operating table and poked and prodded spots that hurt more after the examination than before. Finally satisfied, he pointed to a straight-backed wood chair with a thin cushion tied to it.

"Sit. And mind your bleeding on the upholstery. I had that brought all the way from Boston last year. It cost me an arm and a leg, but it's worth it."

The doctor settled into a matching chair facing the one Luke writhed about in. Finally finding a pose that didn't make him cry out, Luke took a look around. He was in a doctor's surgery and had no memory of how he got here. A cursory examination showed how his coat, vest and shirt had burned. The three layers of cloth saved his hide. Other than a few raw spots and where the doctor had patched him up, his skin was intact.

"The marshal says that Nelson fellow wasn't so lucky. I always thought he was a damned fool playing with nitroglycerin the way he did. He fancied himself quite the chemist, always mixing this with that. This wasn't the first time he blowed himself up, either. When I was a sprout I worked in a tin mine. Just like Nelson, the blaster thought he was smarter than his nitro." The doctor got a distant look in his eye. "I was only twelve and he was my first patient." The look went away and he sighed. "He was the first one I lost, too. Blew his fool arm off and would have left him crippled in both legs if I had saved him. I reckon that made him luckier than he deserved."

"I'm glad you learned your trade enough to save me."

"You weren't in any danger. The explosion blew you into mud. That plugged up the worst of your bleeding wounds. I checked for broken bones." The doctor shook his head. "There weren't any I could find, but you're going to have one bruise."

"One?" Luke hardly believed that.

"Only one, but it'll be all over your danged body."

"It feels as if my chest has been crushed." Luke delicately probed and traced the outline of the shrapnel inside him. He wondered if it had saved his life again. Somehow, he doubted it from the way he hurt now.

"I saw plenty of scars all over your body while I worked. Were you a soldier during the war?"

"I got shot up by the Border Ruffians. By the time I healed enough, the war was over." Luke kept the bitterness from his voice. Charles Hamilton had led the Ruffians on the raid, but his right-hand man, Rollie Rhoades, had been responsible for the explosion that blew the piece of heavy metal into his chest. Rhoades had blown up an entire townful of civilians just to watch the fireworks. There hadn't been any real strategic reason, other than to frighten Free Staters.

And Crazy Water Benedict had learned well from his boss. He must have lit the fuse that blew up all of Nelson's supply.

"But he got away with a sackful of . . . explosives?" Luke remembered more of the fight now. Nelson. Benedict riding past and detonating the dynamite. And he stole a bag of something from Nelson's shack before blowing it up, too. Every detail came to him etched in acid and flame.

"What are you yammering about? I know you fellows get your brains all shook up. You're not seeing ghosts or having double vision or anything like that, are you? I can give you some laudanum if your head hurts."

"Save it for the town whores." Luke's bitterness boiled over. He stood and flexed his muscles. Everything that didn't outright hurt ached horribly.

"No need to get snippy, sir. Why don't you just leave me twenty dollars and go on your way?"

Luke haggled a bit with the doctor over the price of fixing him up. They settled on half that. Finding his money was harder than he expected since all he had in his vest pockets was worse for wear and tear. Piecing together some scrip like some burned puzzle let him pay the doctor without having to open a seam in his coat and squeeze out a few grains of gold dust.

He stepped outside into the sultry late afternoon. The sun was setting and bugs buzzed around, taking special glee in finding the bandages soaked with his blood for an evening feast. Swatting them did no good. For every one he crushed, two more landed. Walking briskly helped keep off the worst of the swarm by creating a small breeze around his body. He tired fast at this pace, but his mind turned over all that had happened—or that he remembered.

As the sun sank under the horizon, he pressed into shadows to avoid being seen by the marshal. The lawman patrolled with a deputy at his side. Luke wondered what the marshal thought about the explosion. Benedict had found Geoff Nelson. Explaining everything that had happened would only land him in jail again.

Making his way to the stables, he saw that his horse was being taken care of properly. Digging in his saddlebags replenished his cash. He looked at the stack of gold coins and considered going to one of those fine-looking hotels for the night. When he heard the stableman approaching, he clenched down hard on the coins and turned.

"You satisfied with how we're tendin' your animal?" The question could have been belligerent. Somehow the giant of man delivered it in a soft enough tone to make it sound like he really cared about the answer.

"You've done a good job, but I intend to hit the trail real early in the morning. So, do you mind if I . . ." Luke's voice trailed off as he let the man finish the question.

"Ain't supposed to let nobody sleep in the stables, but if you clear out before sunup when the boss gets here, I don't see why you can't roll up in your blanket in the stall next to your horse."

Luke piled extra straw on the floor and used his saddle as a pillow. The blanket came up to his neck, so he was cozy enough, though the night was warm. His brain turned over and over everything he had learned and kept him from sleeping, but when he finally drifted off he knew what had to be done.

FOUR DAYS," LUKE raged. He sat astride his horse and stared into the hill country dotted with trees and meandering creeks filled with runoff from the frequent showers. Travel was easy enough. His horse never went hungry, plenty of game fell to his hunting and water was clean and sweet. And it was nothing but a maze of winding hills and shallow valleys where he got lost more than once.

He dismounted and dropped to one knee. A rider had passed by recently. It took him only seconds to identify the trail he followed. These were his own tracks. Luke tugged on his horse's bridle and walked along, trying to remember the terrain. It all looked the same to him. He had spent his life as a farmer, not a tracker. If there hadn't been plenty of rabbits and other small critters, he would have starved on this trail.

It would have been better if he had gone hungry early on. That might have forced him to hire a guide. After all, the Rhoades gang had become expert at hiding their trail from posses. His own overconfidence had wasted the better part of a week. For all he knew, the bank had already been robbed and the gang was in Montana or the far side of the moon or even farther out of his grasp.

The sun sank fast. The few clouds provided no sunset artistry. The glumness he felt had transferred to the very heavens. Crushed under his continuing failure, he slogged along until he found a spot for a decent campsite. For a brief instant his spirits rose. An old firepit showed someone had been here recently.

His spirits crashed again.

"Me. It's one of my old camps." He kicked at the ashes in the firepit and even found a couple lengths of dried wood he had gathered days before but had never used. His eagerness to get on the trail had sent him along his way without breakfast that morning.

It took him only a few minutes to pitch camp. The firepit was ringed with rocks already. The spot where he had scooped out dirt for his shoulders and hip while he slept hadn't had time to fill in due to wind or rain. And not twenty yards away a small stream ran fast and furious. If he bothered, a few fish might make a decent supper.

After hobbling his horse near a patch of succulent

grass it had missed before, he stretched out, hands under his head, and watched the stars pop out in the fierce black sky. Patterns emerged and vanished as his imagination worked to turn randomness into order. His mind slipped out of gear, and he began thinking about the future. What would he do after he rescued Audrey? He had money left from the sale of his farm to the railroad. They could go to a big city and start over.

St. Louis? Kansas City? He wasn't sure what job a sodbuster could find there, but with Audrey by his side, it hardly mattered. He was a quick learner, even if he was too old to be taken on as an apprentice.

But freeing her after so long meant they'd have to adjust again to each other. He hadn't known her all that long, but everything about her was perfect. She was loving and understanding. More than this, she put up with his moods. Not once had she balked when his fiery temper flared. She was a peach.

The stars whirled about and eventually put him to sleep.

The insane shriek that cut through the still night brought him upright, six-shooter in hand. At first he thought he had been dreaming, but what horrible nightmare caused such a ringing in his ears? The shriek came again, only this time another, more curious sound sneaked along with it, twisting about, lilting and even melodious.

Singing. A woman was singing.

He pulled on his boots, wiped sweat from his face and slowly homed in on the music. The half-moon cast enough light for him to proceed cautiously and not make too much noise, but the volume of the song drowned out his clumsiest steps. Turning a stone or stepping on a dried limb was smothered by the strains of "Lorena."

As he neared, he found himself humming along until the singing abruptly stopped and another scream cut through the night. Not knowing what he got himself into, he turned cautiously. As much as he wanted to rush ahead, he carefully put down each step and remained alert for a trap. Luke came out by the stream and for a moment thought a mermaid had washed up on the bank.

Glowing a pale silver in the moonlight, a woman stretched across a large rock, her head thrown back and one hand waving in the air to direct an unseen orchestra. As she shifted, he got a better look at her. What he thought was glowing skin—scales!—proved to be a wedding dress. Tatters of lace dangled into the water and ripped patches showed bare skin below the cloth.

"Audrey?" He rubbed his eyes. But it wasn't his missing wife.

She turned her face to the moon and let out a heartfelt howl like a wolf. Then she screamed again. Luke clapped his hands to his ears. "Soul-ripping" was the only way to describe the sound. Before his ears stopped ringing, she returned to the familiar lyrics.

Stepping back a couple paces let him watch and listen from deep shadows. Try as he might he couldn't make head nor tail out of what happened in front of him. She serenaded the sky like a lovelorn wolf and then burst into song. The quality of her singing left much to be desired. Her voice cracked now and then. At worst it sounded as if too much whiskey had seared her throat and brain. Her best notes carried a plaintive quality that made Luke feel even more alone in the world.

Either way, mournful or shrieking, she was someone to avoid.

As he started to retrace his way to his camp, she stopped singing again and called out, "Please, please don't go. Please! I need you so!"

He froze. How had she seen him? It had been impossible for her to hear him rustling through the bushes as she sang so loudly. All he could think was his camouflage skills, like his tracking ones, were fine for a farmer. To sneak up on anyone without being spotted he had a lot more to learn.

"Come, come sit beside me." She beckoned to him.

Luke stepped forward into a brighter-lit stretch along the stream. If this had been a trap designed to kill or capture him it would have been sprung now. She came to her knees on the rock and motioned for him to approach. He touched the butt of his six-shooter to reassure himself that this wasn't entirely stupid on his part. He stood a decent chance in any cross fire.

Walking carefully, he looked around. The woman had not picked this spot for an ambush. If she knew he camped nearby, shooting him while he slept made more sense than singing and screeching and sounding crazy to lure him.

"Who are you?" He stopped a few yards from the waterside. She had few options to attack if this was a trick. Splashing around in the water to get to the other side gave Luke a chance to retreat. Or if she ran either way along the stream she would be exposed to his gunfire.

"You know me! Don't tease me, Lucas."

He tried to make sense of her answer.

"My name's Luke, not Lucas."

"My Lucas, my dear, darling Lucas. You've come back!" She stood. He got his first good close-up look at her.

She was almost as tall as he was, but razor thin. Her face looked like the blade of a hatchet and her deep-sunk eyes turned into shadowy black pits. Only occasional lunar reflections showed she wasn't blind. Moonlight gleamed off eyes turned silver and intense with emotion. The wedding dress had seen better days—better years. It hung from her emaciated body like tinsel from a Christmas tree. When she moved, the streamers floated, making her into a ghost.

"Who are you? What are you doing out here?"

"Out here? Why, you're right, my dear. I must get you something to drink. Food! It's been so long I've forgotten my manners. You must be exhausted from your trip."

"What's your name?"

She laughed. An undercurrent of madness made Luke even uneasier. She came to him, her feet hardly touching the ground. She floated like some ethereal being and took his arm. The touch was featherlight and yet insistent. He let her steer him away. As she linked arms with him he caught her scent. It both repelled and attracted him. Sweat and dirt mingled with sweet smells of cooking and the flowers she wore in her ratty, tangled brown hair.

"You silly billy, you know my name." She pulled him close and laid her head on his shoulder. In a voice almost too soft to hear: "I'm your loving Sarah. You haven't been away so long that you've forgotten me. I've waited for you, Lucas. How I've longed for you to come home."

"I'm not Lucas. Not *your* Lucas."

"I told you not to go traipsing off with your musket to kill some of them Johnny Rebs. I told you, but you wouldn't. Listen, that is. You told me it was your moral duty, and I didn't have any choice but to let you go off to war. But you're home now. You're home!"

"You know I'm not your husband."

"You're joshing me. That's new, Lucas, and I don't like it. You never had much of a sense of humor. Don't you go now and pull my leg about such a thing." She steered him to a game path. After a few minutes of her cooing and Luke remaining silent, they reached a cabin almost overgrown in the forest.

Luke wondered if she was completely daft or enough in touch with reality to know he wasn't her husband. She had been singing "Lorena," which made him think she understood she was a widow.

Life's tide is ebbing out so fast.

. . .

'Tis dust to dust beneath the sod.

"If I'd a-knowed you were coming I'd have fixed you your favorite."

"What's that, Sarah?"

"You're kidding me again, Lucas. A pot roast! With greens and carrots. I've got the carrots, but the rest . . ." Her voice trailed off. Luke saw the carrots were almost all she had in her pantry. She lived off what she scavenged in the forest. That explained her thinness.

"I ate before I heard you singing by the stream," he said. Taking even a carrot from her seemed a crime he had no desire to commit. "Do you hunt? There are plenty of rabbits in the woods. And squirrels."

"You took the musket, Lucas. I gather what I can."

"You should have gone into town. There's Crossroads not that far away. And Preston. Or you could have gone to Kansas City after the war."

"The war is over. You've come home. You're a hero, my darling Lucas. I know you are. Now let's celebrate with a toast."

All she had was water in a china pitcher. That suited Luke. It gave her something to do, getting out bone-china cups and saucers and acting as if this was a real homecoming. The war had ended seven years back. From the look of the cabin, she had waited the whole time for a man to return who never did. Maybe he had been killed. Maybe he chose to drift on after the war. Or had there been another woman he had come to love more? Whatever the truth, Lucas was not coming to rejoin Sarah now or anytime in the future.

Luke had no idea what to do. He had a wife of his own to find and outlaws to bring to justice for their terrible crimes.

"You looked so glum there for a minute, Lucas. Are you feeling well?"

"No, not too good," he said. "I need to rest. It's been a long way—a long time since I was here."

"Our bed," she said proudly. She pointed to a crude bed with a straw-filled mattress on it. The expression as she looked from it to Luke told him how she wanted to use that bed. For her, it was a homecoming.

"Let's rest for now, Sarah," he said. "In the morning

we can . . . we can head into town. Crossroads is only a day or two off."

"I don't like being around people. They aren't nice to me when I go there to ask after you. The boys throw rocks at me and the old people say terrible things about me. But I never gave up trusting that you'd find your way back to me. And you did! That shows them. Every last one of them! You're a hero, Lucas, a real hero to me."

"Lie down, Sarah, lie down and sing to me. A lullaby. Can you do that?" He sipped at the water in the fancy china cup. Coming up with a way to get her to sleep so he could sneak off proved harder than he expected.

"I will, Lucas, if you hold my hand."

He saw no way around it. If he tried just walking away, she would follow to the ends of the earth. This way he had a chance of getting a head start. Where he rode when he got back to his horse was a bridge to cross. He might even return to Crossroads to see if the marshal had heard any rumors about Benedict or others in the gang, though that was a faint hope. After Benedict blew up Geoff Nelson, he wasn't likely to show his face around town again.

That he had killed Nelson told Luke that the robbery was imminent. By now it might have happened and any chance of tracking the outlaws was gone.

Sarah settled down. She looked up at him with adoring brown eyes.

"I love you, Mister Youngblood."

"So you're Sarah Youngblood," he said softly.

"Forever and ever." She began singing and grasped his hand fervently. After a while her grip eased.

Luke laid her hand on the bed and quietly stood. He backed away, then stopped when she began muttering to herself. He waited to be sure she wasn't coming awake.

The words sank into a low hum. He reached the door and froze when she said plainly, "We can start a stud farm. With those horses all penned up, we can have the best horse farm in all of Kansas."

Luke stared at her. The only horses likely to be corralled around here were the ones Rhoades had taken from the way station. Another possibility existed. What ghosts haunted her mind? Lost husbands and phantom horses?

"Those horses?" he asked. "When did you see them?"

"Not a week back. Are the men watching over them your partners? They are such a rude bunch. You should fire them, fire them so we can be alone."

Luke wanted to believe that Sarah Youngblood had stumbled on where the outlaws kept their spare horses intended to speed their getaway. There was too little else to keep him hunting for his wife.

He returned and sat on the low stool beside the bed. He hated to do it, but he put his hand on her bony shoulder and shook her awake.

"Tell me about the horses, Miz Youngblood. Tell me everything about them."

CHAPTER NINE

"WERE YOU GOING out to look at the horses, Lucas? They'll make fine breeding stock." Sarah Youngblood stirred and rubbed sleep from her eyes. Her nap had been only a minute or two long. "You weren't leaving me again, were you, Lucas? I couldn't stand it if you did."

Luke came back to the small table and sat, staring across it to where the frantic woman fluttered about on the bed. She tried to move left, then went right and finally threw her hands up in the air as if surrendering. Then she began to sing. Thinking her lost husband had returned did nothing to restore her sanity. Luke was beside himself knowing what to do. He hated to keep on deluding her, but she knew things he had to find out.

"They're just waiting there, all tied up and all. Not like mustangs running free. These have brands. I saw the brands."

He had no idea how the stage line's horses had been branded. Many way stations bought animals from several nearby breeders. A few horses were added to the remuda by swapping stagecoach rides for the horseflesh. Although it hadn't sounded like it with the Tomlinsons, some stationmasters weren't above horse stealing and running a brand. It was a dog-eat-dog business and cutting corners by adding a few "free" horses to the corral enhanced profits. Some stage companies even encouraged such behavior by their employees.

"Are they far from here?"

"A mile or two," she said. She swung her legs off the bed and lifted her skirt to midthigh. "Come back to bed, Lucas. You've been away so long and I've missed you."

"We need to plan for the future. How many horses are there?"

"A dozen. I don't know. They looked like bad men."

"Men? Are there guards? How many?" She shrugged. Then she started singing again. He leaned back in the rickety chair. "Can you draw a map so I can go look?"

"I'll go with you! That'll be fun. We can take a picnic lunch."

"It might tire you out. You . . . you can fix a special meal for when I get back after looking over the horses. I'd like that."

"A special meal. A homecoming meal!" She got to her feet and clapped her hands like an excited child thinking about her special birthday party. "That will be ever so much fun."

"It will." He found a scrap of paper and a pencil stub in a cabinet and put them on the table. "Draw me a map. Go on, Sarah. It'll be fun. After I get the horses, we can be together."

"We can be together now. The horses will be there later. They've been there forever."

"Forever? Or just a week or so."

"Almost two weeks. The bad men brought them then."

Luke frowned as he considered the times. That would be about the time Rhoades burned down the way station and left three bodies behind.

"Why do you say they're bad men? What have they done that you don't like?"

Sarah pouted and shook her head.

"I shouldn't tattle."

"Tell me. Tell your Lucas." The lying words burned his tongue. Taking advantage of a woman not right in the head bothered him, but bigger things were at stake.

"I was picking berries. I hid when I heard them cursing, and one shot another. He shot him in the back!"

Good riddance was all Luke could think, but he saw why Sarah would be so upset. She lived a solitary life. Such cruelty had to shock her.

"Did you know the man who got shot?"

"It was Tommy. I've seen him and his sweetheart out in the woods doing . . . things."

"They were married," Luke said. "Tommy Zinn and Beatrice Willum." It took all his concentration to dredge up the names. When he heard their story he hadn't thought it was important, other than being names added to the list of murders committed by Rhoades and Benedict. What brought the names back was remembering the wedding ring the Preston coroner had taken from the charred body. The initials had proven he hadn't brought in his own Audrey.

"He was helping them herd the horses. For an hour

after they built a big rope corral, he curried and fed and tended the horses. Then when he was done, one of the terrible men drew his gun, walked over and shot Tommy in the back of the head."

The outlaws had forced Tommy to help them steal the horses and herd them to the hiding spot. Had the boy even known his wife was already dead back at the way station? Beatrice and the couple he'd worked for? Luke hoped the boy had died hopeful and believing he was being set free. Knowing how underhanded the outlaws were, they weren't above promising him nothing would happen to his loved ones if he cooperated.

"I watched for a long time. I don't know why. It wasn't like Tommy'd come back to life. He just lay there drawing flies until a little boy came. He chewed them out and made them bury Tommy."

"Little boy?"

"He was short and had a face like an angel. Even when he was shouting at them, he looked like a cherub."

"This angel carried a six-gun?"

"A big one. He ordered the others around and then he and an ugly brute of a man left. I don't know where they went. They were too far away for me to hear what they said."

Rollie Rhoades and Crazy Water Benedict. "Cherubic" and "brutish" described each of them well enough if they were seen from a distance.

"Here, Sarah, draw me a map. This is where we are now."

"This is fun," she said, taking the pencil and licking the tip. She bent over. She chewed her tongue as she worked, explaining every landmark to Luke as she drew.

"This is a stream, and the clearing in the woods where they have the horses is here." She made a careful X on the paper scrap. "That's only a couple miles away."

He turned the paper around and around to be sure he had all the important landmarks memorized. His camp was a half mile in the opposite direction. Fetching his horse gave him added speed and mobility, but he was anxious to see if everything Sarah told him was right. Trusting her to report faithfully was a big stretch. What she'd seen could be explained in a lot of other, more legal ways. There were ranches all around. Cowboys sent out from one of those ranches to find strays explained everything.

Everything except seeing Tommy Zinn gunned down. She knew the boy and hadn't said "someone who looked like Tommy Zinn." Cowboys working to round up horses had no reason to shoot anyone in the back. Even more damning, the description of the angelic man matched too well with Rhoades.

"You get to fixing that fancy meal for us, Sarah. I'll see to the horses."

"They're our future, my darling Lucas. We'll be rich and those hoity-toity women in Crossroads won't lord it over me anymore. I'll be able to buy and sell the lot of them all because you came back to me!" She lunged over the table and threw her spindly arms around his neck. She hugged so hard he lost his balance. If he hadn't wormed his way free of the embrace, she would have bulldogged him down.

"I won't be long," he told her, wondering if that was a lie. If he found and freed his wife, Audrey's safety came first. If there had to be more tracking, going after

Benedict, life got more complicated. He refused to believe it was possible for him to run afoul of the gang and end up like Tommy Zinn. They didn't know he was coming, and turning his back on those rattlesnakes wasn't in the cards.

He'd deal with them, and if he couldn't, Crossroads was nearby. The marshal hunted for the Rhoades gang. Recruiting a posse took less time than Luke snapping his fingers if the reward offered was big enough. If Marshal Wilkes couldn't put up the money, Luke had enough left to make the fight worthwhile for even the most craven hanger-on at a saloon.

"It's been so long, Lucas." Tears streamed down Sarah's cheeks. "Don't make it much longer."

He smiled weakly, then his resolve hardened. He felt sorry for Sarah Youngblood, but she was secondary to his real job of bringing the outlaws to justice. He stepped out of the cabin and studied the stars. It was an hour before sunrise. The map Sarah had drawn showed the horses to be a couple miles off. If he hurried on foot, he'd reach the encampment just before dawn. That was perfect time for scouting the situation. If he had to move then, twilight gave him cover for an attack. Luke was sure he was accurate enough to take out any number of outlaws before they knew they faced only a single gunman.

As he made his way along a narrow game trail, he checked his Schofield. All six chambers carried rounds. A quick touch to his coat pocket reassured him he had a full box to back up the cartridges already loaded. His progress slowed when he lost the trail in the darkness. Closing his eyes, he imagined the back trail and where it headed. He lacked the skills of a real woodsman but he had learned enough to keep a sense of direction, even in dense woods like these.

He plowed through bushes, then slowed when he found the trail. Or another one running in the right direction. Cocking his head to one side, he listened hard. The stream burbled along not too far away. Doubly sure of his directions now, he picked up the pace. By the time he stepped out into a clearing, false dawn lit the trees.

The smell of horses and the sound of two men arguing stopped him dead in his tracks. He backed up to take cover in the thick brush beside the game trail. Straining, he listened to the argument over whose turn it was to boil the coffee. After a full minute of swapped invectives, one man agreed to get the water and prepare the morning brew. Luke took this as his opportunity to approach the camp. He thought there were only two men, and if one wandered down to the stream to get water, this gave better odds.

Skirting the clearing, he saw the campfire had burned down to embers. A dark figure poked the coals and added dried oak leaves to bring up the flames enough to eat away at dried twigs. Before Luke got within twenty yards, a decent cook fire blazed. The light revealed the man on the far side of the firepit. The outlaw's name eluded Luke, but he was certain he recognized him from a wanted poster. He slipped his six-shooter from its holster and sighted in on the man.

Luke let his finger relax when the other outlaw returned with a coffeepot and two canteens.

"It'll only take a couple minutes to fix the coffee."

He fished in his vest pocket for a watch, snapped open the case and tipped it toward the fire to better read the face. "We got time."

"I'll fix the coffee. You go water the horses."

This sparked a new argument. Luke shifted his attention from the two bickering outlaws to the woods beyond them. A puff of morning breeze came from that direction, bringing the earthy scent of horses mingled with woodsmoke from the campfire. Being downwind served Luke well. The horses wouldn't get spooked by the scent of a newcomer, and any sounds he made were carried away from the bickering outlaws. He moved closer.

Within ten yards of the fire gave him his first good look at the horses. A quick count showed ten tied down to a rope strung between two trees. This would hardly have been much of a start for a stud farm like Sarah Youngblood thought, but Luke suspected she knew as little about raising horses as he did.

He still worried that these were the only two men in camp. A third or even fourth outlaw posted nearer the horses made sense, both to keep the animals quiet and to guard against predators. He had seen ample spoor warning him how many wolves prowled throughout the Flint Hills. Those horses would make a delicious meal for a wolf pack. After another minute of watching and waiting, Luke decided he only faced two men. They had continued their argument about who watered the stolen horses. He got a better look at the second outlaw. As with the first, he remembered seeing his likeness on a wanted poster but couldn't remember the name.

If they followed Rollie Rhoades, they were dangerous, killers both. They were likely the men Sarah had seen gun down Tommy Zinn.

Luke found himself hesitant about shooting them down from ambush. That was something Benedict would do, and he wasn't lowering himself to the man's level. Another consideration came quickly to deter him. He needed to know where Audrey had been taken. She wasn't in this camp, so that meant Rhoades's hideout was elsewhere. Creating a distraction made more sense. If he released the horses, the outlaws had no choice but to go after them. This accident might cause them to send a warning to Rhoades and postpone whatever robbery they had planned. Delay worked for Luke and against the gang.

Edging around even more toward the tethered horses, Luke found himself in thicker bushes. Thorns tore at his coat and then dug into his skin. He bit his lower lip to keep from crying out when a particularly long thorn drove deep into his forearm and opened one of the wounds he'd already sustained from the dynamite explosion. Pulling free caused the bush to rattle loudly. He looked up and saw both outlaws going for their six-shooters.

Discovered!

He yanked free and, ignoring the blood running down his arm, fumbled to draw his own pistol. Then he froze. The two men hadn't heard him. They reacted to another ruckus from across the clearing.

Luke ducked behind a thick-boled cottonwood. If a shootout started, the sturdy trunk protected him. Poking his head around, he saw the two outlaws separating, moving to get whoever approached in a crossfire.

He heard the singing before he spotted Sarah Youngblood. She came across the clearing, arms flailing about like windmill blades in a high wind and singing "Mister Froggie Went a-Courtin'" at the top of her lungs.

The nearer outlaw aimed carefully as Sarah made her way closer. Luke cocked his six-gun and braced his wrist against the tree trunk. The trigger moved back and then he released it an instant before the recoil.

"Get 'em ready to ride! We got a posse on our tail!"

Luke looked past Sarah to a rider galloping from the woods. He blinked. Crazy Water Benedict had joined the other two. He rode a lathered horse that stumbled and almost threw its rider. Benedict kept his seat and yanked hard on the reins to bring the horse to a halt.

"Who's that?" Benedict pointed to Sarah, who ignored him and the others.

"She just showed up, Crazy Water. We was gonna shoot her." The outlaw closest to Luke rushed forward to take the reins Benedict dropped.

"Don't go shooting. The marshal is right behind us. The boss sent him off on a false trail, but a gunshot will bring that posse down on us like flies to cow flop."

"What should we do with her?"

Benedict glanced over his shoulder. The second man from the camp dragged Sarah forward. Luke lowered his six-shooter. He had lost his chance to take them out. The woman had been captured and the best shooting in the world wouldn't save her now.

"You want us to leave her? Or cut her throat?"

"Bring her with us. We got to find out what she knows." Benedict worked to get the saddle off his exhausted horse. He heaved it over his shoulder and ran to the fresh horses. Without being too choosy, he began saddling the first horse he came to.

"What can she know? She just showed up a minute or two back." The outlaw wanted to argue the point with Benedict.

Crazy Water Benedict turned from saddling his horse, took a step forward and backhanded the man. The impact of hand against cheek sounded like a muffled gunshot. The outlaw stumbled and sat hard. He rubbed his wounded cheek. He started to draw his six-gun when Benedict turned his back to finish saddling his new mount.

"The rest of 'em is comin'," called the outlaw dragging Sarah along. He shook his head when he got his partner's attention and saw he foolishly intended to shoot Benedict. "The boss won't like it."

Luke knew what the outlaw meant. Having his right-hand man shot in the back wouldn't set well with anyone. For Rollie Rhoades such betrayal signed a man's death warrant.

"Go on, fling her over a horse. Tie her down," the offended outlaw said, standing. He rubbed his cheek. If looks could kill, Benedict would have been a dead man. As it was, Benedict wheeled his horse around and trotted back into the clearing.

"I can ride. Where are you taking me?" Sarah tried to jerk free. The outlaw who had been slapped passed along the punishment. He started to vent even more anger by beating on the woman, but his partner stopped him again. Silently pointing, he waited for the men to appear from the forested area by ones and twos. Each rider led a horse.

Luke caught his breath. They had robbed the bank

of so much gold it required four packhorses to move it. The entire gang came into the clearing. Any chance Luke had before of saving Sarah or even potshotting Benedict was long gone now. The gang hit the ground running and began switching their gear to the rested horses. Moving the gold from the pack animals to others required two men.

Luke drew a bead on the outlaw who kept a sharp eye on Sarah. If he knocked the man from the saddle, Sarah's escape was possible. But the woman had lost herself in crazy fantasies again. Crying out for her Lucas won her a backhanded swat that missed. She reared back in the saddle to avoid the blow, but as she rocked forward the outlaw tugged on the reins of her horse and trotted away. In seconds they disappeared across the stream.

Turning his attention back to the gang, Luke saw how efficient the outlaws were. Like a well-trained militia, they worked together to transfer the gold in what had to be record time. Rollie Rhoades supervised the gang from the back of a fresh horse.

"Crazy Water, drive the horses south." He waited until his lieutenant rounded up several of the horses the gang had ridden into the ground, then threw him a mocking salute. "See you at the hideout." Rhoades smiled. For a man with such a baby face it should have been precious. On him it carried more than a hint of cruelty.

"Don't go giving my share to any of those other owlhoots," Benedict said. He played out a couple yards of rope and applied it to the rump of the nearest horse with a loud whack. He started the small herd trotting along to lay a false trail.

In a few seconds Luke stood staring at the empty camp. All the horses were gone and the gang had ridden off. Benedict was the last of the gang to vanish. The silence tore at Luke.

"Oh, Sarah, why'd you have to follow me?"

Luke peered into the distance where the gang had ridden. That was his trail now. Firing a shot to draw the marshal and his posse from Crossroads was a possible tactic, but he doubted they shared his goals.

Freeing Sarah Youngblood mattered more than all the gold Rhoades had stolen from the bank. And trumping even the brainsick woman's safety was rescuing Audrey.

Luke slipped back into the trees, found the game trail and jogged along, intent on reaching the ramshackle cabin and then getting to his camp where his horse grazed. He hoped the animal was well enough fed and rested to gallop the entire way to Rhoades's camp. Catching the outlaw gang was only the first part.

Shooting it out with them would be one monumental firefight. He put his head down and ran hard, in spite of his strength fading with each step.

CHAPTER TEN

LUKE HADLEY KEPT his head down, sucking air into his tortured lungs. He'd been through too much for this exertion. Every muscle in his body told him to stop. He slowed from his stumbling run to walk along the trail back to Sarah's cabin. His thoughts bubbled and boiled. Following the outlaws only started the chore ahead of him. He had to rescue Audrey and Sarah. He held his breath at the notion of killing the man who had put the shrapnel in his chest, until he gasped and missed a step, stumbling. Keeping a steady pace covered more ground than the way he trooped along. A deep breath settled his nerves. A little. But his chaotic thoughts returned to confuse him.

Kill Rhoades. Kill Benedict. Kill the rest of the road agents. All that pleased him, but it had to be secondary.

He arrived at the cabin. Saving Sarah mattered now.

The crazy woman had blundered into the outlaw camp. Whether their not gunning her down was good luck or bad presented a question he couldn't answer. Her fate seemed worse than even wandering the woods bemoaning the loss of her husband—or expecting him to return after so many years. The outlaws showed no respect for life. She would be kept alive as long as the gang found a use for her.

Luke leaned against the cabin wall to catch his breath. More than a few seconds passed until his breathing settled down. Hating every instant it took to recover, he finally hurried off to retrieve his horse. Barely a hundred yards into the woods, he felt a sense of being watched. No definite clue warned him. No unusual smell or sound. Not even a flash of movement in the thick undergrowth. But the hairs on the back of his neck rose and a shiver passed down his spine.

Moving fast, he jumped to the side and went for his six-shooter. Thorns tore at his arms, and bushes crushed as he bulled through to take cover behind a fallen log. For a second he saw nothing. Then came the flash of red plaid. A man took cover behind a black walnut tree. Carefully taking aim, Luke waited for the other man to show himself. It had to happen eventually, if he waited long enough.

A few inches of the man's hat brim poked out from behind the tree. Luke held his fire. This was a ploy to make him waste ammunition and make him reveal his hiding place. Rather than aiming at that side of the tree, he moved to the far side of the trunk in time to get off a shot when his stalker tried to dodge to better cover.

A curse left his lips. He missed by a country mile.

At least he pinned the man in place behind the tree. Scooting back on his belly, Luke flipped over and got to his feet. The shot held the man in place for a few more seconds. With a surge, Luke got his balance and started running. The longer he spent in the woods, the farther away the gang rode. Why the outlaw coming for him hadn't joined his partners wasn't anything Luke wanted to consider. Lives depended on him going after the outlaws.

He burst into the clearing where he had camped. His horse looked up, annoyed. The grass was succulent and only a small patch had been nibbled. Luke scooped up his bedroll and saddle. The hobbled horse tried to put distance between them, then gave in to being saddled and resigned itself to having a rider once more.

Luke secured the belly strap, then dropped to his knees to unfasten the hobbles. He froze when he heard the metallic click of a hammer being pulled back. Somehow the man in the forest had circled around and sneaked up behind him.

"Don't go reaching for that hogleg," came the sharp command. "I don't want to plug you, but you took a shot at my deputy."

"Deputy?" Luke looked over his shoulder. Benson Wilkes had his six-gun leveled and ready to shoot, given any more provocation. Playing for time was the only way Luke came out alive—or out of the Crossroads jail. "What do you mean?"

Footsteps pounded and a man gasping for breath joined the marshal.

"It's a good thing you got him, Marshal. He took a potshot at me."

"That's because you're such a clumsy tracker, Moynihan. I should never have sent you. Denny is a better choice."

"Denny? He couldn't find his—"

"Shut up." Marshal Wilkes reached down and plucked Luke's six-shooter from his holster. He tucked it into his own belt before lowering his pistol. He didn't holster it in case he needed to use it again fast.

"They're getting away!" Luke pivoted and got his feet under him. This earned him the right to stare down the barrel of the lawman's gun again. "Put that down! The outlaws are—"

"They're nowhere to be found, that's where they are. What I want to know is why we found you out here and didn't catch sight of them?" Wilkes signaled with a shrill whistle. A dozen men rode up from hiding places around the clearing. Luke was trapped by the posse hunting for Rhoades.

"They used the horses stolen from the way station as fresh mounts. You'll never catch them now." A quick look showed how right he was. The posse rode lathered horses. More than one of the deputies wobbled in the saddle. They had ridden all night and had tuckered themselves out. More than likely, Marshal Wilkes had recruited men from the saloons, many of them already half-soused when they stepped up to do their civic duty.

"You surely do know a great deal about how the gang operates," the marshal said. "That's what I call curious. Wouldn't you say so, Deputy Moynihan?"

"You mean to say this yahoo's one of them? But we lost their trail. Why's he still here and not ridin' with them?"

"You tried following the trail to the south?" Luke

perked up. "That was a false trail Crazy Water Benedict laid by—" He snapped his mouth shut when he realized he only dug himself a deeper hole. He knew details of the robbery and escape Marshal Wilkes didn't. Or did he? The lawman bounced his gun up and down, as if trying to decide where to shoot his prisoner. Foot or head. Either meant trouble Luke wasn't willing to endure.

Riding after the gang would be hard enough. Doing it with a bullet in him turned the task into one bordering on the impossible, as bunged up as he already was.

"Yes sirree bob, he does know things only one of the outlaws could know." Wilkes waved his gun around. "Go on, climb up. We're going back to town."

"Crossroads? But that's in the opposite direction. Rhoades has the gold. And . . . and he has a hostage. He took the woman that lives in the cabin down this trail." Luke turned to point. For his trouble he got a pistol barrel laid alongside his head. The impact drove him to his knees.

"Don't figure you can escape. Go on, Deputy. Truss him up good and proper."

"Wait, wait." Luke shook his head. Bees buzzed inside and his vision doubled. He rubbed the spot where Wilkes had struck him. The bruise had already turned tender and sent new stabs of pain into his skull. "I'm one of you. Look."

He reached into his coat pocket and was rewarded by Moynihan kicking him in the ribs. He grunted and tried to roll with the blow. Landing flat on his back, he held up the shiny tin star. "I'm a Pinkerton. Here's proof I was after the Rhoades gang, just like you."

"You got to the count of three to step up on your

horse. One. Two." Wilkes sighted along his barrel. Again Luke stared into the .44 bore. Each time it grew in size. Now he was sure a freight train would fit just fine in that gaping, dark tunnel with the bullet at the end.

"Don't shoot." He got to his feet and used his horse to support himself. While it did him no good, he dropped the tin star back into his coat pocket, gripped the saddle horn with both hands and pulled himself up. Astride his horse, he felt as if he had climbed the tallest mountain in the state. He looked down on the marshal and two deputies. All three men had their sidearms trained on him. A glance around showed several of the mounted posse pointed rifles in his direction.

"Everybody back from getting lost in the woods?" The marshal did a quick count. He shrugged. One or two must be missing. Luke hoped they had stayed on the trail.

"The woman in the cabin," he began. "Rhoades has taken her as a hostage."

"The cabin's empty, Marshal," Denny confirmed. "This is where the crazy old heifer lives. The one who comes into town every once in a while and causes a big commotion."

"Sarah Youngblood," Luke furnished. "And she's skinny as a rail. Starving. She thinks her husband'll come back to her. She sings to the moon."

"I knew him. His name was Lucas. He got hisself killed fightin' the Rebs. If he was batty like her, he walked into a cannon, thinking he was goin' home." Moynihan chuckled at the very idea of someone dying in such a grisly fashion.

"For a newcomer, you've learned a lot about the people and countryside," Wilkes said. "Almost as if you scouted for the outlaws. Rhoades, you say? That's the Rollie Rhoades gang?"

"Yes, yes!"

"Was that a confession that he's one of 'em, Marshal? Let's string him up here. There's a sturdy post oak tree back there."

Luke didn't see who called out the desire to hang their prisoner. One of the posse. Wilkes shot his gun into the air to get their attention. The report echoed into the distance. Luke knew there was no longer any chance for it to warn the outlaws. They were long gone.

"We caught him," said Wilkes. "He gets a fair trial. If there's any hanging to be done, the judge is the one who says so."

Luke cast a quick look of thanks in the marshal's direction, but he saw no mercy there. The lawman had been made a fool of by the robbery and escape and wanted the trial made as public as possible to show he wasn't entirely incompetent. Otherwise, there might have been a body twisting slowly from a limb, caught by the humid breeze and drawing crows to peck at his eyes and dead flesh.

The posse circled him. They rode slowly. Still, in spite of their close attention, Luke considered making a break for it. Their horses were tired. His was rested. But the number of deputies riding with their rifles resting across the saddles in front of them kept him from doing anything that foolish. The men and their mounts were tired. Their bullets weren't.

"How much gold did Rhoades get away with?" For an answer, he got a cold stare. "Did he blow the place up? Rhoades enjoys using dynamite."

"He blew the whole danged building up. There's

hardly a brick left whole. The bank vault was twisted open."

"Wouldn't that destroy any greenbacks?"

"You know it did. Every bit of paper money burned to filthy ash. The gold coins in there were all from cattle sales. There must have been close to a ten thousand dollars."

"Woulda been worse. If he'd struck a couple days earlier, the money from the Circle Bar Circle woulda been there. Mister Platt took his money out to buy another thousand acres up north." Moynihan sounded pleased he knew this bit of gossip.

Luke settled down and rode in silence. Rhoades had made off with a king's ransom. If he had struck a few days earlier, his take would have put him in the headline of every paper in the state of Kansas. Whether the outlaw leader cared much about the gold or just enjoyed the robbing and killing—and blowing up buildings—gave Luke something to chew on until they reached Crossroads just after the sun sank behind the horizon. A cool breeze did little to ease the anguish he felt.

"Marshal, I—"

"Shut up. Not a word out of you or I'll hog-tie and gag you." Wilkes pointed to the jailhouse.

Without any recourse, Luke dismounted under the watchful eyes of half the posse. Wilkes paid them off. They whooped and hollered as if they'd been successful in their hunt and raced off to the saloons. Luke had never been much of a drinker—until Audrey's kidnapping. Then he tried too much to snuff out the pain with just one more shot. All that had gained him was a headache in the morning and enduring heartache every instant of the day. Once on the trail of the outlaws, he had wanted a clear head and steady hand not possible with too much popskull but wished right now he went with them rather than into the jail. A six-gun muzzle shoved into his spine got him moving in the direction desired by the lawman.

"You get the same cell. I should never have let you go. That would have saved me a passel of trouble." Benson Wilkes shoved his prisoner in and slammed the cell door. It clanged with utter finality, punctuated with a metal click as the key turned the lock.

"We're on the same side, Marshal. I can help. But if you keep me in the cell, please, I'm begging you, send out a party to find Sarah Youngblood. Those men will do terrible things to her."

"She's not right in the head. She probably threw in with them."

Arguing got him nowhere. Luke finally gave up and sank onto the bed. Dejection washed over him like a drowning tide. If the marshal felt like a failure, Luke shared the feeling in spades. He had been so close to bringing the outlaw to justice. If only Sarah hadn't butted in. If only–

"If only," he muttered. The marshal's failure only meant the bank lost money. His cost Sarah her life.

He had nothing to do but stare at the marshal and Moynihan playing cards. Every turn of the pasteboards made him cringe. Every card was a loser and he had played them all.

When the outer door opened, he turned away. A woman carried a tray covered with a red-and-white-checked napkin.

"Here's dinner for your prisoner." The woman kept

her face down and hardly whispered the words, as if they burned her tongue.

"Nothing for us?" Moynihan reached to lift the napkin. He got his hand slapped for the impertinence.

"Rules," the woman said. "Prisoner's got to be fed. You can get your own food."

Wilkes motioned her to the back, not even looking up from the cards. Moynihan grumbled and paid attention to the game again. The woman shuffled back and stopped a step away from the cell door.

"I'm not hungry. Give it to the deputy." Luke felt like vomiting. Food was the last thing he wanted right now.

"Take it." She rested the tray on the small opening in the bars designed to pass food to the prisoners. "Take it." Her tone carried the whipcrack of command that made Luke sit up and take notice. She lifted the corner of the napkin to give him a quick look at the pearl handle of a derringer.

"Why?" He moved to take the tray.

She swung away and rushed from the jailhouse, head still down and not saying another word to either Luke or the lawmen.

He held the tray awkwardly, then scooted it into the cell. Carefully placing it on the edge of his bed, he pulled back the napkin. His eyes hadn't deceived him. A two-shot derringer rested against the china plate brimming with some smelly goulash. Quick as a flash, he slid the gun off the tray. The cold metal restored his energy better than the dubious food ever could have. He went to the cell door and peered out. Wilkes and Moynihan were lost in their gin rummy game.

"Marshal, take a look at this," he called. Luke clutched the derringer tightly. It took all his willpower not to curl his finger around the trigger and send a round off into space. Both rounds were needed. Two lawmen, two bullets. He closed his eyes for a moment, then opened them. It took a considerable amount of courage to do what had to be done.

"What is it? That slop's all you're going to get."

The marshal stared at the derringer. It was his turn to peer down a barrel that looked to be the size of a train tunnel.

"Open the cell," Luke said.

"The key's in my desk."

"Stay put. Have your deputy fetch it." He held the derringer outside the iron bars to get a better shot. "I've got nothing to lose. You do."

"You miserable, no-account . . ."

Luke cocked the derringer to shut off the flow of invective.

Wilkes got the idea. "Moynihan, bring the key to the prisoner's cell."

"Why, Marshal? He can pass the tray out the same way he took it."

"Do it!"

The deputy grumbled but brought the keys. He turned to stone when he saw the derringer clutched in his prisoner's hand. Silently, he opened the cell. Luke gestured the two men in. He relieved both of their sidearms as they came in, then secured the cell door. He almost sank to the floor in reaction, shaking like a leaf. He hadn't realized what a strain the jailbreak put on him.

"Would you have shot me?" The marshal hung on the bars. Luke stepped back farther to prevent a sudden grab that would deny him escape.

"You'll never know." He dropped their six-shooters on top of the cards and looked for his own piece. Wherever the marshal had stashed it, Luke couldn't find it. A tentative knock on the door stopped his search.

Almost fearfully, he opened the outer door a few inches to peer out. The saloons were filled to overflowing with celebrating posse. The rest of Crossroads was as silent as a grave. Whoever had knocked was gone. Or had his nerves gotten the better of him?

A new sound around the side of the jail convinced him to hightail it. The two lawmen were in a pickle. They had to be heard over the tumult from the boisterous crowds in the saloons, but sooner or later someone would get curious and come investigate. Luke considered going back and gagging the men. More scuffling sent him around the corner, the derringer thrust in front of him and ready to fire.

He pointed the small gun at the woman who had rescued him. He realized right away this wasn't a mirror situation. She held a six-gun in a steady grip pointed right at him. Hers was bigger.

"Looks like we've got a standoff," he said.

"Nope. Your gun's not loaded."

Luke shifted his aim and pulled the trigger. The hammer fell on an empty chamber.

"Mine's got six rounds, all waiting to ventilate you." She cocked the six-gun and fixed a steely eye on him. He believed her. Luke slowly raised his hands.

CHAPTER ELEVEN

"OH, PUT YOUR hands down. You look foolish." She gestured with her six-gun for him to relax. Luke did so slowly. His palm sweat so much the derringer almost slipped out of his grip.

"Who are you?"

"Our horses are around back. Come on." She indicated where she wanted him to walk, using the gun as a pointer. Her manner was brusque, but he doubted she would shoot him. After the risk she'd taken to get him out of the jail, she wanted more from him than his corpse rotting in the sun.

"I will, you know. You've caused me nothing but trouble."

"What?" It was as if she read his mind.

"You're not the first man I've gotten the drop on, and you wouldn't be the first to catch an ounce of lead from my six-shooter. Move faster. The marshal is going to start yelling soon enough."

"I don't know why he hasn't already," Luke said. He rounded the building. Out back two tethered horses tugged at their reins. One was his. He stepped up and waited for her to mount. She did so with a short hop that got her foot in the stirrup and she reached the saddle horn to pull herself up the rest of the way.

While she was mostly cloaked in shadows, he recognized her as the woman who had rescued him before. And the one who had sprung Nelson so he could march off to his death at Benedict's hand. As they rode, she put on a floppy-brimmed hat and pulled it low to shield her face as effectively as any bandanna mask might. From the way she mounted, she couldn't be much over five feet tall but moved with grace and power. The unwavering grip on her pistol told of familiarity with the weapon. The way she had looked at him made Luke believe every word she said about him not being the first man she'd shot—if it came to that. No obvious reason entered his mind why he shouldn't do as she ordered. He needed allies, even if they insisted on pointing six-shooters at him.

He bent low and put his heels to his horse's flanks. The mare rocketed off. The woman followed on her gelding, matching his speed. He caught a glimpse of her profile. A long, straight nose and firm chin more than hinted at her determination. The set to her jaw told how she was a woman capable of getting what she wanted. If he had to guess, and he was poor at such things, she was in her late twenties, not too much younger than him. When she turned to look in his direction, he caught the light reflected off a thin pink scar on her left cheek. A knife left such a reminder.

As feisty as she was, it wasn't much of a stretch to imagine her in a knife fight to the death. If she had won the scar, her opponent had bought himself some real estate and currently resided six feet under.

She struck him as that kind of woman.

Once outside Crossroads, they slowed. The stars above in the clear sky shined down with enough intensity to light the road. She pushed back her hat and lifted her chin. The silvery starlight turned her into a work of art. But this marble statue moved and gestured with a deadly gun.

"That way. Off the road."

"Will the marshal come after us?"

"After *us*?" She laughed. It carried a mocking tone that worked its way into his brain like a saddle bur. "You're the criminal. He has no idea who I am or how I'm involved."

"I'm not a bank robber, and I'm after Rhoades. I intend to bring him to justice."

"Keep riding." She herded him north until they were out of sight from anybody traveling the main road.

After almost an hour, she signaled for them to stop and dismount. He felt stiff all over and could barely straighten his legs without wincing. It had been a terrible few days, and he had spent far too much time in a cell. That had to come to an end. Capturing Rhoades and Benedict meant staying clear of the law. Somehow, the tables had been turned. Luke felt he was more notorious than the actual road agents. They had killed, stolen horses, robbed a bank and kidnapped. All he had done was try to stay alive. And he was the one Marshal Wilkes was most likely to come after. It wasn't fair.

The woman dropped to the ground and came over.

He had been right about her height. She was around five-foot-one, though she looked taller when she wore the high-crowned hat. Other than the hat, she was dressed in trail gear, a split riding skirt and a blouse buttoned up high around her slender neck. Her boots were fancy-tooled and expensive. Matching the work there, her gun belt hung on her hip, the holster still empty. She never took the gun off him as if he were the worst desperado in all of Kansas.

"You've sprung me out of jail a couple times," he said. Her brown eyes narrowed as he spoke. She pushed her hat back and a lock of chestnut hair escaped. A quick move pushed it out of her eyes. "I want to thank you, but I don't know your name."

"There's no reason for you to."

"Look," he said, exasperated at her curt demeanor. "We're both after the gang. I'm a Pinkerton agent. See?" He pulled the star from his pocket and held it out on his palm. With a move faster than a striking snake, she snatched it from him and held it up. Stars reflected off it.

She sneered at him.

"You're no Pinkerton agent. This is a fake. I don't know or care where you got it, but it's not real. Pinkerton isn't even spelled right. At least have the decency to have a good counterfeit made. You left out the 'e-r' in the middle. Pinkton Agency. Pah." She flung the badge and its latigo strap away. It left a silvery spiral in his vision as it sailed into the night.

"Don't! You can't throw that away!"

"It's my right. It's my duty." Face twisted into a scowl, she reached into a skirt pocket and pulled out a leather wallet. With a quick flick of her wrist, she opened the wallet to show a brass badge inside. "This is a real Pinkerton badge. I'm Special Agent Marta Shearing and I ought to have let you rot in the Crossroads jail."

"Why didn't you?" Luke stared at the badge. It had been stamped into a brass sheet and then trimmed neatly. He had never seen a real Pinkerton badge before, much less met a dyed-in-the-wool real agent. Never had he expected it to be a fiery woman like Marta Shearing.

"Tell me everything you know about the robbery. And I mean everything." She closed the wallet with an expert, practiced flip and tucked away the badge. The gun in her other hand never wavered from its target, dead center on Luke's chest.

"I figured Rhoades was going to hit the bank when I heard how much cattle money was deposited there. I saw Crazy Water Benedict and followed him, but he got away. The man he spoke to was probably another gang member. We both got tossed in the clink."

"Do you mean Geoff Nelson? I got him out to follow him. That didn't work too well. He ended up dead, blown up out on the edge of town."

He nodded. That explained why she hadn't bothered getting him out. He didn't know where the gang was but the man Benedict had met would. Rhoades had used the local salesman to furnish dynamite, and then killed him to snip off a loose end.

"What about the robbery?" From the set to her mouth, her patience disappeared quickly. She wanted what he knew. Giving it to her cost him nothing, Luke decided.

He shook his head. "I wasn't there. I only saw a map drawn up by the marshal over in Preston."

"Hargrove," she said. "He got a bee in his bonnet about finding Rhoades after the way station massacre. Only he couldn't do anything about it except make that map. I never saw it, but he knows the country like the back of his hand. Getting a posse formed to go after Rhoades cost too much, and Preston is close to being a dead broke town. If any more people leave it, there'll be nothing but ghosts and the whisper of wind left blowing through deserted buildings."

"Hargrove's map," he went on, "had the places where he thought Rhoades might be holed up. At the time it meant nothing, but I think the map has valuable information now. They robbed the bank while I hunted for the spare horses." He quickly explained how he had followed the trail from the destroyed way station. "They stash the fresh horses and use them to get away from posses."

"Why'd they blow the bank sky-high?"

Luke turned grimmer at that.

"Call it a hobby with Rollie Rhoades. He enjoys seeing buildings—and people—go up in a big bang. I heard tell he used to set fires until he discovered how much more fun dynamite was."

"A bad feller," Marta Shearing said, her lips thinned to a razor slash. "It's going to be hard bringing him in."

"You were on his trail before the robbery. What's the Pinkerton Agency's interest?"

"He held up a Central Pacific train we'd been hired to protect. He killed two agents and made off with more than five hundred dollars."

"Did he blow up the mail car?"

She shook her head.

"He filled the sides of the car with so many rounds that it looked like a termite colony had taken up residence. The wheels and floor were about all that survived. Then there're others in his self-styled 'family' Allan especially wants brought to justice. It's a personal matter with him, especially one of them." She stepped back and made sure he saw the six-gun in her hand. "You were on the gang's trail when Marshal Wilkes nabbed you?"

He explained about Sarah Youngblood and how Crazy Water Benedict had driven the horses used in the actual robbery south to make it seem the gang headed for Indian Territory.

"So Rhoades and the rest of the gang took the gold and rode north? Or northwest?"

"More toward the northwest." He took a deep breath. He had one more card in the hole to play. "I saw a spot marked on Marshal Hargrove's map in that direction where they might rendezvous. We can—"

"There's no 'we' in this, Hadley. Step back. Another step." She fished around in her saddlebags and pulled out his six-shooter.

"But if you're giving me back my gun, that means we're partners. We are going after Rhoades together. Only I want to be the one bringing down Benedict, for what he's done to me." He found himself tongue-tied when he tried to explain about Audrey. Those words disappeared and a surprised cry escaped when Marta flung his gun into the night. He heard it land in a mud puddle with a loud splash.

"I ought to keep your sidearm, but this is dangerous country and I don't think you'd gun down the marshal or any of his posse." She bounced up into the saddle and swung around to grab the reins to his horse. "I am taking this nag. As much as it pains me to say it, Rhoades is a clever owlhoot. There's no reason I can't learn from how he does things and use them to my advantage. Your horse will come in handy as my spare."

She touched the brim of her hat with the six-shooter's barrel, then applied her heels to the gelding and galloped off to the northwest, Luke's horse obediently following. He stared after her, too many emotions colliding for him to know whether to be furious or to laugh. He settled on cursing under his breath, turning around and putting his boots smack in the footprints she'd left when she threw his Schofield into the night. He tromped out until the ground turned muddy, then slowed and finally dropped to hands and knees to search the mud.

"Yes!" He lifted the filthy Model 3 and wiped off as much mud as he could. Finding a stump, he sat and broke open the action. He used his bandanna to clean the gun the best he could. It needed oiling, but the Nye's sperm-whale oil he used for that purpose rode off in his saddlebags, along with his spare ammunition and everything else that he needed to tackle Benedict and Rhoades.

He wiped off his holster and settled the Schofield, then started after Marta Shearing. Barely ten paces on his way, he stopped.

"I need more than my six-gun," he said, determination filling him again. He returned to the spot where Marta had thrown his bogus badge into the field. It took the better part of an hour to find it, but when he did, he wiped it off and tucked it back into his coat pocket. Then it was time to start hiking.

Dawn crept up on him. By the time the sun poked above the horizon, he saw a farmhouse. His nostrils flared when he smelled cooking meat. The family must be ready to eat breakfast after starting their chores. He looked down at his clothing and knew he looked as if he had been pulled through a knothole backward. There was nothing he could do about the dirty, torn clothing or his lack of belongings. Dusting himself off, he walked, shoulders back and proud, to the farmhouse. Two small girls sat on the back steps, counting eggs they had collected.

"Good morning," he said, hoping his appearance didn't frighten them.

They accepted him as he was. One yelled, "Pa! We got a visitor!"

The other added, "He ain't got no horse but he's got a big iron strapped to his hip. Looks to be a S&W Model 3."

Mumbled words from inside provoked the response from the girl, "Naw, he ain't no gunslinger. Just somebody on foot."

The girls' pa came to the door. He nodded to the pair that he accepted their appraisal of their visitor. Luke marveled at how clever they were to size him up and how the man trusted them.

"Morning, sir." Luke wondered what visitors stopped by this farmhouse. The man filling up the entire door frame with broad shoulders and height topping six feet hadn't bothered to fetch a shotgun or rifle.

"Top of the morning to you, too, pilgrim." The man eyed Luke from head to toe. "You have the look of a man down on his luck."

"That's so. I had my horse and tack stolen, and I've been walking the livelong night."

"Coming from Crossroads?"

Luke got a mite antsy at this. Any suggestion of reporting the alleged theft to Marshal Wilkes would land him in a heap of trouble. Marta Shearing had moved on and wasn't in the business of springing him from jail any longer.

"I'm on the trail of outlaws, sir." He pulled out the strip of leather with his fake badge fastened to it.

"It says he's a Pinkerton man, Pa." The more vocal of the two girls peered at the badge over her younger sister's shoulder, then stared up at him. Her cornflower-blue eyes never blinked. "I'm in the third grade and I spell real good."

"I bet you do," Luke said uneasily.

"You really after crooks?" She studied him like a bug under a magnifying glass. He felt as if she moved the lens around and focused the sun's rays on him. He got hot under the collar and flushed.

"I am after the Rhoades gang. They robbed the bank and stole horses from the way station east of Preston."

"Did they, now?" The farmer stepped down and put hands on his daughters' shoulders.

"The Tomlinsons were murdered," Luke said. "And a youngster and his bride."

"Beatrice and Tommy?" The shocked question came from behind the man in the doorway. A woman with the same piercing blue eyes as the little girl pushed past the mountain of a man onto the steps, a rifle cradled in the crook of her left arm. Her easy familiarity with the weapon warned Luke that she was likely a crack shot. Her husband might not be the shooting kind, but she was.

This family split their chores up different from usual,

but questions got asked and answered and no one risked their life without being protected.

"We heard about them. A crying shame, it is," the man said. "This gang, they stole your horse?"

"That's a long story," Luke said. His belly grumbled loud enough for the two girls to notice and snicker, hiding their mirth behind their hands.

"Susanna, set a place at the table for this here traveler. If you'd care to eat, that is."

"Much obliged," Luke said. He followed the man into the kitchen. What he saw shouldn't have surprised him, but it did. The man went to the stove and began fixing eggs and frying up a thick slice of ham while his wife rested her rifle against the wall. He didn't hesitate to unbuckle his gun belt and hand it to her. "If you'd take care of this, ma'am, I'll be more comfortable while I eat."

She gave a curt nod and hung his gun belt on a peg.

"Sven is the finest cook in all of Kansas," she said proudly as she took a china plate from a cabinet and let her husband pile on food. With a deft spin, she swung about and put the food in front of Luke. Before he had the chance to ask for silverware, the girls furnished it, along with a glass of cool water pumped from the well in the corner of the kitchen.

"We owned a restaurant in Fargo before moving south," Sven said.

"Sven is the best cook west of the Mississippi," his wife boasted.

"In all the world, too. Pa is from Stockholm. That's in Sweden," the younger girl said. Her compliment earned her a punch in the arm from her older sister.

The two began to squabble and were shooed out by their mother.

Luke had trouble remembering his last meal. The food Marta had brought in the jail had only served as a way to get the derringer into his hands. Before that, dinner the night before had been a mess of beans and a strip of jerky.

"Fargo lost a fine cook," Luke said from between mouthfuls. "This is about the best I've tasted in . . . ever!"

"Spices," Sven said in a confidential tone. "No one on the frontier takes the time to cook." He heaved a sigh, pulled up a chair and sat across from Luke. "Farming is hard work. With three women to help, it is easier, but a strong son would be a godsend." He looked at his wife, who worked to clean the family's dishes from their breakfast.

"A decent plow horse would be better," she said.

Luke chased the last bits of meat around the plate and forced himself not to lick off the grease. That would be rude. He pushed the plate away. Susanna snared it and began scrubbing it clean to stack with the others.

"This horse isn't good for plowing?"

"An ox would be better."

"If you have a mind, and the horse is broken for riding, I need a mount."

"To go after the robbers?" Sven eyed him shrewdly.

"They are also murderers." Luke saw this struck a responsive chord with the woman. She must have known either Beatrice or Tommy. Out here, neighbors had to be close to stand any chance of survival.

"I cannot give you the horse. I planned to sell him

in town and use the money to buy the ox from Mister Gottfried."

Luke patted his coat where he carried the money from the sale of his farm to the railroad. The lumps showed gold dust was still sewn into the lining.

"What's the cost of Mister Gottfried's ox?"

Sven shook his head. "More than we have, even with selling the plow horse."

"I would like to buy the horse and what gear you have for one hundred dollars."

Sven's and Susanna's eyes went wide. Before the man could protest, she said, "You have this money? You should check the horse to see what you're buying."

Luke had no other option. Either he rode or used shanks' mare. His feet already hurt after only a few hours trooping along. More than this, he had to put distance between the Crossroads marshal and himself. Even a slow horse added miles to what he did on foot.

"We can give him the old saddle. The one left here by that traveling sales fellow. And trail rations. How's that sound?" Sven looked eager and his wife dubious.

"If you cook the food, it's a deal."

Luke began opening the seam of his coat to draw out thin tubes of gold dust. Measuring proved difficult, and he probably paid more than the agreed amount, but he knew the family would put the money to good use. And he had victuals fit for a king, even if the sway-backed horse only plodded along at one slow gait.

CHAPTER TWELVE

THE PLOW HORSE had one speed—the one used to pull a plow. The clop-clop-clop and rolling gait put Luke to sleep after a few miles. He jerked awake often enough to be sure the swaybacked horse stayed on the trail. Or the trail Luke thought he followed. Marta Shearing had come this direction. That was all the information he had, other than a brief look at Marshal Hargrove's map filled with guesswork and potential hideouts for outlaw gangs.

Eyes blurry, he let his chin drop again as the horse soothed him to sleep. When he came awake the next time, his hand flashed to the Schofield at his side. Distant voices alerted him he wasn't alone on this trail.

"Whoa." He tugged harder on the reins. The horse refused to stop. It plodded on no matter how he sawed at the bridle.

Rather than blunder ahead into an ambush, though

how the two arguing men had any chance of laying an ambush for any man with hearing better than using an ear trumpet was hard to say, he jumped to the ground. The horse turned and stared at him. But it stopped. The draft animal was used to obeying commands issued from behind it, not from its back. Luke led it off the trail he followed and down into a gully where a sluggish stream flowed. While the horse drank its fill, Luke crept forward and found a spot behind some black chokeberry bushes. Using a twig, he pushed aside a branch and got a better look at two men crouched beside a small fire where they boiled coffee. Their gear spread around them in wild disarray. If they plotted an ambush, they were careless doing it.

When the wind changed and he caught a whiff of their witch's brew, he almost gagged. How any human drank such vile-smelling coffee was a tribute to cast-iron bellies. The men downed the contents of their tin cups, then began matching pennies. It took a few minutes until one accused the other of cheating. This sparked a shouting match between them.

From all he saw, arguing was all the men did. But something put him on guard. As one of them half turned, he exposed a low-slung six-shooter. The holster was tied down with a rawhide strap. The wood grip showed wear. If Luke had been closer, he'd have bet there'd be notches carved into the pistol grip. This one looked the world like a gunslinger.

A rabbit exploded from hiding not ten feet from the men. The second gunman came to a crouch, drew and fired so fast that Luke hardly saw a blur. Even more impressive, the shot caught the rabbit just above its shoulder. It let out a high-pitched screech as air gusted from its lungs, kicked once and then flopped over dead.

"We got ourselves lunch," the shooter said. He lifted the muzzle and blew the smoke away. "I shot it, you can skin and cook it."

"There's not enough meat on its bones for two of us."

"You expected me to kill two rabbits with one shot? I'm good but not that good."

The pair continued their petty disputation. Luke backed off, then hurried to his horse, still drinking noisily from the muddy stream. It took considerable tugging to get the horse away. If it'd drunk any more it would have started to bloat. Enough problems piled up around him without having to wait for the bloat to go down. With the luck he'd had so far, the horse would develop colic and die.

He tried to figure how to circle the two gunmen and get back to finding Rhoades and his gang, but this section of land was flatter than the hilly area he'd just ridden through. Sitting and thinking got him nowhere. He needed a decent map to pull off the run around the two men. Since he hadn't seen their hoofprints along the soft dirt of the trail he followed, they were coming toward him. If he waited long enough, they'd ride past him and never be any the wiser that he was here.

But they argued endlessly over fixing lunch. That meant another hour to fidget and hope they—

"Howdy, mister."

Luke jerked upright. Both gunmen stood a few yards away, hands resting on the butts of their well-used weapons. They had sneaked up on him while he was daydreaming about avoiding them.

"Hello." He forced himself to sit still and not reach for his six-shooter. The ease with which the one had drawn and the accuracy of his marksmanship warned Luke how close he was to dying. And he wasn't anywhere near as fast as a jackrabbit.

"You one of them?" The man on the right fixed a steely gaze on Luke, demanding an answer.

"I'm not sure who you mean, but if you intend to throw down on me if I answer wrong, let me set your mind at ease. I'm not 'one of them,' whoever that is." He smiled disarmingly.

The men exchanged looks, then laughed.

"Wouldn't matter none if you was a lawman. You out hunting for the ring-tailed varmint?"

Luke realized then that the men were bounty hunters. They had no quarrel with a posse, other than that the posse might grab their quarry and steal away a reward. In a sense, both they and Luke were on the same side of the law, though he had never heard of a bounty hunter who didn't steal away a reward from someone more deserving if the opportunity presented itself.

"I don't know who you mean."

"One of the Rhoades gang escaped from the jail over in Crossroads. The marshal won't talk none about it, so it must have been real embarrassing for him." He spat, then asked outright, "You a bounty hunter?"

The tin star weighed a hundred pounds in Luke's pocket. More. Showing it to the bounty hunters wasn't a smart move. He shook his head slowly.

"Can't say that I am. I'm out here looking for a woman name of Sarah Youngblood. She's not got a reward on her."

"Looking for a woman?" The men laughed until tears ran down their cheeks. The one who had shown his prowess with his iron added, "The three of us are looking for a woman, I'd say. Only we're not overly picky. Don't care what her name is. So far, we ain't had much luck. Seems the purty ones don't want to catch our cooties and the ugly ones cost too much."

"She's wearing a tattered wedding dress." Luke watched their reactions. Neither of them tried to hide what went on between their ears. They were crude and, if he was any judge, devastatingly efficient at their job.

"She run off during your wedding? That's rich. If she did, you're better off letting her go. Any filly who'd change her mind at the last second isn't fit for any man."

The other chimed in, "Soiled doves are cheaper in the long run, and you can pick a different one every time you get the itch."

"Get the itch? That's what you get *from* a soiled dove."

"You, maybe, like you did over in Denver. You remember the big redhead who gave you the clap? I was lucky you got first dibs. The señorita I had was more than I could handle. Almost!"

Luke held his tongue. The two argued endlessly over anything and everything. When they finally ran down and turned back to him, he realized he had to get away from them.

"If you gents don't mind, I have to be on my way."

"That your horse?" The one pointed. Both laughed.

"Hey, don't laugh. It'll hurt his feelings." Luke patted the horse's neck. The huge animal leaned into him and almost knocked him over.

"You're definitely not a bounty hunter. No self-respecting vigilante rides a nag like that."

Luke nodded and gave what he hoped was an agreeable smile.

"Don't you go insulting our new friend, Zeke."

"Don't go using that tone of voice with me, Deke."

Luke blinked. They acted like brothers but looked nothing alike. From their names, they might have been mistaken for twins. He had grown up with twins named Benjamin and Kenneth, Ben and Ken always, and never their full names. A touch of skepticism made him think that Zeke and Deke were summer names. Bounty hunters changed their names as they went from one part of the country to another because they were as likely to be wanted by the law as the men they caught and shot.

"It's about time for me to ride on," Luke said. He shifted his weight to draw, if it came to that. Neither of the two bounty hunters looked the least bit concerned that he might start flinging lead in their direction. They had already dismissed him as a threat. The sad part was that Luke agreed. He might clear leather but the speed he had seen from both of them would leave him gasping for life. He understood a little better why so many men were killed by getting shot in the back. It was safer.

"Now, boy, you have to be worried something sick riding around the countryside all by your lonesome." The one calling himself Zeke spoke. His partner nodded vigorously.

"Why's that?"

"We're after this escapee, and the Crossroads town marshal says he's a slippery cayuse."

"Dangerous as a stepped-on prairie rattler, too," added Deke.

The two might be looking to rob him, but all they would get would be his gun and boots. The few coins he had left in his pockets hardly bought a shot of whiskey. And neither of them would think to rip open the gold-dust-laden seams on his coat, as battered as it was. They had already passed judgment on the plow horse, and Luke had to agree. That horse wasn't worth leading to the glue factory.

"I appreciate your concern, fellows, but I haven't seen anyone out here. This escaped convict isn't going to be a bother."

"The posse we ran into not all that far back is looking for any solitary rider." The way Zeke dropped that out, as if it was something about it looking like rain or the sun came up in the east every morning, alerted Luke. These two had a good idea he was the man Benson Wilkes was hunting. He had no idea if the marshal had posted a reward, but even a few dollars interested men like Deke and Zeke. That was especially true since they didn't have to go far or risk much to collect enough money to buy a bottle of whiskey.

"A lone rider, eh?" Luke looked northwest. "I came across a trail of a single rider headed that way." He pointed in the direction Marta Shearing had taken. "I'm not much of a tracker and I hadn't heard about escaped prisoners." He hated the idea of putting these two on Marta's trail, but he began to think any subterfuge saved his life. Deke and Zeke had the look of men who took their quarry in dead. Less fuss and they didn't have to feed a prisoner.

Luke shuddered, thinking a bullet in the head might be preferable to drinking their vile coffee. He doubted either of them rose above the level of poisoner when it came to fixing victuals.

"Do tell." The two exchanged a quick glance. "You think you can find this trail?" They tried to keep eager looks off their faces and failed.

"I don't see why not. It was a single rider leading a spare horse." This caught their attention.

"Two horses?"

"One rider, two horses," he confirmed. "All that meant to me was someone has more money than sense. Or if they can afford two horses to ride like that, they're in a powerful hurry."

Luke fell silent and let the men whisper back and forth. Zeke pointed once in his direction, but the lure of two decent horses to steal rather than a swayback plow horse decided the argument.

"Three of us riding along together'll be more than any escapee would want to tangle with. That is, if you'll throw in with us."

He wanted to find out more about where the bounty hunters had run into the posse. Three men riding along attracted no attention at all from a posse. Not like it would if he rode alone. He patted the horse's neck. Outrunning a posse meant leaving the horse behind and trying to outdistance them on foot.

"For a day or two. That is, if we can split any reward." Luke had no interest in rewards, but he saw that the pair expected such a protest. They haggled a bit, them arguing that their tracking skills deserved more. A final split of 20 percent to Luke and the rest split between them was shaken on. But Luke knew he'd have a bullet in the head if that proved the easier road to take for the bounty hunters.

He mounted and got his horse ambling along. Cutting farther north brought him to a lake. Even he found hoofprints in the muddy shoreline.

"Yup, two horses," Zeke said after examining the tracks. "He watered the horses and rode on not more than a day ago." He stood and scratched himself.

"What's the matter?" Luke saw something was eating Zeke, something more than the fleas that infested his clothing.

"The depth of the prints is all wrong, unless we're chasing about the skinniest man alive. Or a boy. Neither horse shows that it's carrying much weight."

"Makes sense if the spare trots along all fancy-free without a rider," spoke up Deke. "Might be the rider's a boy and not a full-growed man?"

Luke already knew the answer. The rider was a small woman. He resisted the temptation to toss out this tidbit to play one-upmanship with the bounty hunters. The dumber he played, the longer he stayed alive. They knew the escaped prisoner was a man if they'd talked very long with Wilkes or any of his deputies.

He let his horse drink from the lake, ready to pull it away if it showed signs of taking in too much. His heart felt as if someone grabbed it and squeezed hard when he saw a line of riders on the horizon. Zeke had already spotted them and saw his worry.

"That's the posse from town," Zeke said. "They either found a trail or are riding in circles. They're not too far from where we crossed paths with them early this morning."

Nervous, Luke stepped up into the saddle and pulled his hat down to his ears. Then he slumped forward to give the impression of a shorter man riding with the other two.

"We might ride along a spell with them," Deke said. The way he studied Luke when he made the suggestion spoke worlds about the bounty hunters. Deke needled him. They had no more desire to ride with the posse than he did.

"You're within a day of catching up, and you said they're riding in circles. Why do you want to give up your share of any reward? Has there ever been a posse that'd split reward money? The ones with the most guns get the bounty." Luke tried getting his horse to a faster gait. It plodded along at the same rate it had since he had first set astraddle. "How much is the reward, anyway?"

"Twenty-five dollars," Deke said.

"It's fifty, but he's already split it up betwixt the pair of us. Split three ways, how we agreed, uh, that'd be—"

"Ten for me and twenty for each of you," Luke said, doing the ciphering in his head. One of his strengths as a farmer had been figuring out costs and yields. He had been so good at doing sums that Mister Dalton at the mercantile had offered him a job as clerk.

"Wave to them," Zeke said. "They're a friendly bunch." He followed his own advice.

"They're friendly because they each had a pint of whiskey given them before they hit the trail. When the rotgut's gone, mark my words, they won't be as sociable." Deke waved.

Luke joined in to keep from standing out as the only one not greeting the distant posse. He felt the tension flow from him when a couple of the deputies waved back and the entire posse kept on riding. They weren't looking for three men together. They wanted a single rider.

That made him wonder if Wilkes had given up on finding Rollie Rhoades and his gang. The marshal hadn't been too eager to continue the hunt when he had nabbed him and tucked him away in the jail cell. One robber who didn't shoot it out was safer to hunt than a gang willing to blow up a bank because the leader enjoyed the carnage dynamite created.

"Looks like we're on the right track," Deke said after walking back and forth along the lakeshore. "The rider went that way."

Luke tried to see across the lake to where Marta might have ridden. He had to believe she followed the gang's trail using her own skills while he depended on the bounty hunters to find her. Luke wished he had the chance to swap riding with her for being under the thumbs of the two bounty hunters.

They mounted and started around the lake. The two rode ahead, eagerly pointing out signs on the ground that Luke barely saw—or had no idea at all what excited his new partners. When he caught up, he asked.

"We got fresh prints. Not more than six or eight hours old, but there's other tracks. A whole herd of horses from the way the ground's all chopped up." Zeke hesitated, then added, "If I laid a bet on this, the rider we're following is after the herd of riders."

"That means a straggler from the gang that robbed the Crossroads bank is trying to catch up with the rest of his partners." Deke rubbed his palms on his thighs, then tapped his fingers nervously. "If we bring in the whole gang, there's plenty of reward to go around."

Both men might as well have spoken aloud. Luke knew what they really thought. Kill the bank robbers, keep the gold stolen from the Crossroads bank. That amounted to a whole lot more than any reward, even for notorious outlaws. While they might gun down the crooks, take the stolen gold and try to collect a reward for the dead bodies, they'd come under suspicion if they claimed the gold had been lost or already hidden.

Luke knew how good Deke and Zeke were with their six-shooters. But were they good enough to take on the Rhoades gang and best them? He knew how treacherously evil Rhoades and Benedict and the rest were and doubted the bounty hunters had a chance unless it involved back shooting or cutting throats in the middle of the night. Worse, Zeke and Deke had to kill Sarah and Marta, too, if they intended to steal the loot. No witnesses.

That included Luke Hadley.

"Audrey." The name slipped out as his mind raced.

"How's that, old son? You say something?"

"I remarked on how close to sundown it is. We ought to camp for the night and get an early start. If we're within a few hours of finding the single rider, we can spot him by noon."

From the way the two exchanged knowing looks, he anticipated what they'd say. He wasn't disappointed.

"You go on and pitch camp. You got to make better coffee than Deke. We'll just scout a ways ahead to be sure this is a safe place to spend the night."

"Yeah, safe," Zeke said. Luke wanted to play poker with this man. His face told every thought running through his treacherous brain.

He stepped down and stretched. As he pulled off the saddlebags containing what gear he had and the food the farmer had sold him, he said, "I swear, you two better not take long. I'm hungry enough to eat a wolf, growl and all."

"Make up a real good fire. Over there, against that rock so's it is out of sight from farther along the trail." Deke inclined his head to his partner. They wheeled about and trotted off.

Luke forced himself to count to one hundred to give them enough of a head start. Quickly slinging his saddlebags back over the plow horse's rump, he mounted again. Before he followed the bounty hunters, he checked the load in his six-gun. He snapped it shut and tucked it into his holster. He wished he had ammunition for the derringer, too, but if he had a wish to burn, he'd ask for a full troop of cavalry to back him up. Whatever happened, he was on his own.

The trail had grown indistinct, but he caught enough trace of Marta's passage to know she had slowed considerably. If she was a mile ahead, he'd be surprised. While he lacked the sharp tracking skills of Zeke and Deke, he had learned a great deal since setting out on Benedict's trail.

As he rode, finally glad the horse picked its way so carefully, not making much sound as it walked, he worried that any gunfire would alert Rhoades and his men. From all the times he had looked along their back trail, the posse was nowhere to be seen. Since leaving the lake, he and the bounty hunters had traveled more than five miles. Even if the posse heard the gunfire, a hard gallop meant they were an hour away unless they killed their horses.

The twilight made the going even more hazardous. Keeping his eyes peeled for the two gunmen ahead, he kept heading in the direction they had ridden. Any chance of seeing their hoofprints—or Marta's—was gone in the dying light of day.

His heart leaped into his throat when he heard Deke drawl, "All righty, little lady, you just keep that hand off your iron."

"My partner's right about that," chimed in Zeke. "It'd be a plumb shame if you did anything stupid and ended up ventilated."

Marta's reply was garbled, but the tone came through loud and clear. She understood what surrendering to the bounty hunters without a fight meant. It would be a long, tortured night for her and eventually they would kill her. Better to shoot it out here and now.

Luke put his heels to the horse's flanks. It kept moving along at the same maddeningly slow gait. A quick exchange of shots echoed back along the trail. He kept raking his heels against the horse's flanks and got a reluctant burst of speed from the animal. It wasn't much but he rounded the rocky prominence and came out on a small pond surrounded by a few cottonwoods. The muzzle flash from ahead showed where Marta made her stand.

But he couldn't find either of the bounty hunters. Unless he did, riding ahead only put him in the cross fire. Ending up dead did nothing to help Marta Shearing or bring any of the Rhoades gang to justice.

Worse, he had no hankering to go knocking on the Pearly Gates. Not yet.

He drew his pistol and looked around. A shadow moving across darkness drew his fire. Whatever he aimed at wasn't human. Twin tongues of flame lanced at him from directions completely unexpected. Luke fell off his horse, which kept on moving at its own pace, leaving him on his back and exposed to hot lead from both the bounty hunters and the Pinkerton agent.

CHAPTER THIRTEEN

LUKE WINCED AS a slug tore past his leg. Another ripped a hunk of leather from his boot. With a powerful kick, he rolled over and kept rolling. Dirt danced in tiny tornadoes around him until he fetched up hard against a fallen, rotted log. This protected him from bullets aimed at him from one direction. He got his bearings and trained his gun on a spot where the muzzle flash momentarily revealed Deke all crouched down and intent on killing something. Three quick shots rewarded him with a yelp. He doubted Deke was seriously wounded, but he had forced him out of the fight for a few seconds.

Flopping onto the other side of the log opened him to attack from where he believed Marta Shearing had taken cover.

"It's me, Miss Shearing. Luke Hadley!"

He propped his gun hand on the log and bided his

time. Patience paid off. Zeke tried to make a dash for where Deke moaned and cursed in pain. Luke emptied his gun. Over the past few months he had developed a sense of when he hit a target and when he missed. The emptiness in his gut warned him he had done nothing more than add wings to Zeke's feet. The bounty hunter reached his partner without paying a penalty in flesh and blood.

Luke broke open the action, ejected the spent cartridges and began reloading.

"Get over here. You're exposed. They've circled!" Marta Shearing's urgent warning carried a hint of fear along with it. He snapped shut the Schofield and started rolling, hands over his head.

Rocks tore at his body and a twig poked into his leg with as much intensity as if he had been knifed. Heeding Marta's warning proved a smart move. Two streams of bullets blasted hunks of the fallen tree into the air. If he'd stayed, at least one round would have found him.

He wiggled and slithered and finally dug his toes into the ground to get some purchase. A mighty lunge carried him forward to land in a grassy patch beside a cottonwood. He located the Pinkerton agent by smell before he saw her.

"That's a mighty fine perfume you're wearing," he said.

She cursed under her breath before saying, "I haven't had time to take a bath. It's the only way I can stand myself when I'm on the trail."

"I can't object." He got his feet under him and crouched on the other side of the rugged tree trunk. She fired now and then. He gauged the direction, moved closer to her and added his fire to hers.

"Stop shooting," she said testily. "Unless you've got a box of ammo in your coat pocket."

"All I have is in my gun belt." He ran his fingers along the tiny cases and made a quick estimate. "A dozen rounds, plus what I have in my pistol." He remembered he hadn't reloaded fully. "Fifteen shots. That's all I have."

"Do you have a rifle?"

He shook his head, then realized she couldn't see him too well.

"My six-shooter is all I have."

"Do you have any idea who we're up against? Are they stragglers from Rhoades's gang?"

He quickly explained how Zeke and Deke were bounty hunters intent on stealing the gold from Rhoades—and leaving anyone who got in their way stretched out on the prairie as buzzard bait.

"You rode with them?" Astonishment filled her words. "Why'd you do a stupid thing like that? You had to know they were going to kill you, too."

"I needed their tracking skills. You didn't leave much of a trail."

"It rained a couple times. That slowed me down finding the gang." She slid back behind the cottonwood and reloaded. "So you expect me to believe you used them?"

"Something like that. I knew when they told me to pitch camp they'd found you."

"So you blundered into the middle of a gunfight to save me?"

"You don't have to be so sarcastic. It looks as if I *have* come to your aid." He got off a couple shots where he saw a shadow move. From the way the bushes moved, he had been decoyed into wasting the rounds. Whatever else he thought of the two men out there, they were cunning and vicious.

"If you had a worry on that score, you should have brought the Crossroads posse along with you."

"I wouldn't want to get you in even deeper trouble."

"Why do you say that?" Marta fired a couple more times, then sank back to let the bounty hunters waste some of their ammunition.

"Who helped me break out of jail by slipping me a derringer? Or have you forgotten that?"

Luke heard her grumble and had to smile, in spite of their predicament. She might have used him just as she had tried with Nelson. Get a crook out and watch where he ran. Only he wasn't one of the gang, and Nelson had been used by Benedict and eventually murdered in a blast that sent blood and body parts sky-high.

"I wish I had a couple sticks of dynamite right now," Luke said.

"Are you letting Rollie Rhoades influence you? Another box or two of cartridges would go better." She chanced a quick look. Neither Deke nor Zeke shot at her. She turned to him. "They're coming around to get us in a cross fire. They think the stream will keep us pinned here so they will attack from each flank."

Luke considered this for a moment, then said, "The way for us to get out is to head that way." He pointed toward where the bounty hunters had initially attacked. If they moved to the right and the left, that meant the center was undefended.

"If I'm wrong, we'll run smack into their guns." Marta looked hard at him. She was mostly cloaked in shadow, but he saw her brown eyes gleaming in the dark.

"Are you wrong?"

"I could be."

"But you don't think so. You're a Pinkerton agent. You know things like this."

"Hold on," she said. "The horses. If we take our horses and get across to theirs, we've got them pinned here."

"Where are they? The horses?"

"Closer to the stream. Cover me."

Before Luke objected, she lit out. He stood and fired off to his right flank, where one bounty hunter might be hiding. The response he produced with his wild shooting warmed him. Zeke cried out in real pain. He had winged the man by shooting at shadows. Luke spun around in a crouch and emptied his six-gun in the other direction. Deke was luckier. He hadn't made it as far around as his partner, causing Luke to guess wrong as to his location.

The thudding of hooves warned him that Marta had fetched the horses. He swung up into the saddle, glad she hadn't taken time to drop the tack to the ground to let the horses rest. Leaning forward, his head near his mare's, he galloped fast and hard to get away. It felt good having a powerful, fleet steed under him again after the plodding draft horse.

Exultation lasted only a few yards. His horse stumbled and fell forward onto its knees, sending him flying over its head. He landed hard. A loud scream while he flew like a bird exhausted the air from his lungs so he wasn't badly stunned when he landed. Every bone in his body ached, but the air hadn't been knocked out of him. He was learning all the tricks needed to keep from taking himself out of a fight. Luke rolled onto his belly and saw that everything had gone wrong with the attempted escape.

His horse had been shot from the rear. The bullet had ripped the length of the horse, killing it instantly. Worse than this, Marta's horse had also been cut out from under her. It screamed and kicked and thrashed about. A back leg had been broken by the bounty hunters' fire.

Luke rose to lay down covering fire for the Pinkerton agent. His hammer fell on empty chambers, one after another as he kept pulling the trigger.

"Run, run!" Marta waved for him to keep going. If they reached the far side of the clearing they could claim the gunmen's horses and strand Deke and Zeke.

"What're you doing?" He almost went to her. She tugged hard to get the saddlebags free from her panicked gelding. "Leave it. There's nothing you got in there worth dying for."

"I told you to run. Decoy their fire!"

Luke realized this was the only course of action left to him. There wasn't time to reload and dying to save Marta Shearing gave him his only possible satisfaction now. Standing and being gunned down served no purpose.

"Here, here I am!" He stood upright and waved his arms, then began dodging. With a lurch to the right, he drew both men's fire. A feint the other way caused them to waste more bullets. But then they figured out his pattern. Twice the sharp, hot bite of lead tore through him. The first grazed his side, leaving a shallow, oozing wound. The other proved more embarrassing than dangerous. It tore a chunk of meat from his left buttock. He stumbled and fell. The wound prevented his legs from moving smoothly—or at all.

He began crawling and found a shallow depression that afforded some cover. Flopping into it, he reloaded his pistol and looked back, praying Marta had eluded the deadly fusillade. She was on her knees halfway to him. He shouted to her, but she ignored him. Leaning forward, she dug like a gopher, throwing dirt into the air.

He had no idea what she hunted for, but he took a couple measured shots past her, hoping to drive the bounty hunters out where he had better targets. The answering orange tongues of flame from their six-shooters were nowhere near where he expected them. He shifted aim but held his fire. Marta was in the way.

"Get down!"

"Get their horses," she ordered. "We can strand them if you get their horses!" She slung the saddlebags over her shoulder and finally ran to join him.

There wasn't room in the shallow earthen bowl for both of them. She dodged and then raced past, shouting, "Cover me!"

He did his best, but his six-gun came up empty too fast. His sense of hitting his target told him he needed more practice. After the first couple times he winged Deke, every shot had been a clean miss.

She dodged and ducked and came back to lie beside Luke. A bump of her hip moved him a little out of the cavity. Neither of them had total protection from the steady rain of lead coming at them. Twisting around, she dumped the saddlebags in front and rested her gun hand on top. Twin holes in the leather showed that the saddlebags had already stopped bullets intended to kill her.

"I'll run to the left and draw their fire. You get to the horses." Luke stared back at his dead horse. It had served him well. Marta's horse still thrashed about, in pain from its shattered back leg. He ran his fingers over the hot barrel of his Schofield, wishing he had one final bullet to put the horse out of its misery.

"You'd shoot the horse instead of saving yourself?"

He looked at her and nodded.

"I'd rather plug those owlhoots." She scooted forward and pressed against the saddlebags, aiming down the barrel of her pistol.

"You looking to tend to your horse?"

"I've got one round left. I ran through my ammunition about the same time you did."

"You don't have more in your saddlebags?" Luke deflated. She had risked her life to retrieve the twin pouches. He expected more from that wild act of bravery.

She didn't answer. Like a statue, she held her position. Her concentration was total and blanked him out of the world. One shot remained. Luke wondered if Deke or Zeke would be on the receiving end.

Even in his nightmares, he had never expected his life to end this way in a wild shootout. Luke decided it could be worse, but great regret weighed him down. Rhoades and his gang deserved nooses around their necks for all they had done, during the war and after. Sarah Youngblood might be crazy as a loon, but she didn't deserve her fate at the hands of the outlaws.

And his biggest regret came from not facing Crazy

Water Benedict. The man deserved personal justice, not that meted out by some judge and an executioner. Luke wanted to see the man's face as he shot him down. It wouldn't be a killing like Benedict had expected at the wedding ceremony. His last thought would be seeing Luke Hadley pulling the trigger and thinking he had made the mistake of his life trying to kill a helpless groom and kidnap the bride.

"You have any ammo left at all?"

Luke checked a final time. He came up dry.

"If we both make a break, that'll force them to divide their fire," he said.

"They've had plenty of time to get the range. And from the way you're bleeding, how fast can you run?"

Luke winced as he touched his buttocks. The grazing wound on his side burned like fire but wasn't too serious. Trying to run was out of the question. With half his ham all shot up, walking proved chancy. Blood already caked his pants and made movement painful.

"I'm not going anywhere. You save yourself."

"Do you have a death wish?" She scowled. "Never give up. Ever. There's always hope."

"You expect the pair of them to come at us single file so you can drill both of them with one shot?"

She laughed, and it was an ugly sound.

"Something like that. Yeah, exactly like that." She pressed forward even more and held her six-gun with both hands to steady it. When she cocked it, Luke peered over the lip of dirt to see what the bounty hunters were up to.

Deke waved a bandanna and called, "A truce! We want to parley."

"Say what's on your mind." Marta tensed even more.

Deke stepped out, still waving his red-and-white truce flag. Zeke joined his partner. They exchanged a quick whisper, then walked slowly forward.

"There's no call for us to waste bullets on each other," Deke called. He shifted the truce flag to his left hand.

"He's getting ready to go for his piece when he gets close enough to see us. So's Zeke." Luke felt empty inside. The end of the trail had come too soon for him. He glanced at Marta. For the Pinkerton agent, too. The bounty hunters had figured out they had to make a move now, dangerous as it was, or they'd lose their horses.

Luke looked around for a rock to throw. That was as close to retaliation as he could get. Zeke and Deke would walk right up and gun them down. He wished Marta used this slow advance to get away while it was still possible. If the gunmen got much closer, they'd have a clear field of fire.

"I know," she said. "Wait. Keep down and wait."

Luke called out, "Do the right thing and put the horse out of its agony. You shot it, you should put it down."

The men exchanged another quick whisper.

"I'm not wasting my ammunition. It's your horse. We'll let you come out so you can do the right thing. Or are you out of ammunition? You trying to make us run out, too?" Zeke took a couple steps closer.

"They've guessed we don't have any way of stopping them," Marta said. "I've got one shot. One shot." She muttered over and over that she had one shot. Luke had no idea how winging one of the bounty hunters helped them. The remaining one would rush them.

He saw he had been right about Deke being wounded, but compared with the hole in his own butt, the other man was unscathed.

"This is it. Get ready," Marta said softly. She settled down and called, "You two no-accounts. Don't come any closer. You stop right there! I'm warning you!"

Deke and Zeke looked at each other, grinned, tossed aside the bandanna, drew their guns and started toward their victims.

Luke wondered at Marta. She counted backward from five. When she got to one, she pulled the trigger.

The report made Luke cringe. The explosion that came almost instantly after deafened him. A shower of dirt and rock cascaded down over him, blinding him. He sucked in a mouthful of dust and choked. Through ringing ears he heard Marta shout, "Get 'em now. It's our only chance."

She swarmed over the saddlebags she had used as a bulwark. Luke tried to follow as she ran hard toward the crater dug in the ground by the explosion, but his leg refused to work right. He began dragging it behind him, using both hands to pull it forward. Pain shot the length of his leg, but he ignored it to keep moving after Marta.

He came to the edge of a shallow crater. At one side lay her dead horse, put out of its pain by the explosion. He hobbled forward through the settling dust and bumped into the Pinkerton agent. She shoved something into his hands.

He fumbled and almost dropped a pair of six-shooters.

It took a few seconds to realize she had stripped the guns from Deke and Zeke. Luke held one in each hand, then limped forward to where the men lay sprawled on their backs, staring up into the sky. They moaned and thrashed about weakly.

Luke trained the six-guns on their former owners.

"Don't move, either of you. Nothing'd give me more pleasure than to shoot you."

Marta worked to relieve them of their gun belts and the bullets carried there. She performed a quick search and tossed aside a couple knives. Only when she assured herself they were stripped of weapons did she step back.

"I've got handcuffs in my saddlebags. Keep them covered, Mister Hadley."

Luke felt giddy. Whether it came from the sudden reversal of fortune or the loss of blood hardly mattered. He was strong enough to pull the triggers if either man moved a muscle. It might have been an hour or only a minute but Marta Shearing returned with her shackles. The sharp metal click as she fastened them brought Luke back from wherever he'd drifted to.

"Let me have this one." She tugged harder to get him to release the pistol he held in his left hand. He finally relented. She whispered in his ear, "You go on over to the stream. I'll get you patched up as soon as I secure these two, so they don't go running away."

He nodded. He understood her but other concerns bubbled up that seemed more important.

"What blew up? What—?"

"I had a couple sticks of dynamite and used my last bullet to detonate it. Now go. To the stream. Get those jeans off."

"Been a while since a woman said that to me."

Luke wondered why she laughed. He hadn't realized he was joking. Dragging his gimpy leg behind, he started hobbling toward the gentle sounds of a running stream. Not even sitting in the icy water brought him back to full consciousness, but feeling the woman's fingers fumbling to undress him came close.

CHAPTER FOURTEEN

A BUG TRYING TO crawl up his nose woke Luke. He batted at it, missed, then sneezed. That sent the offending insect sailing. He wiped his nose off on his sleeve. Then memories flooded him. He sat up and immediately regretted it. All his weight pressed down on his rear end. Pain shot through his loins and up into his side.

"Stay flat. You must hurt all over."

"Felt worse," he said, and he had. Collecting shrapnel in the chest had been bad, but having Crazy Water Benedict try to murder him had been worse.

Now there was pain, but not the horrific view of a man destroying a future.

Luke eased onto his right side and stared at Marta Shearing. She went about fixing a meal. It didn't smell like much, but Luke's grumbling belly wasn't in the mood for fancy food with French names he couldn't pronounce. Anything he kept down would be the best meal ever.

She sat on a low rock, giving him a view of her profile. She wasn't the loveliest woman he'd ever seen. That had to be Audrey, but Marta was far from ugly. He saw a few scars on her right cheek. She turned to face him and he saw the tiny pink lines that showed up on both cheeks.

"Knives," she said, answering his unspoken question. "I get into knife fights a lot."

He shook his head.

"The scars are from something else."

She took a deep breath, her breasts rising and falling under her blouse and the tan duster she wore open in the front. She dished out some of the stew she'd been poking at and brought it to him. He started to use his fingers to eat but she stopped him. Fishing around in her gear, she found a spoon.

"Thanks." He took a deep whiff. "Smells good."

"It'll go down better with a couple of these." She popped a pair of biscuits from a pan and dropped them on his plate. He gobbled down the food as if he hadn't eaten in a month of Sundays.

When she handed him a second helping, she said, "It was my first case working for Allan. Allan Pinkerton. And yes, I know him, I've worked with him personally on more than one case. And yes, he's a master of disguises. He taught me how to fade from sight without trying. When I put on a real disguise, I become someone entirely different."

"It's hard to add height to a disguise." He watched

her reaction over the top of his plate. He pushed what remained of his second biscuit to mop up the juice. She silently took the plate and refilled it.

"You're right. You've got a good eye."

"How's that?" He stopped shoveling the food in. His belly began to ache from too much food too soon rather than the quality. It felt good aching somewhere other than in his butt or side.

"It's hard to look taller, but I know ways. And you're right. The scars aren't from knife fights. My first case didn't go well. A counterfeiter caught me and tortured me to find out what Allan knew about the operation."

"You kept quiet, right?"

"I sang like a canary. He used a heated nail to mark up my face. I held out for almost an hour. It seemed like a century. But I told him everything he wanted to know." She smiled crookedly. "It turned out Allan expected me to spill the beans and had set a trap. The counterfeiter fell into it and the Secret Service caught him and stopped the flood of phony money throughout Chicago."

"So you helped catch the crook."

Marta laughed at this.

"For a man on a mission to exact vengeance, you are an optimistic cuss. I suppose you could say I helped catch the counterfeiter. All it did was extend my apprenticeship for another six months."

"How long have you worked for Pinkerton?" He pushed himself up and found a way to sit that didn't make him dizzy with pain.

"Four years now. I wanted to be a schoolteacher, but this suits me better. When I level a gun, I can use it. Killing a schoolroom full of misbehaving kids, as gratifying as that would be when they acted up, is frowned on in most places. Shooting a bank robber or killer wins approval of a job well done."

"And a reward."

"Pinkerton doesn't accept rewards for its agents. That's all right. I get paid well. And I get to shoot outlaws."

Luke pulled himself upright and looked around. His hand went to the pistol resting on the ground beside him.

"Don't get your dander up. Zeke and Deke are chained securely."

For the first time Luke noticed his pants were different. Momentarily panicked, he hunted for his coat with the gold dust sewn into the piping. He grabbed it from where it had been thrown over a log and pulled it to him. Quick strokes along the sides assured him the gold dust that financed his hunt for Audrey hadn't been touched.

"You might toss away that coat of yours. It's worse for wear and tear. As hard as it is to believe, Deke had a better one. I reckon bounty hunters have to present themselves as successful."

Luke laughed. Both men had been on the trail too long and had not bothered bathing. Telling what color their coats were under the heavy layers of dust challenged the eye of even the best artist.

"How much money did they have on them?"

"Not much. You claiming it as your due for getting shot?" Marta scrounged through her saddlebags and pulled out a leather pouch. "There's close to ten dollars here."

"You ought to keep it as your doctoring fee. You patched me up real good."

"I ought to keep it because I had to get your jeans off you."

"I can see that would be a chore." He tried not to blush thinking about it. Sometimes it was better to be unconscious. Then he started to consider what it would be like if he hadn't been shot and she . . .

"It was quite an undertaking, the way the blood caked onto the cloth and glued it to your flesh. I looked for a fillet knife, thinking to skin you. It was easier letting you soak in the stream until the dried blood washed away." The smirk on her face irritated him.

"I'm not used to such treatment."

"Don't you have any sisters? I've got four younger brothers. When Ma got the grippe I had to ride herd on them. The oldest was ten." She turned pensive. "Ma died. Pa remarried a year later, but by then I was the woman my brothers looked to for everything."

"That was a burden, but I'm sure you did it well."

"Are you being sarcastic?"

"Not at all! I can't see you doing anything you're not good at."

She snorted and shook her head.

"You don't know me or you wouldn't say that. And it looks as if I don't mean getting caught and tortured to spill my guts was a learning experience." She looked mad at herself for revealing even that small detail about herself.

"Sorry. I promise never to bring it up or tell anyone. My lips are sealed." Luke worked his way to standing, using the cottonwood for support. He took a tentative step. White pain flashed through him like he'd been hit by lightning. The second step wasn't as bad. In a few minutes he found the right gait to keep the agony at a minimum. He wasn't going to run any footraces but walking no longer stymied him.

While he practiced walking, she cleaned the plates in the stream and packed away the gear.

"You up to riding? We've got both their horses and the one you rode in on." She snorted again. This time it told him she thought little of the plow horse. He took offense at her attitude.

"It got me here, and it's the best choice for me getting on. It's got a steady gait and is gentle."

"You're not giving up on finding the bank robbers? I need to know what's driving you so hard to get Rhoades."

"And Crazy Water Benedict." Luke haltingly related his wedding day and how he felt in his gut that Audrey was still alive.

"You're just saying that to give yourself a reason to find the gang. You want to kill Benedict and Rhoades. If you're honest with yourself, you know they wouldn't have kept your wife alive all these months. Considering the moral character of the gents in that gang, she's better off dead."

"She's alive. I know it."

"Do you believe in Pecos Bill, too? And Paul Bunyon's big blue ox?"

Anger filled him. He began gathering his gear. Strapping on his six-shooter proved uncomfortable until he twisted it around so it rode a bit in front. He rested his hand on his left buttock. Marta had done a good job sewing him up, but riding would be the next challenge.

"Did you take all their clothes?"

"Deke and Zeke? I stripped them down to their long johns and tied them to a tree a dozen yards in that direction." She pointed back toward the clearing where the shallow crater stretched as a reminder of the deadly fight there. "They'll get free eventually, but without horses and boots they won't travel too fast. Why do you ask?"

He showed her by putting on a second pair of jeans. The added padding helped. Folding a shirt and putting it between him and the saddle acted like a thin pillow. Every move came slowly, but he didn't cry out in pain. He was ready to get back on the trail of the robbers.

"I've got two horses and can travel like the wind," she said. Marta brushed her brown hair back and trapped it under her floppy-brimmed hat. With a jump, she got up into the saddle. "You just head in some other direction and let me bring Rhoades to justice. I know you've got a bur under your saddle, and with good reason, but you're in no condition to fight it out."

"You thought I wasn't in any condition before I got shot. It doesn't matter what you think." Luke slid his boot in the stirrup, tested the muscles needed to mount and found them lacking. He gripped the saddle horn and pulled himself up, hardly using the muscles in his left side. Settling down, he vowed to keep pace with Marta Shearing, no matter what it cost him. He felt fine now but a few miles on horseback changed that, even when he wasn't all shot up.

"Real Pinkerton agents are trained. Because you had a fake badge in no way qualifies you to chase down men as vicious as Rollie Rhoades."

Reflexively, he put his hand in his pocket. His fingers traced over the tin badge there. Marta hadn't noticed it when she took off his coat to tend his wounds. She might be right that it was bogus, but it made him feel as if he was on the right side of the law. After the wedding massacre, he had felt lower than a snake's belly and unable to cope with simply living. During his recovery, he had read a few dime novels about Allan Pinkerton's exploits and how everyone looked up to him. Carrying a Pinkerton badge was just the thing to bolster his own confidence and open doors to information people normally wouldn't give up to a stranger. So far, the fake tin star had worked its special magic for him. That was something she couldn't understand because she was a real agent, trained and ordered by her boss to bring in the gang leader.

He took his hand out of his pocket and settled the reins in his left hand. The horse refused to budge. Gingerly, he tapped his heels into the plow horse's flanks. It looked back at him. The way its ears flicked caused him to sit straighter and use his own senses.

"Riders," he said. "The horse felt the hoofbeats through the ground, but I hear them coming."

"They're not riding fast. That means they're following our trail—or yours and the bounty hunters'. Come on."

"What about Deke and Zeke?"

"They'll talk their way out of anything Marshal Wilkes throws their way. If they don't, then good riddance. They're both scoundrels." She snapped the reins and set off at a brisk walk.

Luke was hard-pressed to keep up with her. They splashed into the stream and followed it for a quarter mile until the sounds of the posse finding the two bound men behind them echoed over the rush of water. Marta urged her horses up a steep slope and onto a level area. Luke followed with more difficulty. When he came to a halt beside her, his heart sank. Rolling hills gave way to prairie.

"You can see four or five miles from horseback," she said. "We need to put that much distance between us and the posse."

"Why are you running? I'm the one they want. I'm the escaped prisoner."

"Don't play that song again. Stop being so noble and offering yourself up as a sacrifice. They'll know who they're after when the bounty hunters tell them we stole their horses. They might even figure everything Deke and Zeke say about the gunfight is the truth."

"That reminds me," Luke said. "How'd you come by the dynamite?"

"If Rhoades enjoys blowing things up, I thought fighting fire with fire—or dynamite with dynamite—was a possibility. I forgot that you needed blasting caps to set off the sticks."

"A bullet works just as well," Luke said. He admired her resourcefulness, especially since it had saved them. But the brief respite from being in a gunfight had to be used wisely. They had to keep away from the law.

"What are you doing?"

Marta Shearing dismounted and pulled up several clumps of Canada bluegrass by the roots. Tying them into a large bundle at the end of her rope, she mounted and motioned for him to precede her. He saw right away what she intended.

"Will that erase our tracks?"

"Not if they have a good tracker." She snorted. "Maybe not if they have a lousy frontiersman, but we have to try. Ride fast. Three miles, maybe four, and try to follow the contours of the land."

He gave the horse its head and rode half turned in the saddle. It took only a few minutes before pain jabbed him in the side, then worked down the length of his left leg. The whole time he saw nothing in the heat haze behind them. Marta worked to keep the grass bundle directly behind her horse for the best effect. Even from his position, Luke saw it wasn't working well enough to fool anyone.

"Clouds are gathering," he said, "for a late afternoon shower."

"That might save us. Head northwest."

"The direction the gang took when they changed horses."

He strained his eyes hunting for any spoor left by the fleeing robbers. All he saw were timid creatures peering out of their burrows and more aggressive predators coming out for an early supper. The gentle rise and fall of the land became more pronounced the longer they rode. He began seeking out the hillocks to give some small protection from pursuers' eyes.

"We might be running for no reason if they decided not to chase after us."

"Think about that, Mister Hadley. Deke and Zeke will make us out to be the worst of the gang, just to get even with us. The marshal might even get a decent description of you and know you were the one who broke out of his jail."

"What are the chances they described you well enough for him to identify you as the woman who gave me the derringer?" He touched his pocket. The empty two-shot pistol weighed him down. Marta saw him press his fingers against the pistol in his vest pocket.

"There's a cartridge or two for that gun in Deke's gear. When we make camp, I'll give you a couple shells."

"We have to keep riding. Put as much distance between us and the posse."

Luke rambled on, only vaguely realizing how close to exhaustion he came. After a few minutes he realized they were retracing their trail, heading back toward the posse. He protested.

"Let me worry about it, Mister Hadley. You work to keep from falling out of the saddle."

"Oh, you're confusing them. Doubling back to make them unsure where we've gone." He swatted at a fly. His hand came away wet. Holding it up as if beseeching the heavens, he hunted for the spot of bug juice. Or blood. Only water trickled down his palm. He pushed his hat back and looked into the sky. He recoiled when a raindrop hit him smack dab in the eye.

"Ride faster," she urged. "The storm will erase our tracks." She cut loose the bouquet of weeds she'd been dragging behind to mask their trail. When he didn't respond, she reached over and grabbed the reins of his plow horse.

Luke clung to the saddle horn. The world spun around him as the horse plodded along. Rain began fitfully, then picked up determination to soak him to the bone. In the back of his mind he rejoiced. They changed direction again. If the posse rode ahead, thinking they weren't deviating from a straight line, they'd miss them entirely.

"Get down. Don't fall. I'm not strong enough to carry you."

"You did back there." He gestured vaguely. "From the stream when you patched me up. You got me out of the water."

She laughed at him.

"You may not remember it, but you did most of the walking. I just nudged you in the right direction. Dismount here. We're going to camp."

Rocks. He saw rocks suddenly illuminated by a vivid flash of lightning. There wasn't much shelter, but with the wind kicking up and blowing harder, the rain slanted in. The rocks gave some protection. He leaned forward and slithered from the saddle. Hanging on to the plow horse kept him from collapsing.

"No fire, not in this rain. There's no dry wood out here anyway, and I'm not going to hunt for buffalo chips."

"Cow chips," he mumbled. She looked at him quizzically. He pointed. "Somebody drove a herd of cattle past here."

"Even half-dead, you've got a good eye. Sit. Pull your slicker around you."

He did as he was told. She tended the horses, hobbling them so they wouldn't bolt and run as thunder rolled across the prairie. He drew up his legs and bent over them. The slicker created a tent that kept him only a little drier than being out in the storm. He snapped alert when Marta pushed up the edge of his slicker and joined him. Their bodies generated more heat together than either separately.

"Does this mean we're partners?" He had no idea

why he asked. Luke didn't expect an answer, but he got one.

Marta Shearing snuggled closer, held the edge of his slicker and rested her head on his shoulder. The last thought flitting across his mind as he slipped into a half sleep, half coma was this would be the closest answer to his question that she was likely to give. And that was just fine with him.

CHAPTER FIFTEEN

WHEN MARTA SHEARING moved away from him, he reached out to keep the slicker from falling off his head. Luke came immediately awake when he realized the sun was up and shining brightly. The rainstorm had passed, leaving the air fragrant with prairie and the sky scrubbed of even the wispiest of clouds. He tried to stretch and regretted it. Aches froze his joints. Sleeping all doubled up with Marta beside him through the night froze his knees and elbows into place.

"Move slower," came Marta's advice. "Are you hungry? I hope not."

He moaned softly as he worked his legs straight on the wet ground in front of him. He yawned, stretched his arms and began working shoulders and other joints around. In spite of sleeping in an awkward position in the cold rain, he felt better and moved better. Using the rock that had provided a bit of shelter from the rain, he edged upward until he stood on shaky legs. Walking around, he gained strength.

"Your butt still hurts, doesn't it?"

He nodded. There was no need to answer such an obvious question. For whatever reason, she tried to irritate him. Then everything clicked in his head.

"Are we partners? Tell me."

"No!"

Her quick, vehement denial told him she found the notion unsettling—and yet she wasn't quite able to simply ride away, leaving him behind. She had two sturdy horses. Trying to keep up with her on his plow horse was the kind of thing he read in the penny dreadfuls. All heroism and strutting about and utterly impossible feats. More important than having faster horses, she had better tracking skills. In spite of the rush and crude techniques, he thought her attempt the day before to hide their hoofprints from the posse using dragged vegetation would have worked.

"Why no breakfast? Didn't Deke and Zeke pack any victuals?" He paced now, testing the limits of his sore body.

"We have to hit the trail ahead of the posse, if they kept coming this way. There's no way they can find our spoor after the rain, but I've never counted on good luck and always assumed others do. It's kept me alive." She hesitated, then added, "And those others? Some of them aren't alive."

He thought she tried to scare him off with hints of men she had killed and desperate situations she had survived. If it came down to matching story for story, his was more dire. All she wanted to do was make him quit his hunt so she could go after Rhoades on her own terms.

She worked to get their gear assembled. Catching at the yellow slicker, she tossed it to him. Watching her closely, he rolled it up and fastened it at the rear of his saddle. Testing the extent of his healing, he bent and hefted the saddle. Momentary giddiness passed. He slung it up over the plow horse and cinched it down. He was ready to ride.

"Where do we go?"

"We?"

"We're in this together. You can't leave me behind. What if the posse caught up with me?"

"You'd set those hounds on me when I'm the one best able to arrest Rhoades?"

"I want more than that from him and the gang. From Benedict." His hand twitched and moved involuntarily toward his six-gun. She squared off, as if she thought he was going to throw down on her. They both relaxed.

"I know. You told me about Audrey." She cinched the belly strap on her horse a little tighter to secure the saddle and mounted. Looking down on him, she said, "Well? Are you coming or not?"

Her attitude irked him, but he needed her. From the way she acted, she needed him, too. Separately, they would have been shot up and left for the coyotes by the bounty hunters. Together, they had escaped. That partnership went further when they came up against an entire gang like the one led by Rhoades.

"How do you know where to go?"

"I'm making a calculated guess. Do you have any better idea?" She looked hard at him.

"Those rolling hills yonder? See them? They showed up on Marshal Hargrove's map. He had marked them with a circle and maybe an X as if he figured they'd make a good hideout for a gang on the run."

"If he's leading the posse, he'll make a beeline for them, then. We should, too." She waited for him to object.

"Hargrove's back in Preston. I doubt he gave Marshal Wilkes a copy of the map. Even if he did, what're the odds Wilkes will believe in such guesswork by another lawman? He struck me as hardheaded and too sure of his own abilities."

"I read him the same way," Marta said, nodding slowly. She lifted her gaze and tapped her horse's flanks to get it moving. From her attitude she really didn't care if Luke came along.

Luke settled down in the saddle. He used the spare shirt as a pad beneath him. Riding felt more comfortable today than it had yesterday. Getting the horse moving at its one gait, he started for the distant hills. Oak and walnut trees dotted the landscape, but this region was less hilly and more prairie, where grasses predominated. They rode through hock-high vegetation. With so much rain, the grass would be shoulder-high in a couple weeks. Making their way through grasses like this left a trail.

He stood in the stirrups and scanned the countryside, hunting for the route taken by the outlaws. The rain had caused the grass to spring back up. If the rain hid their trail from the posse, it also disguised the outlaws' from them. He felt desolate at seeing no distinct direction to explore, but he hadn't counted on Marta's skill. Less than an hour riding, she veered from the direct route into the hills and worked her way down into a muddy wash.

"We can get caught by a flash flood in the gully," he

said. "The sides are steep and will crumble if we try to climb back."

"There," she said, pointing. "Do you see it? Up against the bank? A couple old firepits. The rain didn't wash them away."

"So they were built after the rain stopped. I don't know when that was last night."

"You snore," she said. "So much noise from that honker of yours drowned out the sound of the rain. It stopped after midnight." She rode back and forth, studying the ground. It had started to dry out already in the morning sun. "Several riders came this way, made camp for a few hours, then moved on well after midnight—recently. You can see faint outlines that were made after the rain stopped and the ground began to firm up. From the look of the campfires, they can't be more than a few hours ahead of us."

Luke considered this and how long he and Marta had taken reaching this point. Rhoades should have been a couple days ahead of them by now.

"He waited for Crazy Water Benedict to join him," Luke said, working through the logic of the situation. "They had an agreed-upon rendezvous. Benedict tried to divert the posse. He must have failed since the posse is likely hot on this trail."

"For a robbery that big, and blowing up the bank so only a few cracked bricks remained, the marshal would send out more than one posse." She nodded to herself as she worked over other reasons.

He added one she might ignore.

"Having a prisoner bust out of his jail in the way I did must have made Wilkes hot to recapture me and corral the bank robbers."

"To his way of thinking, you're one of them. Catch you, catch one of the gang. Rhoades can't like it that you helped stir up that hornet's nest. Wilkes has to be spitting mad. Definitely more than one posse out hunting for the fugitives, you included." She swiveled around to face him and after a brief thought on the matter said, "This ravine leads to their camp. It starts in the hills. The outlaws follow it this time of year, and any rain wipes out their tracks. There's no need to see the hills for a landmark if it's stormy or it's nighttime. Just stay between the banks. They wouldn't even need a compass."

He had nothing to add to her logic. She understood how crooks' minds worked better than he did. Riding in a gully prone to flash flooding struck him as dangerous, but Rhoades willingly took the chance. Such a tactic had to have worked for him in the past, just as using stolen horses to add distance between the robbery and their hideout had been successful.

"The posse isn't likely to get down into the gully, either," she went on. "The risk Rhoades takes getting washed away is less than being spotted by the law, if they got this close."

Luke rode with his right knee brushing the bank, warily looking deeper into the sprawling Flint Hills for any sign of a storm ahead. Water pouring across the sloping hills there filled up a ravine miles away, even if there weren't clouds directly above. He glanced up and appreciated the pure azure dome.

"They'll have sentries out watching for pursuit," he said. He wanted to bull right in. Waiting for nighttime to mask their approach meant a half day wasted. Still, if he truly believed Audrey was captive in the outlaws' camp, a few more hours to ensure her safety was minor, but logic be damned. He still wanted to *do* something. Blazing guns and falling robbers and dead kidnappers meant he had accomplished something.

"Whoa. Hold up." Marta held up a hand to stop him. That was a good thing since he wasn't listening to her, lost deep in thought about how best to attack.

He looked to the heights on the left side of the ravine and caught his breath. Her keen eyes had spotted the faint curl of white smoke rising straight into the calm air. A hidden guard sat there, smoking. He betrayed his position as surely as if there had been a breeze sending the scent of tobacco downwind.

Marta wheeled about and pressed close. Faces only inches apart, she whispered, "We won't get past him if we stay in this ditch. Follow me."

She led the way a quarter mile back the way they'd come to a break in the bank. Her horse scrambled up amid a cloud of dirt and mud and stones. Luke's plow horse lacked such agility. He got off and led the animal to the top of the bank. Simply walking caused new aches to bedevil him, but the pain had disappeared. Discomfort he withstood. Being so close to finding the bank robbers' hideout made this bearable.

"We skirt the sentry and head into the hills. Their hideout can't be too far off. Are you up for it?" She studied him for any reaction that put her life at risk. Capturing even one of the outlaws posed a real danger. Going after Rollie Rhoades was worse. But Luke had Crazy Water Benedict in his sights. She deserved the accolades Allan Pinkerton would heap on her for a successful job. Getting Audrey back was all he wanted.

"You go first," Luke said. "I'll come along at my

own speed." He patted his horse's neck and was rewarded with a big brown eye winking in his direction.

"The guard's finished his smoke. Chances are good he will take a siesta. Quiet." She put her finger to her lips to caution him. Marta turned back and judged the direction, the small valley in the foothills and how to approach it. A quick snap of her reins sent her horse forward.

Luke started to call out to her, then clamped his mouth shut. She left one horse behind. There wasn't any reason to take a spare. The bounty hunter's horse was stronger, quicker and broken for riding. He patted his plow horse's neck again.

"I'm sticking with you, partner. We got this far together. Let's go the rest of the way."

He made sure the spare horse was secured to a sturdy bush. Leaving it behind struck him as wrong. Audrey might ride out on it. When he played all the possible problems in his rescue, he knew the horse was better left here. With a quick tap of his heels, he started the plow horse walking. His body ached more than it had earlier, but he knew tension built and caused his muscles to knot in anticipation.

Marta had a few minutes' head start. He followed her tracks for five minutes, then cut away to make an even wider approach to the shallow valley. The horse plodded along, making enough noise to raise the dead. Luke sucked in a deep breath and let it out slowly. The clop-clop wasn't that loud. He was keyed up.

He almost jumped out of his skin when he heard voices to his right, from the direction of the ravine.

". . . reach for the sky, little lady. I'd hate to plug you, you bein' such a purty filly."

Luke leaned in the saddle and used his legs to steer the horse while he drew his Schofield. Marta answered, but her reply came muffled. The sentry had been more alert than she'd expected, or there might have been another man on guard duty. Luke got ready for either problem. When he came within a few dozen yards he dropped to the ground and weighed his horse's reins down with a rock. A simple toss of the head freed the horse, but for the moment it contented itself with munching at some succulent grass.

Marta's horse reared and pawed at the air. He saw only the top of Marta's head. She stood to one side, hands raised as she'd been ordered. Rather than rushing forward, Luke cut toward the ravine at an angle. Every word came clearly now. Unless a second sentry remained mute, only one had caught the Pinkerton agent as she tried to ride past. Luke came to the brink of the gully and went along it so the sentry's back was exposed. The outlaw was too engrossed in taunting Marta to notice she had a rescuer on the way.

"Look, we know what happens to women who get caught by the Rhoades gang," she said. "I don't mind one . . . man. Especially if he's as handsome as you are. But the five others?"

"Seven others," the sentry said. He puffed up and his gun wavered from its target. "You think I'm handsome? Of course you do. All the women do. I got them lined up around the whorehouse to just meet me, much less—"

Luke crept forward, intent on swinging his pistol and landing it on the side of the outlaw's head. If the sentry paid no attention to anything but Marta, Luke similarly made the mistake of being single-minded. He never noticed his shadow stretching out in front of the outlaw—and spooking Marta's horse.

The horse jerked away, pulling her off balance. The sentry glanced down, saw Luke's shadow in time to throw himself to one side and avoid the worst of the blow intended to knock him out. Shock rippled up Luke's arm as his gun barrel collided with the man's right shoulder. The outlaw dropped to his knees and lost his six-shooter, but he hadn't lost a speck of fight.

Snarling like a wildcat, he twisted around and grabbed with both arms. His right gave way because of the damage Luke had meted out, but his left tackled Luke powerfully enough to force him to the ground. They locked in a wrestling match, rolling over and over. When Luke's gun hand hit a rock, he dropped his six-gun. The two men grappled, grunting and straining to gain the advantage. Luke ended up on his back with the man straddling his waist. Strong hands clamped around his throat and squeezed.

The guard had been injured, but compared to Luke's bullet wounds, he was fully functional.

"Gonna choke the life outta you. Gonna have fun doin' it. You cain't blindside me like that and—"

The rain-softened embankment gave way. Both Luke and the outlaw plunged downward. Startled, Luke jerked to the side. As he turned he broke the grip around his neck. When the pair landed, Luke was on top. One knee crushed into the outlaw's belly and a flying elbow caught him on the side of the head.

The outlaw gave a twitch and then lay still. Luke stared down at him, confounded. One instant he had been having the life choked out of him. The next he won the fight by breaking the man's neck. He pushed up and wiped mud and dirt off himself. Noise above made him whirl around. His hand went for his six-shooter, but the holster hung empty at his side. He peered up into the bore of his own gun.

"Is he done for?" Marta Shearing peered over the edge. "Here. Catch." She dropped his six-gun.

Luke caught it in shaky fingers and stuffed it back into his holster.

"He won't warn the others."

"His death will be noticed when a replacement comes to relieve him. Don't just stand there. Come on!" Marta waved anxiously, urging him to join her. The climb proved more difficult than getting to the bottom of the arroyo. The more Luke climbed, the less energy he had. When he was almost to the top, the woman reached down, grabbed his collar and pulled him the rest of the way.

"Thanks. Climbing up was harder than I expected."

"You ought to stay put. Wait for the owlhoot coming to relieve him and take him out. I'll scout ahead."

Luke considered it. He had started into the gang's hideout feeling strong enough to come out of most fights. His brief wrestling match drained him. As he stuck out his hand, it shook like a leaf in the wind. Aiming with such weakness was dangerous. Hitting anything—anyone—looked to be impossible. But letting Marta risk her life going in alone rankled. Worse, this was his fight. She was a legal agent for a respected detective company, but she only did what she was ordered.

He did what was necessary.

"Getting yourself killed won't help Audrey." Marta fixed him with her stare. Her set jaw warned him not to argue.

He didn't have the vitality to do more than sit cross-legged and look up at her.

"Go on. But just to scout," he ordered. "Get the layout of their camp and come back for me. We'll both go in. I'll be rested up by then."

She glanced up at the sky and nodded.

"It'll be sundown in a couple hours. You get ready. I'll be back then and we'll go in under cover of twilight."

She mounted and set off. Luke watched her until she disappeared down a draw, heading directly into the foothills. He knew a lie when he heard one, and that had been a whopper. She intended to take on Rhoades by herself.

Luke tried to stand, but his legs gave way. He cursed getting shot, cursed being so close and unable to do more, and then he cursed Marta Shearing for being so diligent in doing her job.

CHAPTER SIXTEEN

HE FELT LIKE a ghoul robbing a grave. Luke spread the dead outlaw's belongings out on the ground and picked through them, setting aside anything useful. When he finished his inventory, he dumped what he couldn't use over the embankment to land around the dead man. Staring down for a moment gave him vertigo. He closed his eyes and stepped back from the verge. Weak. He was so weak. And he felt guilty stealing from a dead man.

A dead man who tried to kill you. Luke rubbed his neck. Hot streaks remained where the outlaw had throttled him. It had been a case of self-defense. That made him feel a tad better. Especially when he remembered who the dead man was.

Any of Rhoades's gang he put six feet under—or in this case left for coyotes and buzzards, already circling overhead in the twilight—the fewer he had to fight when he found Audrey. Self-defense or not, kill them. They were murderers, each and every one of them. What chance did a simple farmer have against cold-blooded killers unless he ambushed them and otherwise hoodwinked them? After all, his killing was for a good reason.

Audrey.

He let out a howl of rage. That broke his self-pity. Everything was a flight of fancy until he learned the truth. And he would. He would.

He picked up a box of cartridges and stuffed them in his coat pocket. Then he tucked the outlaw's pistol into his belt. He wished the calibers had matched between his Schofield and the Colt, but carrying a second six-gun increased his firepower. He had heard tell that William Quantrill and his filthy guerrillas rode into a town carrying six or seven loaded six-shooters. That gave them the firepower of an entire company of Federals. Luke pressed his fingers against the shrapnel in his chest. He had been the victim of an explosion. Over the years, knowing Rollie Rhoades's penchant for such things, he imagined the outlaw had set off the explosion as part of a Border Ruffians' raid. It made sense to him. Charles Hamilton, the leader then, had been like Quantrill. He enjoyed watching the frightened faces of his victims as he shot them.

The outlaw had left his horse saddled. Luke tended it the best he could. Moving about helped keep his leg and side from getting stiff. Now and then he felt a little jolt of pain, but ignoring it became easier as it grew darker. The sultry heat remained but direct sunlight no longer tormented him.

When the sun sank entirely behind the hills, he

knew it was time for him to move on. Marta wasn't coming back with her reconnaissance. She had either abandoned him to finish her assignment or been caught. Either way, he was on his own. He slung his fully loaded saddlebags over the plow horse and stepped up. All the moving around had kept him limber enough to ride without pain.

"Let's go, old friend." He patted the horse's neck. The horse tensed under him and began dancing about. A few seconds later he heard what spooked his mount.

The steady hoofbeats coming straight for them might be those of the Pinkerton agent. Relying on his gut, Luke doubted it. Carefully reaching down, he drew his six-shooter and cocked it. If he had time, dismounting and finding a good spot for an ambush made more sense than staying in the saddle. But the rider was almost on top of him.

His instincts proved right when the rider called out, "Where are you, Dutton? I'm here to relieve you. Stop foolin' around."

"Here." Luke hoped the grunt he uttered along with the word hid the difference in voices. The still night air carried sound far too accurately for him to hope to fool the dead man's partner.

"You all right? You sound like you got a frog in your throat."

Luke coughed to carry out the deception. When he heard only the sound of the other man's horse, he knew he had been discovered. Without hesitation, he slid his leg over the saddle and dropped to the ground. He grunted again as the pain swept over him. The now riderless horse neighed and started walking. Not for the first time, Luke appreciated the horse's single-minded gait. If it had taken off at a gallop, the approaching outlaw would have been alerted. The slow pace drew him in.

Luke had to make that unwitting deception work in his favor. He rushed forward, gun leveled at the spot where he expected the rider to appear. When he didn't, Luke ducked and sprinted away.

"Dutton? Dutton? Where'd you get that nag of a horse? And where are you?"

Luke flung himself to the ground. He drew a bead on the outlaw, who snared the plow horse's reins and led it back. For a moment the man sat astride his own horse, outlined against the twilight sky. What might have been an easy shot went unfired. This close to Rhoades's camp, any shot would alert the others. Not only did that put Luke in danger, Marta's scouting would be put into question. Getting her shot because of his own stupidity rankled. He stuffed his six-gun into his holster.

"Dutton?"

The outlaw dropped the reins and rode closer to where his partner had watched the trail along the bottom of the gully.

Toes digging into the ground, Luke rose and rocketed forward. The man wasn't on guard, but his horse reared. Luke launched himself into the air, trying to drag the outlaw from the saddle. His fingers slipped across the man's duster. Between missing a decent handhold and the rearing horse, Luke's attack failed. He crashed into the horse's rump.

Knowing what had to follow, he threw himself to the side in time to avoid the horse landing on its front legs and kicking out with the rear. He had failed to pull the rider down, but the bucking, spinning horse kept its rider occupied with trying to stay in the saddle.

Luke landed hard, rolled and came to his feet. He watched the horse spin around like a top. He jumped and grabbed the rider's leg. As the horse continued to turn, he pulled the outlaw from the saddle. Unfortunately, the man came off the horse and landed atop Luke. For a moment, Luke found himself pinned down and unable to move. The only saving grace was that the outlaw was too shaken to fight.

They rolled over and over. Luke flashed on falling into the gully again as he had done with the sentry. Digging his toes into the soft ground brought him up short. The outlaw kneed him in the stomach and scrambled to his feet. Stunned, Luke lay there gasping for air. With a lurch he got to his feet in time to see the outlaw astride his horse once more. Luke touched his gun, then remembered what catastrophe a single report would cause.

He stumbled along to the sentry's horse and pulled himself up. The plow horse was reliable. It was also slower than a rich man's charity. He bent forward in the saddle and brought the captured horse to a full gallop. Following the other rider in the dark proved easier than he expected. Dust clouds and chunks of flying mud showed the way as surely as if he followed a map.

He overtook the other rider just as he turned through a sparsely wooded area and headed for the gap in the hills leading to what had to be Rhoades's camp. Arm swinging out, Luke caught the other rider on the shoulder. That blow didn't unseat him, but it did make him veer away from the valley. Luke leaned in and his horse responded perfectly. It must have been trained as a cow pony. Using his knees, he steered the horse closer.

Both hands grabbed for the rider. He leaned far out and clamped down on the outlaw's gun hand to keep him from drawing his six-shooter. A huge heave lifted the man from his horse and dumped him to the ground. Luke kept his balance and wheeled around. It was a foolish thing to do but he never thought about it. Arms outstretched, he dived from horseback.

The impact as he hit the outlaw made him see stars. For the outlaw it was worse. His six-gun went flying and he sat heavily.

Luke shook off the shock and started to draw. The other man tackled him, arms circling his legs and lifting. Crashing to the ground in a flailing heap, they swung and kicked and tried to connect with their opponent. Neither had any luck until the outlaw came to his feet. He reached to the top of his boot and yanked out a thick-bladed knife.

"I don't know who you are, but you're gonna spill your guts."

"I'm the man who killed Dutton."

The use of his partner's name confused the outlaw just long enough for Luke to bat away the knife hand and deliver a right cross. He pressed his advantage and wrapped his arms around the other's body. Driving hard, he tripped the outlaw. This time Luke landed on top. But as he swarmed up to keep punching, he saw the other man had given up.

"Better you than me," Luke muttered. As they fell, the outlaw's knife had turned. The weight of Luke's body drove the tip into an exposed heart. Without intending to, Luke had killed another of Rhoades's gang.

He stared at the body. Not a twitch. Not a muscle spasm. The heart thrust had skewered all life in the man and left him a fleshy husk.

"How many men? Marta tricked Dutton into saying seven others. Who was he counting?" No matter how many the gang member considered, one less faced Luke now. Six? Was Rhoades in that number? He thought so. A minor follower and toady included his boss in any count.

Reaching down, he pulled the knife from its grisly berth and wiped it off on the man's vest. A quick search found the sheath inside the boot top. Luke transferred it to his own boot. The more weapons he carried, the quicker he killed the men who had brought such misery to his life. With that thought, he stripped off the dead man's gun belt and slung it over his shoulder. In addition to his own pistol and the knife, he had two captured six-shooters. That gave him eighteen shots before he needed to reload. Facing down six killers, he'd need that firepower and more.

A quick touch to his vest pocket reassured him that he also had the derringer Marta had used to break him out of the Crossroads jail. This time it carried two chambers loaded and ready for use.

"I hope it's not the marshal I need to use it on again." He took a few steps and got his balance before hunting for his horse. It had run off. So had the one ridden by the man lying dead at his feet.

He was lucky to be alive, but he threw his hands up in despair. Going into the enemy camp on foot was loco. As he started back to the spot where he had killed two of the outlaws, he heard a familiar clopping sound. Standing stock-still, he waited. The plow horse came up at its own speed.

Luke snagged the reins and patted the horse on the neck.

"I wish I had a sugar cube for you. Wait." He rummaged through the saddlebags and found a dried apple. "It's not much, but you deserve it for not making me walk."

The horse took its sweet time nibbling at the apple as he held it out in his hand. When the horse finished, Luke stepped up and found stars to guide himself. He let the horse keep its own pace, which was slower than he wanted but gave him plenty of time to listen for any other rider on the trail. Marta was hours overdue, and for some reason the gang hadn't moved on. If he had been Rhoades, packing the hideout's corral with even more horses would have been the smart thing. Relay using the stolen horses to reach this spot, switch a second time and scatter throughout the West.

That they hadn't done this meant the gang felt secure here. Safe from the law.

But they would never be safe from Luke Hadley.

He found a trail mashed down in the grass where several riders had passed recently. A check on the stars confirmed he still headed in the right direction. Dark hills rose slowly around him. This was the place where danger lurked. Posting a sentry back at the gully made sense only if Rhoades expected a posse to approach from that direction. An alert gave him time to retreat deeper into the hills, but a guard on either side of the valley leading into the maze of shallow canyons and wooded areas made sense to catch invaders in a cross fire.

He drew rein and listened rather than stared into the darkness. Then he took slow, deep breaths. No flare of a cigarette or smoke from a careless sentry anywhere. He gave the horse its head and let it set the deliberate pace into the mouth of the canyon. Looking for tracks without using a torch required him to dismount. The pressure of finding what had happened to Marta Shearing wore on him. There hadn't been gunfire, but that meant little. He had been occupied killing outlaws and missing a pitched gun battle wasn't out of the question.

Or she might have ridden smack-dab into an ambush. Having three or four rifles leveled at her convinced even the most stubborn Pinkerton agent to surrender without a fight.

As he rode, he closed his eyes to concentrate on sounds. Only those he expected came to him. Crickets chirped and distant wildlife moved about, finishing dusk meals and returning to burrows—or hunting for the slowest to return to their burrows.

The distant scent of firewood alerted him to the presence of others. He came to a fork in the canyon. Riding to the heights on either side afforded a chance to look down and be sure what he faced, but the woodsmoke wafting down from the left-hand branch now carried a hint of savory stew with it. His mouth watered. Even his horse responded by pulling away from the right valley floor and straining to the left.

He let the horse set the pace again as he drew the pistol carried in the gun belt slung over his shoulder. In less than ten minutes he caught sight of smoke curling upward. The still night allowed it to rise straight to the heavens. Following it back down, he found a small cabin partly hidden by a ring of oak and maple. A window in the side was covered with waxed paper. The door hung crooked on its hinges, letting light ooze out around the frame. Cracks in the walls leaked light that looked like shiny claw marks, in spite of what had to be only a single coal oil lamp inside.

Luke caught his breath when the light flickered in just the way it should if someone moved about inside.

He gripped the pistol more firmly and rode closer. When he got within fifty feet of the cabin, he dismounted. The smart thing to do was circle the cabin and find out how many he faced.

He threw caution to the winds when the door opened and a woman was silhouetted.

"Audrey!"

CHAPTER SEVENTEEN

LUKE HADLEY FORGOT about the aches and pains in his side and leg. His head had been battered about during his hand-to-hand fights and he ignored it all. It had been worth every cut and bullet wound.

"Audrey!" His voice came out a hoarse croak. Emotion choked him.

He ran halfway to the cabin when the woman turned and went back inside. She hadn't seen or heard him. The door closed, once more showing light around the frame and even through the cracked, half-rotted door itself. Before he called out to her more loudly, someone called his name from behind. He skidded to a halt and whipped around, the captured six-gun coming up. Shadows moved.

"Marta? Is that you? I found her! My wife!"

"Don't leave me. Please, Lucas. Don't leave me or I'll have to tell them."

He went cold inside. Sarah Youngblood had been far from his mind. He had forgotten she had been kidnapped by Benedict and the gang.

"Quiet. Don't cause a ruckus."

"Don't leave me. I love you so!"

The shadow shifted and then turned darker as the woman retreated into the woods. Luke heard her sobs as she ran from him. He glanced over his shoulder. Getting Audrey away from here was foremost in his mind, but what chance did he have if Sarah, in her pain of his supposed betrayal, warned the gang? He had no idea how many armed men he faced, but if only Rhoades and Benedict showed themselves, the opposition was formidable and deadly. They had proven themselves to be cold-blooded killers. Defending the gold they had just stolen would add to their viciousness.

Luke didn't fool himself. If Benedict recognized him as the gunned-down bridegroom, he would take extra glee in a shootout.

His plan for rescuing Audrey had been faulty. Worse. He realized it had been nonexistent since deep down he struggled constantly to quell the niggling doubt that she had survived. No matter how he had lied to himself, he always feared she had died horribly at Benedict's hand. And if not him, any of the others riding behind Rollie Rhoades showed plenty of brutality. A single word, a careless glance, not enough fear, those were reasons enough for any of the outlaws to kill her.

He looked into the woods, then back at the cabin. Audrey still moved around inside. There hadn't been any hint of Benedict with her. From everything he saw, she was alone. The gang thought she was safe enough to leave alone and on her own. He looked around the darkened terrain. How close were they? How far? If he didn't stop Sarah right now, she would bring the whole gang down on his and Audrey's heads.

In the distance came Sarah Youngblood's sobs, loud enough to wake the dead. Why did they let her roam freely? Or were they confident enough that both women were bottled up in this camp? That made him even more skittish. Pulling Audrey up behind him on the plow horse hardly made for a speedy escape. Carrying two riders was a snap for the strong horse. But its speed never varied. How long before the rest of the gang missed the owlhoots Luke had killed?

And where was Marta? Had she run afoul of the robbers and was now their prisoner?

Too many questions tore at him. He had to find answers fast or they all might die.

Sarah began keening like a banshee. The normal forest sounds disappeared like mist in the morning sun. As still as the night was, that screech carried for miles. The outlaws had to be deaf not to hear Sarah and come investigate.

A desperate look at the cabin convinced him he had to deal with Sarah before going to Audrey. He had never thought he had woman troubles before the day of his wedding. Since then there hadn't been anything but trouble. While he had never signed on for the job, he now had to secure the safety for three.

He plunged into the darkness, stumbling and trying to keep a sharp eye out for any of the gang. The night cloaked his way too fully. He slowed to better home in on Sarah's mournful cries. Before he reached the top of the hill, she had switched to a song he didn't recognize. This did nothing to ease his concern. She ran free—crazy free. How the outlaws allowed that puzzled him, unless she had escaped. And if she had, everything she did provided a way for them to find her.

At least she hadn't been murdered.

A smile came to his lips. Neither had Audrey.

Almost knocking himself down by colliding with a sapling in the dark, he recoiled and chanced a call to the crazy woman.

"Sarah! Sarah Youngblood! It's me. I've come to take you home. You want to go home, don't you?"

"I waited, Lucas. I waited for you. Now you want *her*. I saw how you were when you saw her! After all I've done, you're leaving me for *her*."

"You're wrong." The words burned Luke's tongue. He lied and wished that the woman believed him. She might be crazy, but she wasn't stupid.

"No, I'm not. You are a bad man, Lucas. Bad! You lied."

"Quiet down. Come here and let's talk. You want to talk, don't you? Make me come back?"

He worried that she might do just that, yet he had no other choice but to capture her. Maybe if he hog-tied her and left her gagged somewhere in the woods, it would give him the chance to rescue Audrey and get away before Benedict and the others noticed. Then he could come back to cut her loose. Or send the posse in. As long as Sarah was out of the line of fire, she'd be safe.

He told himself that and wondered if she wasn't right about him being a liar.

She rustled about in the undergrowth but made no effort to obey. He turned slowly and pinpointed her location amid the sparse trees. Walking with a deliberate step, he pushed into the bushes. He felt her presence rather than saw her cowering behind a tree. As gently as possible, he spoke softly to coax her out.

"Hello, Sarah. It's good to find you all safe and well." He held out his hand. She didn't budge from her safe spot. "How did you get away from Rhoades? He stole you away from me. You haven't taken a shine to him, have you? You're not giving up on me so you can go with him?" His stomach churned at such tactics, but their lives depended on him catching her before she drew unwanted attention from the outlaws.

She sobbed. "I waited so long for you, Lucas. You went to war. It took forever until you came back."

He made his way through the foot-tangling brush and came out onto a game trail. A dark figure a few yards away moved. When she moved into a spot letting starlight shine down, he caught his breath. Sarah still wore the disheveled wedding gown. If anything, she was even more skeletal than before, as if no one fed her—or she never noticed food in her search for a long-dead husband. But what stunned him was the way she momentarily looked like his wife on her wedding day. It was all illusion, he saw now. He saw what he desired most. Sarah Youngblood looked nothing like Audrey. Nothing. His own journey here had been taxing and his senses reeled.

"I want you to get away from here. We can go home."

She said nothing. Sarah whirled about and darted into the night. He went after her, doggedly refusing to give up. Too much rode on silencing her before she alerted the gang. He dodged trees and bushes as he went along the hilltop. Somewhere he lost her trail. Panic flared as he stopped and turned in a complete circle, hunting for her.

A heavier tread breaking twigs and crushing leaves warned him someone else prowled through the trees. He drew his pistol, then returned it to the holster. An accidental discharge now ran the risk of hitting Sarah—or worse. He might bring down the gang on his neck. Stooping, he felt for the knife sheathed in his boot top. He had killed to get this knife. He had even more reason now to use it.

Blade in hand, he went toward the noise, then slipped behind a tree, back pressed hard into the trunk. His heart hammered as the footfalls came closer. As the indistinct figure passed, Luke acted. He was no killer, not like those in the Rhoades gang, but too much depended on him right now. Driving the knife forward as hard as he could, he grabbed for the man's chin to hold him in place.

His coordination was off. He dragged one leg slightly and failed to get a secure stance. The reasons for his attack to fail became greater than he dared count. The knife missed a clean kill by several inches. Blood still spurted over his hand, making his grip on the handle too slippery. The weapon went sailing as his would-be victim let out a bull roar, spun and drove an elbow back into Luke's face.

Staggered, he fell back against an oak tree. The jolt stunned Luke and gave his opponent time to draw his six-gun. Looking down the barrel wasn't something

Luke relished. He had done it too much lately, and now his enemy had no reason not to pull the trigger.

"You cut me bad. Who are you?" The outlaw held his gun in a shaky right hand and tried to stanch the blood flowing down his left side by pressing with his other hand. "The boss said to bring anybody we found in, but I'm gonna shoot you."

"Do you intend to talk me to death?" Luke's fear evaporated. He had faced death too many times to let this scare him now. His only regret lay in not saving the women from their fates. "Or are you waiting for her to come back?"

"What? You talkin' 'bout the loco we picked up?"

"Her name's Sarah Youngblood."

"You know her? If you care for her, you're as loony as she is."

"Take me to Rhoades. He'll want to find out what I know." Luke shifted his weight. His legs refused to move exactly right. To draw and fire before the man facing him squeezed the trigger wasn't likely.

"You got yourself a passel of guns. One in a holster, one slung over your shoulder and another tucked into your belt. You fixin' to fight a war?"

"Looks like," Luke allowed. "You should take the guns from me."

"It's startin' to hurt something fierce." The outlaw wobbled now from loss of blood.

"She'll take care of you. Behind you."

"I ain't fallin' for any trick like that. It's the oldest one in the book."

"Hello, Lucas." Sarah floated ghostlike to the gunman's left side. She distracted him enough for Luke to press his foot against the tree trunk and shove himself forward. He collided with the outlaw. His hand circled the man's brawny wrist. Even wounded, the man's strength was greater than Luke's.

They hit the ground and rolled over and over. Luke tried to get to one of his guns. The man had dropped his own six-shooter and used both his hands to pin his opponent. Luke grated out, "Help me, Sarah. Help me!"

She started singing "The Sow Took the Measles." The rising notes distracted the outlaw again long enough for Luke to press his hand into his vest pocket. His fingers traced the derringer's outline. Jerking around, his right side pressed into the ground, he cocked the derringer through the cloth and pressed the trigger.

The report drowned out Sarah. For a moment Luke wasn't sure who had screamed. His throat felt raw. He had not been quiet. The lead slug ripped open his vest and kept going upward, through his coat and into the outlaw. The man slumped over, dead. The slug had entered under his chin and blasted smack-dab through his skull.

"He's dead," Sarah said. "You killed him." Her voice was neutral. She might have remarked how many stars were in the sky or how lovely the sunset had been.

"For you," Luke said. "All for you." He lay sprawled on the ground until he regained both senses and strength enough to push the dead outlaw away. No sense of accomplishment went with these deaths. The men were only faces on wanted posters he had seen in sheriffs' offices. He had killed three men and it hadn't been personal. Not like it would be when he finally found Rhoades and Crazy Water Benedict.

"We can be together finally, Lucas. I waited for

you." Sarah began singing, the words lost in the ringing in his ears. Discharging a derringer so close had taken its toll on him in ways he hardly realized.

"Come here," he said, sitting up. The aches and pains had returned. Worst of all was sitting on the hard ground. He rubbed his butt, then levered himself to his feet. All the energy fled and his bones turned to water when he looked around.

Sarah had gone off again.

He started to call to her, then worried the derringer shot had been heard by others in the gang. The ringing in his ears died down, making him wonder if the sound had been all that great. His body muffled its report as he had pressed close to the dead man.

Letting faith take over, he loped into the woods, hunting for Sarah. She couldn't have gone far. His hearing returned, but she wasn't singing. For once he wished she'd belt out a song or two for him to find her. This time, he vowed, he would rope and gag her so she'd be safe. If he failed to find her soon, he faced a new decision. Let her be and go back to Audrey or keep looking.

Sarah had somehow been free and roaming the woods on her own. The Indians believed crazy people were possessed by spirits and, if not venerated, were considered holy. He doubted Sarah was somehow possessed with spirits of the dead or had wisdom to impart, but he felt responsible for having gotten her into this mess.

"There you are! Stay put, Sarah. Don't move."

She sat on a stump, legs crossed and one foot kicking back and forth. She leaned on one hand and stared at the stars above. Luke made his way to her, then froze. He wasn't alone.

They weren't alone.

A quick glance to his right made him curse his impatience. A rifle barrel poked through the foliage and pointed directly at him. He slowly raised his arms in surrender.

CHAPTER EIGHTEEN

THERE'S NO NEED to shoot." Luke Hadley tried to figure how to decoy the gunman's aim away from Sarah so she could escape. But there wasn't any way he could be sure she would see his sacrifice as something to take advantage of. She turned her face skyward, as if basking in the rays of the sun. The moon wasn't even up. Only the stars shined down on her, turning her into a thin, ghostly silver statue.

"Why would I shoot, you fool? The saints know it would put you out of your misery, but that's not my job."

The question shocked him. A quick turn spun him around to face Marta Shearing as she came from the darkness, a rifle held in her hands. When she saw him staring at it, she lowered the muzzle.

"I took it off one of the gang. He wasn't in any condition to use it anymore."

"I . . . I've killed three of them. How many are left?"

She stopped a few feet away and looked up at him. Her brown eyes were wide and she started to say something. She clamped her mouth shut and shook her head. The look of surprise forced him to explain—or was it confess? The men he had killed deserved their fate, and Luke only wished he wasn't the one to take justice into his own hands.

"Two of them outside the valley and one in the woods, when I tried to catch up with her." He pointed to Sarah Youngblood. The woman jumped up and stood on the stump, struck a pose and burst into song. Both he and Marta cringed at the loud sound blasting out across the valley.

"Can you shut her up?" Marta lifted her rifle just enough to let him know how serious she considered the noise.

"Don't shoot. I'll try to quiet her. She's not right in the head."

"She's not the only one." Marta glared at him. He wondered if she meant him or herself.

He edged closer to Sarah and held out his hand. She looked down from her perch on the stump, smiled and then took it. Her song died as she let him help her down. With a deep curtsy in his direction, she recovered and tried to run. He caught her and spun her into his arms. She looked up. The contrast between her and Marta startled him. The Pinkerton agent was calculating, sharp, intelligent—and deadly. Sarah Youngblood's eyes reflected the stars and a gentle insanity that tore at his heart. Nothing returned her to the real world. She was doomed to drift in her own mind, thinking only of dreams, for the rest of her life.

"Kiss me, Lucas. It's been so long."

"Later. When we get back to your cabin."

"Our cabin." She clung to him so hard he winced. His side hurt and the bruises accumulated during his wrestling matches with the outlaws began to throb and ache something fierce. He guided her around to where Marta watched him like a bug under a magnifying glass. For some reason, her scrutiny made him even more uncomfortable, as if he had to explain everything to her.

"Our cabin, my love. Let's go there now."

"That's a right fine idea, Sarah. Why don't you let Miss Shearing escort you there?"

"Hold on!" The Pinkerton agent grabbed him by the arm and yanked him aside. "I'm not a nursemaid. If you want her out of danger, you take her. She's taken quite a shine to you, unless I miss my guess."

"It's not like that."

"Look at her making cow eyes at you. She's in love."

He saw Marta enjoyed this a little too much.

"We've got our own trails to ride. I can't let her get in my way, not when I found Audrey."

Marta stared hard at him. If he felt she was examining him before, his very soul had pieces torn away now.

"You're not lying, are you, just to get me out of the way? You found your wife alive?"

"In the cabin at the mouth of the valley."

"I skirted it," Marta said, chewing on her lower lip. "I followed one of the owlhoots in that I thought was Rhoades. He turned out to be another of the gang, but he led me to their main camp. It's a ways from that cabin."

"How many did you find?" Luke found Sarah to be

more than a handful. She twisted and writhed about as if all the bones in her body had evaporated. Trying to escape was the least of his problems with her. She licked her chapped lips and hummed, ready to begin her loud singing again. He considered punching her to knock her out. As frail as Sarah was, he worried he might kill her.

"I didn't get a chance to count noses," Marta said. "There were three campfires. Usually that'd mean a dozen or so, but nobody's ever reported the gang having that many riders."

"They must be waiting for something. The bank's been robbed, but they aren't acting like they have to put miles between themselves and a posse." Luke pushed Sarah down. She sat on the stump. A bug crawling up a worn strip of cloth on her wedding dress occupied her attention for the moment.

Marta shook her head. "My best guess is that they're scattered around. I tried to figure how many were here by the horses in a big corral. It looks as if they intend to ride on soon, each of them taking a spare horse or two and getting as far away as possible from Kansas as they can. There's no sign of the gold they stole back in Crossroads."

"But that doesn't matter to you, does it? You were after Rhoades and the rest before they held up the bank." Luke put his finger to his lips when Sarah held up the bug and started to serenade it. Silencing her produced considerable pouting. She would break down and cry or bolt in a few minutes if she wasn't taken away. Letting her go would be wrong, but not saving Audrey was worse.

"You're right. Rhoades is wanted for train robbery

and other crimes. And it's not only him Allan wants brought in." She nodded slowly, her floppy hat rippling as her head moved. She started to say more and stopped. When she did speak again, Luke thought she was leaving out key details of her assignment. "I don't know where Rhoades is. I didn't see either him or his partner."

"Crazy Water Benedict."

"Yeah, him. Look, I see you're telling the truth about finding your wife. That's nothing less than a miracle. Since I didn't get a chance to arrest Rhoades, here's my plan. My new plan." She pointed at Sarah. "I'll escort her out of the valley. If she keeps on like she's doing, she's bound to stir them up. Get her out, don't give the gang any reason to start shooting at anything that moves."

"Like us," Luke said. "That's a good plan. You take her out, and I'll do the same for Audrey. Once we're out, you can come back in for Rhoades. They won't even know we've been here." He didn't add "until they find a passel of dead bodies."

Such an explanation wasn't lost on Marta. She knew all hell would bust loose when the sentries were discovered dead.

"Go save your wife." Marta gripped his upper arm and gave it a squeeze. Then she went to Sarah. The two women stood shoulder to shoulder. Luke had no idea what was said but Marta convinced Sarah to come with her.

Sarah blew him a kiss. He waved, a weak gesture but all he was up for. Stringing her along only made the hurt worse when he left. He wasn't her Lucas.

He was Audrey's Luke.

They melted into the darkness, leaving him alone. He looked up at the moonless night. Stars began to disappear behind wisps of clouds moving in from the north. A new storm blew in and would pelt the land with rain before morning. That'd cover his and Audrey's tracks, if they left soon enough.

He got his bearings and returned to the top of the ridge. Retracing his steps, even in the dark, proved easier than he expected. He even came across the outlaw's body in the wooded area. Hiding it gained him nothing. Already bugs and a coyote or two had come to dine. There was a reason bodies were buried six feet under. It took that much earth to hide the smell of a decaying body from the keen-nosed scavengers.

Time weighed heavily on him. He rummaged about and added another pistol to his armament. Search as he might, the knife he had lost in the fight was nowhere to be found. Reluctantly he gave up his hunt for it, but he did check the derringer in his vest pocket. The dead outlaw gave up a cartridge that fit the small hideout gun. Once more primed with two rounds, the gun soothed him as it pressed into his chest over the spot where shrapnel rode within him.

Both had saved him. If Lady Luck rode at his shoulder, each had served its purpose and only his skill prevailed from now on.

He kept walking through the trees, growing more tired by the minute. When he found himself stopping every few minutes to catch his breath, panic consumed him. Not having a good look at the sky robbed him of the chance to figure out how long he had until sunrise. He took out his pocket watch but it had been smashed. The only thing he had to go on was the feeling of hours passing. The sooner he saved Audrey and got on the trail back to Crossroads—or anywhere as long as it was away from Rhoades and his "family"—the safer they'd both be. Heaving to his feet, he changed his tactics. Rather than retracing his steps, he'd go to the valley floor. The going had to be easier there and chances of missing the cabin decreased.

As he came out of the forested area, he worried at the hint of false dawn working its way into the eastern sky. Real dawn was an hour off, but he had spent far too long blundering about saving Sarah Youngblood. Finding Marta and having her escort the crazy woman out of the valley took some pressure off. But not much. Not as much as he expected.

A small stream meandered along the valley floor. He splashed water on his face. The cold shocked him alert. He drank, then tried to get some of the blood off his clothes. Showing up looking like he'd blundered through a slaughterhouse would scare Audrey. He gave up after a few minutes. Explaining his condition had to be easier than cleaning off the dried blood and gore.

"At least most of it's not mine," he said softly. He almost started laughing hysterically. The strain wore at him from too many directions.

"Time to get out of here."

He checked his stash of six-shooters and hiked along the stream for almost a half mile before seeing the cabin. The weak glow inside showed Audrey had turned down the coal oil lamp to barely a flicker. Emotion told him to rush in. Logic warned him to be sure he didn't put them both in danger. For all he knew the rest of the gang slept in the cabin.

A quick circuit showed that they had removed any chance for Audrey riding away. He found an iron ring set in a stump where horses had been tethered, but not recently, not within the last day or two.

He went to the rickety door and reached out to open it. His hand shook. Months had passed since Benedict had shot him at the wedding and kidnapped Audrey. Months. But he had lived centuries since then. In spite of his bravado and insistence that Audrey was unhurt, some tiny rotted black spot deep inside had told him she was dead.

Or better off dead than Benedict's captive.

The door creaked as he tugged at it. When it came free, almost falling off the hinges, it made an earsplitting, shrill sound. A nail pulled out of rotted wood and the latch fell off. He stepped inside and pushed it closed the best he could.

The cabin's darkness stole away his vision. The pale yellow flame in the lamp on the table did nothing to illuminate the corners. And in the far corner a lump under a blanket moved.

"Audrey?"

The lump erupted. The blanket went flying and the woman sat up with a start. He made out Audrey's face in the dim light.

"Mal!"

"No, not Mal. Not him," he said quickly. "Stay quiet. I didn't see any of them outside, but as still as it is, your voice carries a long ways. They're camped somewhere near. They must be."

"You . . . you're not Mal."

"No, my darling. It's me. Luke."

"Luke?" She shifted in the bed, pressing into the

wall. Her eyes blinked. She rubbed them and then squinted to get a better look. "Luke? It *is* you!"

"I vowed to find you. I promised till death do us part. I never doubted you were alive." He rushed on, even though that was only mostly true. "Is there a horse you can ride? I scouted around but didn't see one. Mine is slow and old, but it'll carry both of us if it has to."

He vowed to go back and pay twice what he already had to the farmer for the use of the plow horse. It had been better than any quarter horse working on the range. Its strong, slow-gaited dependability would carry him and his wife to safety.

She shook her head vigorously and said, "We can't go. Not yet."

"We have to!" He went to her. She looked so small and vulnerable. "I can't fight off the entire gang."

"We have to eat first. Food. I can fix you breakfast."

"Throw something into a gunnysack. We'll eat on the trail." He grabbed her wrist and pulled her to the edge of the bed. She jerked free and shook her head even harder.

"Let me, Luke. You're so brave coming for me. Let me do something for you."

"We'll go to San Francisco. Or Chicago. New Orleans! We can have breakfast in bed at some fancy hotel."

"You can't afford that." Her tone was chiding. She got her bare feet under her. The dirt on the floor made soft brushing sounds as she moved about, going to the Franklin stove in the corner. Audrey opened the iron door and poked at the embers inside, then added a few twigs. Somehow, she got a fire going. Only when she felt the iron side warming did she turn to him. "You can't afford it, can you?"

"I sold the farm to the railroad."

"For a lot of money?"

He held up his tattered coat to show the rigid seams.

"There's plenty of gold dust here to keep us going for a long time, until we decide what we want to do. Now let's go!"

"You carry it around with you? How much?" She came to him and ran her fingers over the seams, moving segments of the dust up and down. A shiver passed through her.

"You're going to freeze to death, wearing that."

All she wore was a thin muslin undergarment. Gooseflesh showed wherever bare skin poked through. But when she looked up, her eyes were hot and sharp as if she had a fever. He touched her forehead. She grabbed his hand and pulled it down so she could kiss it.

"I've missed you so, my dear. We never had time together because of Mal."

"There's no time to talk here. Once we get on my horse and clear out, then we can talk for the rest of our lives." He began worrying that their lives would end quickly if they stayed much longer. It was as if an hourglass dribbled sand, and he watched every grain fall. The pile at the bottom soon enough signaled the end.

"I want to fix you breakfast." She pushed him down into a chair.

Luke fought to stand, but his leg gave way. His side ached and dizziness prevented him from focusing his eyes. Food might not be a bad idea, but he'd rather risk collapsing on the trail.

"You want to know everything, don't you, Luke?"

"Hurry it up," he said. "Nothing fancy."

"You know I'm not that good a cook. But then, you don't really know anything of the sort. I never fixed much for you. Our courtship was so fast, and you never knew much about me at all."

"Not even where you came from."

"Chicago," she said. She put a skillet atop the stove and dropped a spoonful of lard into it. Rummaging around, she found a couple eggs in a basket beside the stove. She cracked them and let the eggs begin to hiss and bubble. Taking a spatula from a hook on the wall, she poked at the eggs until they firmed. With a deft scrape she captured the eggs and plopped them onto a dirty plate already on the table. She pushed it toward him. "Fork's there." Audrey pointed with the spatula at a dirty fork.

Luke took it, hesitated, then began shoveling the runny eggs into his mouth. The quicker he ate, the sooner they left.

"I left Chicago and found you. I thought everything was perfect when I heard how much the railroad wanted to buy the farm."

"So you didn't want to be a farmer's wife," he said. "That's a hard life. A good one, but hard."

"How much money do you have left? You must have spent a lot of it to find me."

"There's some left." He scrapped the plate clean. "Now let's go."

"He found me. I thought I'd gotten away from him in Chicago, but he's a clever, determined man."

"Who? Benedict? You mean you knew him?"

"Mal would have let me go. But Rollie isn't the sort to let anyone go their own way like I wanted."

He stared at her, not sure he understood. This was

Audrey, the woman he'd married so gladly. But she was different. Her attitude was different.

"What have they done to you? After they kidnapped you, what'd they do? What'd Rhoades do?"

"Rollie? Not too much once I was back with the gang."

"Back? You were in his gang in Chicago?"

"Of course I was. He didn't rob banks then. We worked swindles, but it was getting too hot for us there. I got tired of it, but Rollie wanted one more big score. While he was working the sucker, I hightailed it."

"You were one of his gang? Did he . . . did he ever—?"

"Rollie? Of course not. He'd never. Well, let's say I wanted to go straight, Luke. With you."

"Let's go. Now." Both hands against the table, he pushed himself standing. His butt hurt and his side ached, but they'd stop hurting when he got on the trail with Audrey. But would he have to watch his back? Luke's hands shook. She was the woman he married, only that woman was a complete enigma now. He loved her and that was forever, but there was so much more about her he had no idea about. A swindler? A willing participant in illicit schemes with Rhoades? Still, he saw so much to love. He had to come to love, or at least accept, the greater part of her he hadn't known.

"Don't you want to hear what I went through after the wedding? I'm surprised to see you after I watched Mal shoot you. He doesn't miss. He's a crack shot."

"He hit dead center, but I'm tougher than I look." He tapped his chest where the shrapnel rested in his chest.

"You must be. You weren't killed, and you tracked us down."

Luke caught his breath. The way she said "us" put her in with the gang. Again.

"They're going to find us if we don't go." He wondered what she had to say about that.

"It'll be days before they get back. Rollie took the gold north and is hiding it. Mal only got back from decoying the posse to the south." She looked hard at him. "He didn't do such a good job of that, did he? I can tell by your expression. Is that how you found us? You tracked Mal? Is he drinking the crazy water again? He promised to stop."

"What's in the crazy water?"

"He mixes laudanum with alcohol. Or morphine sulfate, he calls it sometimes. If he finds any, he cuts it with branch water. It makes him plumb loco in the head after a shot or two." She laughed. "It doesn't pay to be in the same county when he's tied one on. You can't believe how ornery that makes him."

"It sounds as if you know firsthand. Did he go loco a lot after he took you?"

"Rollie is hiding the gold and then he and Mal are heading for Indian Territory for a few months, until the ruckus over the robbery dies down." Her voice dropped to a conspiratorial whisper. "They're going to double-cross the rest of the gang. Maybe that's why Mal left such a plain trail for you to follow. He expected the law to be hot on his heels and catch the rest of the boys so he wouldn't need to waste his ammo on them."

"You know too much for them to let you live. What if you spilled this to the others in the gang—the ones that are left?"

"The ones that're left? Why, Luke Hadley, have you

taken out a few of them yourself? And you, not even a lawman."

"No," he said slowly. "I'm not." He touched the tin star in his pocket but left it where it rested. He wasn't proud of lying to others. The lies about that star ended now, and he wasn't going to let on to Audrey all he had said to find her. The outlaws' dead bodies spoke loud enough.

He grabbed her and swung her around toward the door. Again he felt time crushing down on him—or the lack of it. They had to leave. Now.

He kicked open the door and dragged her through it. She resisted, then stopped and said, "Lookee there. I reckon I was wrong about how long it was going to take him."

Luke released her and faced Rollie Rhoades as he stepped down from his horse.

CHAPTER NINETEEN

"Now, who do we have here?" Rollie Rhoades cocked his head to one side. A slow smile curled the corners of his mouth. His boyish looks carried none of the cruelty Luke knew was possible. But the eyes did. They were dead as they stared at him, cold and black as coal and . . . dead.

Luke pushed his coat back so his gun rested free and easy to draw. The other pistols he had taken off the dead outlaws weighed him down, but he wasn't inclined to discard them. Any movement on his part now meant the gunfight began. Rhoades's reputation was fast, and Audrey had claimed he was a dead-accurate shot.

"You are actually facing me. From what I'd heard, you really prefer me to turn my back. That's the way you've killed most of the men, isn't it, Rhoades?"

"A pretty speech from a man who's stolen another man's wife." Rhoades shooed his horse away. It went only a few yards off before it discovered a watering trough and dipped its nose in for a drink.

"What do you mean?"

"Dumb and slow. That's you. I'd heard you were slow bordering on glacial with your six-gun, and it surely does seem that dumb goes with that. Dumb and slow, that's—what's his name, Audrey? Never mind. There's time to figure out what to put on the grave marker."

"You talk big. Are you trying to bore me to death?" Luke knew exactly what the gunman was doing. If he got his dander up over the insults, he might make a mistake. If he was as mad as a wet hen, his aim became shaky. More than this, Rhoades enjoyed throwing out the insults. They buoyed his spirits as they tore down his opponent.

"Who in their right mind faces down the fastest gun hand in the entire West?" Rollie puffed out his chest. For the first time Luke saw him up close and realized how short the man was. That added to the false image of the killer being boyish, younger than he was. While much of his face was still hidden in shadow because Rhoades had chosen to put his back to the growing dawn, tiny wrinkles showed at the corners of his eyes. He had to be ten years older than Luke. That made him old, really old, in his forties.

Luke tensed at that revelation. Nobody rode the outlaw trail as long as Rhoades and reached such an advanced age by being careless. Or stupid.

"You and me. We shoot it out," Luke said.

"Why not? It'll do my reputation good that I cut down a man trying to steal another's wife a second time." Rhoades shrugged and moved his hand to rest on his holster.

Luke saw the tension in the man's fingers, curling slightly, but none in his face. The mocking smile remained. And those eyes bored straight through to his soul.

"You keep saying that. I don't know what you mean. I'm here to take *my* wife back."

Luke sensed rather than saw the outlaw draw. Never in all his born days had Luke witnessed a man with such snakelike speed. Rollie Rhoades cleared the holster and brought his gun up before Luke began his draw. A white puff of smoke curled from Rhoades's muzzle. Luke winced as the bullet ripped past his head, cutting the top of his ear.

Then his far slower hand pulled out his Schofield. The world moved as if everything had moved underwater. He saw with utter clarity where he wanted to aim, to shoot his round. His gun slipped free, his hand thrust out and he fanned off a shot. He imagined he watched the leaden slug make its way through the air and Rhoades's vest turn inward in just the size of a .45 caliber bullet. The cloth stretched on Rhoades's chest began to turn red with blood. The outlaw took a step back and then crumpled, as if his legs turned to water.

Before the other gunman hit the ground, the world snapped back for Luke. He lowered the aim to the writhing outlaw. Rhoades moaned. If his eyes had been open, Luke could not have stopped himself from putting a bullet between them. Those dead pits remained hidden, and that saved his life.

"You shot Rollie. That's not good," Audrey said, coming up behind him.

He batted her hand away from the pistol holstered in the gun belt dangling from his shoulder.

"You'll hurt yourself," he said, knowing that wasn't what he meant at all. He stared hard at her. "What'd he mean that I was stealing another man's wife? You're not married to him, are you?"

If she'd said yes there'd have been no way to stop him from putting five more slugs into the outlaw's body.

"Don't be silly. Rollie's not the marrying kind. We were in cahoots, and I double-crossed him. That's all. We were in business together. Our spell in Chicago never went beyond him forcing me to fleece marks."

Luke hardly believed that.

"He forced you to steal for him, isn't that it?"

"He—"

The thunder of a galloping horse spun him around. He saw the rider coming on strong. Luke raised his six-gun but the rider opened fire first. His Winchester barked harshly and tore a new hole in the cabin wall.

"Get in. Now. Get in!" Luke shoved Audrey so hard she stumbled and fell. He stepped over her, grabbed her by the scruff of the neck and heaved. Muscles protested and his leg threatened to give way, but he got her out of the line of fire. Three more bullets tore through the dawn.

He put his weight against the flimsy door and shoved it shut. It fit even more poorly than before. The top hinge had pulled free, causing the door to sag and leave a large gap. He used this space to peer out. The rider halted amid a cloud of dirt and rocks kicked up by his horse's hooves. Through the dim light and debris floating in the air came a face that had haunted Luke's nightmares for long months.

"Benedict!"

"Mal? Is that Mal?" Audrey tried to push past. He

batted her away. She stumbled back into the cabin and sat in a rickety chair by the table.

"Stay down. He'll blow your head off, given half a chance." Luke poked his six-gun through the gap and got off a couple shots. He spooked Benedict's horse and forced the outlaw away from his boss, who still moaned on the ground. Where Crazy Water Benedict had taken refuge was something of a mystery since there wasn't any obvious hiding place nearby.

"I know. That's the way he is."

He hardly paid attention to her. He feared shifting his attention for even a split second gave the killer a chance to rush the cabin. As the sky lightened with dawn, Benedict's hiding place would be obvious. All Luke had to do was stay alive long enough to pull the trigger. He pulled his pistol back and broke it open. Four spent rounds. He ejected them and reloaded, then stuck the gun into his holster.

He had three captured six-shooters to empty before returning to his trusty Schofield. If luck favored him as it had in the gunfight with Rhoades, all he'd need was a single shot.

As if refuting his optimism, wet rivers ran down his neck and soaked into his shirt. He touched his ear and cried out in pain. Rhoades's bullet had ripped off the top of his ear. A fraction of an inch to the left would have blown his brains out.

"I was doubly lucky," he muttered. "I'd better not be running low now."

"You make your own luck," Audrey said somewhat bitterly. "That's why I always end up like this."

"We'll get away. I shot Rhoades, didn't I? You said he was fast, and he was. His aim was off just enough.

Mine wasn't." He dabbed at the blood still flowing from his blown-off ear. It had been a dull ache. Now sharp pain lanced into his head, causing his vision to blur enough to throw off his aim.

Audrey came over. He thought she wanted to patch him up. Instead, she stood on tiptoe and looked out.

"Yup, you ventilated Rollie real good. But he's still alive. See how he's crawling away?"

Luke drew a bead but shooting a man, even Rollie Rhoades, in the back as he crawled off wasn't in him. He saw where the road agent tried to take cover. In the growing light he saw a small woodpile. This had to be where Benedict had taken cover.

He ran his sleeve over his lips. Nerves got to him now. Facing Rhoades had come fast and the gunfight ended even faster, not giving him time to think about it. Now he realized how much depended on him. He was all shot up, weaker than a newborn kitten, not seeing clearly, and more than his own life depended on getting away. He had come to the end of his hunt and found his wife.

"Can you knock out a board in the back wall and get away? No, no, don't do that. You'd be on foot. If Benedict is here, too, the others in the gang are roaming around and would catch you."

"They intended to kill the rest of the gang and keep the gold for themselves," Audrey said. "Since Mal's out there now, the others are dead."

Hornets buzzed in his brain. He tried to make sense of her words. A certain logic warned him he missed something, but Audrey had to be right. The only roadblock between them and a life together crouched behind the woodpile. That obstacle's name was Crazy

Water Benedict. And he was going to kill him rather than run away.

"He'll find you, no matter where you run," Audrey said, as if reading his mind. "One or the other of you's got to die."

Luke poked his captured six-gun out and sighted in just above where Rhoades still inched toward safety. He fired at the same instant that Benedict popped up, only the outlaw appeared on the far side of the woodpile. One rifle bullet after another blasted splinters from the door. Luke emptied the six-gun, dropped it and drew another. By the time he chanced to look out again, he saw Benedict looking over the woodpile at his boss.

"Pull me to safety, Mal. I can't move anymore. It's gettin' dark, cold."

"Won't be that way where you're going, Rollie." Crazy Water Benedict leaned over the woodpile and fired point-blank into Rhoades's back. The outlaw leader jerked once and died, his spine blown into smithereens.

Luke tried to do the same to Benedict. All six shots went low, into the wood barricade. He tossed the pistol down and drew the third one. By the time he had it in action, Benedict had disappeared. Audrey pressed close to him, peering over his shoulder. She chuckled.

"Mal took him out. That's more for us."

He started to ask her to reload the pistols he had dropped, then thought better of it. He hesitated to give her a loaded gun. He tucked the one he used into his belt and reloaded the ones he had dropped. One took its final six cartridges. The other from the belt slung over his shoulder had several more reloads left. Still, he and Audrey were pinned in the cabin, whether she was right or not about Benedict killing the rest of the gang.

No matter the truth in that, he had killed Rollie Rhoades.

"It was an act of decency I didn't expect from him," Luke finally said. "There wasn't any way Rhoades survived the bullet I put into his chest." He traced the piece of shrapnel in his own chest. His finger left bloody tracks. His ear wound still dribbled a stream of blood. It refused to cake over properly to stanch the flow.

"I need to patch up my ear," he said.

"Why bother?" She took a quick look over his shoulder. "Mal is a tricky snake. He'll think of something pretty quick. He's not going to let you go."

After killing his boss, Benedict had a soaring taste for blood. What she said was too true. Worse, she seemed to know how Benedict reacted. Their time together couldn't be a good thing.

Luke looked at the roof. He saw slivers of pale blue sky through it now. Sunrise betrayed how leaky that roof was. Bits of grass and mud showed where someone had done a poor job of patching it. The first real rain washed away the attempted repairs. Luke wished for rain about now to prevent an obvious tactic. A torch tossed onto the roof would send the entire cabin up in flames.

"With Rhoades dead, Benedict's not likely to toss dynamite in here." Luke realized he spoke out loud. "He's not the kind to enjoy explosions. His tastes run more to watching a man die."

"Rollie enjoyed his explosions, that I'll grant him," Audrey said. She stared at Luke, her expression unreadable. He vowed to never play poker with her. She cleared her throat and said, "I can go out and dicker with him. He won't shoot me. At least, I don't think he will." She tried to push past, but he shoved her away from the door.

"He killed a man he rode with for years. If you're right, he did it to get a bigger share of the gold. It must be a small mountain for him to turn on his partner like that."

"Mal's not a man to understand. He operates on, what do they call it? He operates on impulse. If something hits him right, he does it." She gave her little chuckle. "If something hits him wrong, he does it, too. There's never much thought that goes into anything he does."

Luke spun the cylinders in his captured six-guns and then checked his own pistol, more to keep busy than because he doubted everything carried a full load. He took the time then to tie his bandanna around his head, pressing his bloody ear to the side of his head. The rag absorbed enough blood to glue it to his hair. For the first time since Rhoades shot him, the bleeding stopped.

"You really have gold dust all sewed up in your coat? Take it off and show me. I'll open one of the seams, just to be sure it's all there."

"From the railroad," he said. His belly turned over. Head spinning, he worried that the eggs she had cooked for him were bad. It was always better to sop up the yolk with a biscuit. He tried to remember Audrey ever fixing a meal. He sank to the floor when his legs gave way.

"You're in a bad way," she said. She stood.

"Stay there. Where you are. Sit in the chair. Table." He lifted the gun in a surprisingly steady grip. He felt as if one foot kicked dirt into his own grave, yet he drew a bead on his wife. That made no sense, but nothing made sense to him right now.

"There's no need to go all crazy on me."

"Crazy. Crazy Water. That's what they call him. Because of the drugs in his water that turn him loco."

"I got a bottle of his popskull around here. You want a sip? It's not for the weak-spirited. Mal drinks with the best of 'em, and you don't have the look of a man able to hold his liquor."

"Sit!" Luke cocked the six-gun and pointed it at her. He edged up, using the wall as a support. Something worried him. It took a few seconds for him to figure it out. "Where's Benedict? He stopped shooting."

"I told you. Mal's sneaky. He might have shot Rollie as a diversion, then snuck off to do something else. Rollie was the one who enjoyed blowing things up, but Mal can be a quick learner. Maybe he found some of Rollie's dynamite."

Luke snapped his legs stiff and walked around the cabin perimeter, looking through cracks in the wall to be sure Benedict hadn't circled to attack from a side or the rear. The morning light cast long shadows that'd shroud a clever man. They also made certain approaches more difficult to hide. Long moving shadows. Luke hunted for them. That'd be Crazy Water Benedict.

"I don't see him."

"That's because he's back behind the woodpile. I see his head bobbing around."

He pushed past Audrey and leveled his gun. She wasn't lying. Trying to guess where Benedict would pop up was a fool's game. Luke fixed his aim dead center of the woodpile, ready to move either left or right when the outlaw decided to show himself.

A flash of white appeared left of the woodpile. Luke swung his pistol around and drew back on the trigger. Only decent reflexes allowed him to jerk the muzzle up and away. The bullet sailed off into the sunrise.

But he didn't plug Sarah Youngblood.

"Get down!" Luke swung his gun back around. Benedict must be out there somewhere. The movement Audrey had seen was the crazy woman and not Crazy Water Benedict.

"She's staying right where she is," came Benedict's taunting voice from hiding. "I knew she'd come in handy as a hostage. This is the time I play her as my trump card. What is she to you? Two pair? Three of a kind? Something more? A straight flush?" Benedict laughed harshly.

"Who is she?" Audrey pressed close to stare out past him. "I heard tell they brought another woman back to camp after the robbery, but I never saw her. Mal must have chained her up somewhere else."

"I don't know what she's doing here," Luke said. Bitterness tinged his words. Marta had escorted her away from the outlaw camp. Or she had tried. Sarah was clever, and giving Marta the slip if she wasn't prepared was as easy as falling off a log. Warning the Pinkerton agent should have been his first chore.

Or had something terrible happened to Marta? He only heard secondhand how Rhoades and Benedict intended to kill the rest of the gang. His eyes darted to the gang leader's corpse. Rollie Rhoades had paid for trusting Benedict. Were others similarly shot in the back or had Benedict allied with them against his former boss? Nothing mattered now other than escaping. Doing that became more complicated because of Sarah.

Unless he sacrificed her. Audrey pressed closer and laid her hand on his arm, the way she used to do. He and Audrey were married. He owed her a debt of both law and heart. The past months came crashing down in failure if he tried to save Sarah Youngblood and failed. He failed not only her in her ripped and filthy wedding gown but also his own wife.

It wasn't as if he hadn't taken lives. But they had been worthless, criminals, men who'd cut his throat as soon as look at him. Sarah was a free spirit, even if the shackles of insanity held her to a past that could never be broken.

"Shoot her," Audrey said. "He can't use her as a bargaining chip then. Or does she mean something to you?" She squeezed down on his arm. Her fingernails dug into his flesh.

"I know her, but getting you away is what I've got to do. It'd be good to save her, too, but . . ."

"You aren't including yourself on the list of those to be saved," Audrey pointed out. "How heroic."

He looked at her sharply. The sarcasm burned his ears as surely as the bullet had cut away half of one. She smiled up at him, angelic and as innocent as could be. This standoff had to end. Now. He made certain his pistols were close at hand and called out to the outlaw.

"She's not part of our feud, Benedict. Me and you. Face-to-face." Luke hardly expected Benedict to take him up on the offer, but anything that changed the stalemate seemed a good trail to take.

"Winner take all?" Benedict laughed harshly. "I'm looking at a dead man in the dirt."

"You shot him in the back."

"To put him out of his misery. I'd do that to a horse.

He was my boss, and I owed him that much. You're the one that shot him."

"He did it in a fair fight, too!" Audrey yelled past Luke. She chuckled when he shushed her.

"You come on out and throw your six-shooter down or I'll shoot her." Benedict moved fast. His arm circled Sarah's throat and choked her. He held his six-gun in his right hand. The muzzle pressed hard into her temple. "I'm not much for all that counting, not unless it's twenty-dollar gold coins. So, I'm giving you to the count of three. Come out with your hands up or I plug her."

Sarah wasn't the least frightened. She might have been strolling along a quiet meadow. She began singing one of her songs, but Benedict choked it off by tightening his arm bar across her throat.

"That's one, greenhorn. You fixing on coming out? I'll let this one live if you come out. I promise."

"He's not big on keeping promises," Audrey said.

"Get behind me." Luke shoved her back. His mind raced. If he stepped out, he was a goner. Audrey's warning that Crazy Water Benedict was a liar was unnecessary. He figured that out for himself. Any man who'd shoot a man on his wedding day and steal his bride had the sand to do about anything he wanted.

"Let me see her better," Luke called. "Just to be sure it's her and not some whore you brought with you. The sun's in my eyes."

"You know who it is. Your little songbird. We had her in camp long enough for her to tell us all about you bein' her hubby."

"That's not true," Luke said quickly, never taking his eyes off Sarah and Benedict as they moved away from the woodpile. The morning sun made them both glow in a golden light. "She mistook me for her dead husband."

He lifted his gun and steadied his nerves. It would be a hard shot, but he had it in him. All he needed was patience and the right opportunity.

"Two. Or did I already say that? Three!"

Luke exhaled, aimed and squeezed the trigger. At the same instant, something hard and flat smashed into his head, stunning him. His finger came back reflexively. The six-gun fired but the bullet tore into the dirt not ten feet in front of him. It missed Benedict by a country mile. The frying pan landed again on his head. This time the world turned black around him.

CHAPTER TWENTY

SHE SAYS IT'S true, so it must be. Why, by stars and garters, a sweet little thing like her'd never lie. Would you, Sweet Little Thing?"

The voice came from a million miles away. Through a dull ache and eyes that threatened to pop from his skull, Luke Hadley fought to understand what was happening. A blink or two got his eyes open enough so he had to squint into the sun. He lay flat on his back outside the cabin. Crazy Water Benedict snaked his arm around Sarah Youngblood, drawing her close. She tried to force herself away, but he was too strong. As thin as she was, Sarah might never have been strong enough against such a powerful man.

"Let her be. She's done nothing to you." Luke struggled to sit up. Benedict kicked him squarely in the chest, slamming him back to the ground.

"Now, boy, did I ask you for an opinion? I don't remember doin' that, not at all." He drew Sarah to him and planted a kiss on her lips. She went limp and collapsed. He stepped away and stared at her wilted body.

"You always had that effect on women, Mal."

"Audrey?" Luke craned around and saw his wife moving about. She held a skillet in her hand. As she came more fully into his line of sight, she swung it back and forth. The swishing sound reminded him of something. It took a second to finally place it.

He'd heard that sound an instant before something whacked him in the back of the head.

"Audrey? What are you doing?" Luke tried to make sense of what had happened. He was too mixed up to find answers to a heap of questions, about Sarah, about Benedict, about why Audrey acted the way she did.

"See, Mal? Keeping me all cooped up for a month like this sapped me of my strength. I meant to mash his head flatter 'n a pancake. Twice. I had to hit him twice to knock him over!"

"You didn't have to bother. I'd've shot him." Benedict straddled Luke, a six-gun aimed squarely at his face.

He caught his breath. He had been in this same position before. At the wedding. Flat on his back, only he'd been shot a couple times then before Benedict pointed the gun at him. The only thing missing was . . .

"Kiss me, Mal." Audrey spun into the outlaw's embrace and planted a big wet kiss on his lips. She looked down at Luke and grinned. Never had he seen a woman so evil. And memory trickled back. She had given him the same look at the wedding, only he had been too stunned to realize it. All he had seen was how Crazy Water Benedict kissed her, not how she returned her supposed kidnapper's kiss.

"One thing's missing." Benedict swung the woman around and raised his six-shooter.

A flame a foot long spat from the muzzle. A slug to his shoulder drove Luke back flat on the ground. He kicked feebly. The physical impact hurt him bad. The way Audrey kissed the outlaw hurt him even more emotionally.

"I wanted to get away from Rollie. I saw you, Mister Farmer Man. You couldn't keep your eyes off me, but you were dirt poor." Audrey laughed. "Get it? A farmer is dirt poor? I heard about the railroad wanting your land and knew you'd come into a pile of money."

"So you married me?" The words grated as they came out. Anger buoyed him. If he got to his feet, he'd rip Benedict's arms off and beat him to death with them. What he'd do to Audrey was going to be worse.

"She thought she'd cross Rhoades by leaving the gang. Nobody does that." Benedict guffawed. "Nobody *did* that. I'm glad he's buzzard bait now. I never liked him much."

"I only had eyes for you, Mal. That's why I snuck off in Chicago to get away from Rollie. He wanted things from me that I wanted to keep private just for you."

"You're such a liar." Benedict pulled her close again.

"That's why we're so good together. We understand each other just fine."

"I want a divorce," Luke said. He slumped back and stared into the sky. Clouds formed. There'd be rain later in the day. He wanted to see it. He hoped he lived long enough to see it.

Both of them laughed. Audrey bent and plucked a six-gun from where it lay beside Luke. She hefted it, cocked it and fired. Luke winced. The two laughed at him again.

"Darling Luke, I was checking to see if the gun was loaded. I'm a crack shot. I never miss." She snuggled closer to Benedict. "Let me shoot him, Mal. Please. You owe me that much."

"He married you."

"He said he wanted a divorce. Let me give it to him."

Luke looked up at a pair of six-shooters aimed at his head.

"Don't be dumb. He can't divorce you. You're already married. Or have you forgot that night in Chicago?"

"Forgot it? How could I, Mal? It was the best night of my life, all night long." She looked down the barrel at Luke. "It was our honeymoon, our wedding night."

"Wedding? You were already married to . . . him?" Luke thought the pain in his soul had reached a limit before. He found out how wrong he was. She had lied over and over. The worst part of it was that part of him still believed her and loved her.

"Of course she was." Benedict cocked his six-gun. His finger drew back on the trigger and then the gun discharged.

Luke lay on the ground, wondering if this was what it felt like to be dead. His agony hadn't changed one iota. Then he saw how Audrey had batted Benedict's gun away. How she had batted her husband's gun away.

She still loved him! He had begun to doubt her but this showed she would risk her own life to save his.

Then he realized what he should have before. Nothing Audrey did was for him. She thought only of herself.

"I told you to let me shoot him, Mal. You owe it to me. You do."

"Go on. Shoot him. Smack in the middle of the chest like I did before."

"That didn't work out so well for you," Luke grated out. Then he screamed in pain as Audrey pulled the trigger and heavy lead smashed into his chest.

Things happened all out of sequence from the way they should. Her gun spat lead and there was a second explosion and a bullet ripped through his flesh, only it ran across his chest, not through it. The shock knocked him senseless.

"All happy, my sweet?"

"Yeah, Mal, all happy. And I'm glad you finished off Rollie. It saved me from having to do it."

"You'd never work up the nerve. You were scared of him."

Luke heard the argument through the ringing in his ears. He didn't understand what had happened. He wasn't dead. His chest burned like fire, but a sticky stream trickled down his side. Dead men don't bleed. Their hearts stopped pumping their lifeblood. And nobody he'd ever talked to spoke of a dead man feeling such pain.

There'd been a preacher who talked of hellfire and eternal damnation for the wicked. Luke had done nothing to deserve that fate. Killing the outlaws he had in the past day ought to send him to heaven, not the other way. He had stopped killers from murdering even more innocents. And it had been in self-defense. Coming to rescue his wife and then Sarah Youngblood was the right thing to do, too.

His life wasn't perfect, but damnation for what he had done seemed far too extreme.

"What are we going to do, Mal? Rollie wanted to head down into Indian Territory until the law stopped hunting us."

"That was his plan. He buried the gold, then we killed off the rest so we could keep it for ourselves."

"I knew him like the back of my hand. He intended to kill you, Mal. Maybe me, too, and keep it all for himself."

Luke heard the pair moving back and forth. One sound confused him until he recognized Audrey's skirts brushing the ground near him. He held his breath and kept his eyes closed. The impulse was to squeeze them shut tight but he resisted.

"I killed him good and proper. Look at that, Mal. His vest caught on fire. Why'd that happen? I wasn't close enough to him for the muzzle flash to heat him up like that."

Luke kept from grunting as a foot ground down on his chest. Audrey stamped out the smoldering cloth. He hadn't even felt the fire.

"Leave him be. I ought to find some of the dynamite Rhoades always carted around and stick that in his mouth. Blow his fool head off."

"Why'd you go and do a thing like that, Mal Benedict? He's already dead."

"Those are the lips that kissed my blushing bride. I don't share you with anybody, much less a Kansas sodbuster."

"He was a Free Stater, too. He said so."

"All the more reason to blow him to smithereens."

"The gold, Mal. You know where Rollie hid it? If we get it, you and me, why don't we just take it and ride north? It's cooler up in Canada right now. Or heading over to Montana would give us both a change of scenery."

"He had a point about the posse. I tried to decoy

them south. That marshal from Crossroads is one smart cayuse. He didn't buy it for a second. And from what I overheard one night as I spied on his camp, there's a second posse roaming around hunting for us."

"You spied on them? Like an Indian creeping up in the dark? That excites me, Mal. It excites me a whole bunch. Why don't you do that tonight, when we're camped and the fire goes low? Then me and you—"

"Where are we going to camp? Somewhere in the direction of where Rhoades hid the gold?"

Audrey laughed. From the sound, she kissed Benedict again, but Luke dared not sneak a peek. The pain faded a mite, but the blood kept running down his side and soaking into his coat. That meant he hadn't died and this wasn't his punishment in the afterlife. His mind spun about in crazy circles. He wasn't dead, but what if Audrey remembered him telling her he had sewn the gold dust into the seams of his coat? If she searched him, she had to find out he was alive. As weak as he was, fighting was out of the question. Even pulling a trigger was too much of an exertion.

He went limp. The sun burned his face, and the sounds around him faded to nothing.

In his dreams, he swam in a cool lake. Water all around, floating, drifting, going nowhere and not caring. Then he sputtered as he started to drown. He turned his head to the side. Water cascaded down against his injured ear. Every drop turned to acid. The pain jolted him awake. He blinked and got dirt from his eyes and stared up into Sarah Youngblood's admiring face. She held a china pitcher.

"More? Do you want more water?"

Luke sputtered and then croaked out, "Drink.

Thirsty." His face felt like leather and someone had lined his throat with sandpaper.

"Don't choke like you did before."

She lifted his head and rested it in her lap. A trickle of water from the pitcher became a downpour. This time he was ready. Spitting some out, he kept enough in his parched mouth to revive him. Then he wondered if it was worth the effort. No part of him didn't hurt like a million ants crawled along his veins, nipping viciously and biting out hunks of his flesh.

He forced his way to a sitting position. Her hand stroked over his matted hair. When she brushed across his ear, he recoiled. The movement highlighted how many other places he hurt, especially dead center of his chest.

"Why aren't I dead?" He probed the burned spot on his vest. Then he laughed. "The derringer. Audrey's bullet struck the derringer!" He pulled the ruined two-barreled pistol from his vest pocket. Her slug had hit the gun and set off a round, making her think she had killed him. The errant round from the derringer left a shallow groove in his chest and caused the blood to run down his side. The way it soaked his coat fooled both Audrey and Benedict into thinking she had killed him.

"Those terrible Johnny Rebs," Sarah said. "They tried to kill you, and I couldn't stop them."

"You collapsed. Are you all right?" He felt a pang of guilt. He had intended to shoot past her in an attempt to kill Crazy Water Benedict. If he had missed, Sarah's life would have been forfeit. She might be crazy but she wasn't murderous like his wife.

Like his never-wife because she had already married Benedict.

"They rode off. That way. You should warn your commanding officer. This battle isn't over yet."

"No, it's not." He peeled back the matted cloth of his shirt and vest. The blood that soaked into his coat made it feel twice its weight, and that included the gold dust sewn into it. Audrey had been in too big a rush to lay her hands on the gold from the bank robbery to remember what Luke had considered their nest egg.

"I'm not good at bandaging wounds, but I can try. For my hero, Lucas, I can try."

Deceiving her caused him less guilt than he expected. As he leaned heavily on Sarah, they made their way to the stream. He stripped down and began washing off the caked blood. She disappeared for a while, leaving him to his own devices. It gave him a chance to plot and plan. He lacked the skills to track that most of the others showed, but he knew the general direction Benedict and Audrey had taken.

"Mister and Missus Malcolm Benedict," he said with bitterness oozing from every word. That simple declaration, as much as anything else, solidified his plans and strengthened his resolve. Justice would be meted out. They had left him his Schofield. If he thought he needed them, other weapons were scattered around the gang's former hideout.

Chasing after them on his plow horse might be a slow process, but he needed time to heal. He had beaten Rollie Rhoades in a fair gunfight—and it felt good seeing the outlaw with a slug in his chest. The pleasure would be even greater when he gunned down Crazy Water Benedict.

But what about Audrey? He had loved her with all his heart and soul. She had never cared one whit for him. She saw him as a sucker to be fleeced and nothing more. Her time with Rhoades in Chicago and with Benedict for who knows how long had turned her heart into cold, black stone. In spite of that, Luke doubted he had the nerve to return the favor she had shown him. Pulling the trigger if he had the drop on her wasn't in the cards.

When Sarah returned, he felt good enough to be embarrassed by his lack of clothing. He had shed everything down to his long johns, and then had peeled away the torso to reveal all his wounds. After he healed, there'd be an army of scars crossing over his side and especially his chest. He probed the wicked red wound just above his diaphragm where the derringer had exploded. The groove left by the bullet after the pistol discharged was hardly more than a rope burn, but that didn't mean he felt no pain. He winced as Sarah touched it.

"I can fix that. I found some salve." She slathered on some. He almost passed out as pain drove like a knife into his body. "Sorry, Lucas, so sorry. I'm no good at this. I should have volunteered with that Clara Barton lady and learned how to be a nurse."

"You're doing fine." Light-headed, he wobbled about. She supported him. How he had a chance against Benedict in his condition posed a question he dared not answer. He had to go.

Mal Benedict. And his wife. Luke had to go before they reached the gold cache and disappeared for good. He had an idea where they rode now. If they got to Canada or anywhere else, finding them would be a matter of pure chance. He had the feeling that he had used up all the good luck for a lifetime.

"Now to wrap some bandages around you." Her hands lovingly caressed him. If the situation had been different, the temptation to lie and claim he was her dead husband could easily have overwhelmed his sense of right and wrong. She was thin and had worn the wedding dress so long it had become a part of her. He had scraped off his blood-soaked clothing. Her dress clung from years of sweat and grime. They both needed a change of clothing after all they'd been through.

He sucked in his breath as she pulled the bandage tight. Where she had found them mattered less to him than what he said next.

"I have to leave, Sarah. You need to stay here. Or better yet, ride and find the posse. They're out there somewhere."

"I'm not leaving you. Never again, Lucas!" She threw her arms around his neck and pulled him off-balance. It took all his strength to keep from falling over.

"It's going to be dangerous, and I don't want you hurt."

"I won't ever let you go anywhere without me."

For a waif as emaciated as Sarah Youngblood, she had what felt like a death grip around his neck. Prying her loose wasn't possible until he agreed to let her ride with him.

"I'll take real good care of you. I will, Lucas, I promise!"

"Do you have a horse?" Everything about her riding off with Marta Shearing came to him in fuzzy patches.

"I do. That bossy woman found me one. She ordered me around, so I left. I came back here to you." She got him in a headlock again. It wasn't any easier prying her arms loose a second time.

"So Miss Shearing wasn't hurt? What did she do after you left?"

"How should I know what she did when I wasn't there? You're being silly, aren't you? She kept going on and on about finding a marshal. Lawmen never treat me good. They try to put me in jail. I wanted to come back to you."

He walked back to the camp, feeling better and testing the limits of his strength. The new wounds troubled him less than the bullet he had taken in the rump. Now and then he got dizzy, but it wasn't anything he couldn't work through.

"Fetch us all the food you can find," he told Sarah. "Pack our saddlebags. While you're doing that, I'll gather up some guns and ammunition." Having an arsenal tucked in his belt and over his shoulder had worked before. His trusty Schofield still hung at his side. Keeping it in reserve made sense. When he needed a reliable gun, he knew where to find it.

An hour later, they left the gang's hideout. Sarah rode a spirited gelding and he sat astride the plow horse. Finding the trail proved easy.

Then the rain began pelting down to erase the hoofprints.

CHAPTER TWENTY-ONE

"We have to keep riding." Luke Hadley put his head down so the rain dripped off his hat brim. He had given up hunting for Audrey's trail a mile back. The rain wasn't so powerful that it erased hoofprints instantly, but he lacked the skill to figure out which water-filled depressions in the dirt were prints and which were only caused by falling rain.

"I want to stop. I'm cold." To lend emphasis to her plea, Sarah shivered. Water flew off her like a dog shaking itself.

It was cruel forcing her to continue. She would catch her death of cold. Being such a spindly thing, Sarah had to be prone to any disease that drifted by. Luke felt guilty pressing on, but he worried how much longer his strength would last. Anger and the need for vengeance kept him going now. If he simmered down, his energy would drain away just as the rainwater dripped from his hat.

He glanced up and caught a drop in his eye. The drop had beaded on a hole shot in his hat. When that hole had been put there was a mystery to him since it was a few inches toward the rim from ones he knew already had been there. Never in all his born days had he expected gun battles to melt together in his head. He had been in too many over the past couple weeks to even guess.

"Not what you expect from a sodbuster," he said.

"Lucas," Sarah whined.

"Very well. Let's find a dry place to hole up until the storm passes."

"It's going to be dark soon. I want to camp for the night." She flashed him a shy little smile. He tensed, thinking he knew what she wanted to ask for next. She surprised him. "And supper. Food would be so nice. I'll fix it for you real good. I promise."

He said nothing. Scouting for a dry spot dragged on longer than he expected. Sparse stands of trees gave some protection, but once the leaves got wet, the rain dripped endlessly long after the storm cloud passed. He found a bulge in the land promising rockier ground. The rolling hills finally yielded a spot in the lee side that was drier than anywhere else he had seen. Dismounting, he motioned for Sarah to join him.

Silently, they went about setting up camp. He found some branches dry enough to burn. After making a small lean-to, he dug a shallow firepit and got a fire started.

"You learned so much being a soldier," she said. She sat close to him. Luke didn't want her getting the wrong idea. She thought he was her long-lost husband, but he wasn't Lucas Youngblood.

Not for the first time he wished he had figured out

how to leave her behind in the gang's hideout. Tying her up was about the only thing possible. To do so meant she starved to death if she failed to wiggle free or a posse rode past without knowing she was trussed up.

"War made you different," she said.

"Getting shot up will do that." He touched the spot on his chest where the derringer had discharged and the shrapnel beneath that still rode under the skin. Riding for most of the day caused his rear end to hurt. It sounded funny, getting shot there, but he found it increasingly difficult to stay on the trail because of that wound.

A tiny smile crept to his lips. He had been close to unconscious when Marta Shearing sewed him up. He had expected to feel humiliated letting a strange woman see his naked hindquarters. More than that, she had patched him up and applied a bandage to her sutures. Nothing about her made him think of her as a dispassionate nurse. She focused on her job as much as he did on finding Crazy Water Benedict. He just felt more at ease with her.

Or shock had dulled his sense of shame letting a woman he hardly knew see him like that.

"It made me different," Sarah said. "I know what people say about me. 'That crazy woman,' they call me. It doesn't matter. I sing to keep up my spirits. And it works. I knew if I kept singing you'd come back. You always liked my singing and came running for dinner before I ever got to a second verse in most tunes. It worked just fine." She wrapped her arms around him and pulled herself closer. Her body was as warm as the small fire at the edge of the lean-to.

Luke hardly moved. To do so might give her the

wrong idea. She rested her head on his shoulder and stayed like that. Only her gentle breath against his wet shirt told she was there.

He stared out into the drizzle. Any chance of finding Benedict's tracks were gone, but he remembered the map he had seen in Marshal Hargrove's office. There had been several places marked with X's. He closed his eyes and figured out which had been the actual hideout. A smile came to his lips. Another spot to the northwest had attracted Hargrove's attention. If he assumed Rhoades was a man of habit, that possible hideout turned into a hiding place for the stolen gold. That cache possibly lay only a few miles farther.

Luke moved carefully and disengaged from Sarah. She stretched out so that her feet stuck out into the rain. The gentle drops falling on her ankles caused her to curl up so she was completely under the lean-to. He rolled out into the rain, pulled up his collar and tugged his hat into position. They had camped at the foot of a low hill. He tramped to the top, expecting to get a better idea of the landscape.

Mud sucked at his boots, and the rain turned colder. The sun must be sinking, though the heavy clouds hid that daily occurrence. More than once he considered retreating, but he had already climbed more than halfway. Once he crested the hill, a blast of wind staggered him. He put his head down and found a rock to scale, giving him another few feet of altitude.

He scanned the terrain in the direction suggested by the marshal's map. The cold gnawing at his bones turned to fire when he saw a curl of smoke on the far side of the hill.

"Luck's all mine. No matter what's happened so far, it's all mine right now."

He had come across the spot where Audrey and Benedict camped. Moving his coat back, he touched the Schofield at his hip. Darkness and storm masked him. It would take only a few minutes to reach the camp, cock his six-gun and fire twice. Both of them would be turned into worm food as fast as he could pull the trigger.

With a shrug, he let the coat fall back over his six-shooter and sagged in despair. His anger was immense, but gunning both of them down in cold blood wasn't something he could do. Such murder put him on their level.

"She'd have murdered me in my sleep," he said. "Benedict has tried to kill me more than once." Then he remembered how Audrey had begged the outlaw for the chance to shoot him. She had wanted a divorce written in blood and hot lead, not that they were even married. She had married Crazy Water Benedict years earlier.

Everything jumbled in his head. They deserved to die for what they'd done to him, but he wasn't a killer. The outlaws who had died at his hand—all self-defense. Facing down Rollie Rhoades had been a fair fight. But sneaking up and firing into a bedroll to kill a sleeping Audrey or even Mal Benedict rankled.

"Who am I kidding?" He jumped down from his pinnacle and slipped and slid downhill to where Sarah had roused from her sleep and prepared some oatmeal. She dipped a finger in and stirred, then licked it clean of the sticky cereal.

"Supper's all ready. There's some hardtack, too. I can warm it up on the rocks around the fire."

He sank beside her. He took a tin plate with a dollop of oatmeal on it and scooped it into his mouth. It needed brown sugar to make the lumps more palatable, but he ate mechanically. On the way back he had worked out a scheme. Now he had to convince Sarah to go along with it.

"I found them. They're on the other side of this very hill." He stared at her. She paid him no attention as she fussed about with the small cooking pot. "I want you to ride back and find the posse. Bring them here."

"When do we leave? It's still raining." She put the pot out where the rain spatted into it. At the rate it filled, they'd be here another hour. Luke champed at the bit to get moving. The end of all his woe was at hand. Postponing the confrontation only made him more nervous.

"You're not listening. I have to go on. You must find the marshal and bring him here. To support me."

"If we both find the marshal, he can support you sooner." She frowned. "What's that mean? 'Support' you?"

"This is my fight. You have to tell the marshal where the gold is."

"But I—"

He hushed her with a finger on her lips. As he eased off, she started to speak again. He pressed his finger back. This wasn't getting any easier for him.

"If you love me, you'll do this. For me." Luke hated himself for taking advantage of her delusions. "You go, then we'll be back together. Later."

"But I heard—"

"Please, Sarah. Will you do it?" He considered the dangerous tactic of tying her up, then returning to free her. If anything happened to him, she might die. The chances were good he'd get shot up. He touched his damaged ear and flinched. The rest of his wounds were patched up good enough to keep from bleeding. He felt weak as a kitten from blood loss, but his hand remained firm and steady. That's what he needed to deal with Benedict.

He had to decide how to deal with Audrey.

"I don't understand." She drew up her knees and hugged them. A song rose, low at first, then growing in volume. He shook her until she stopped singing, pointed to her horse and gently pushed her in that direction.

"I used my slicker for the lean-to. You wear it. It's bright yellow, and the posse can spot you quicker."

"You'll get wet."

He tried to reassure her that that didn't matter without coming out and warning her of his chances against Crazy Water Benedict. Most gunmen he had heard about ended up being shot in the back. That had always struck him as a cowardly thing to do. Facing Rhoades changed him. At the time he hadn't felt that nervous. A touch of fear, but nothing that kept him from being deadly accurate. In a way he had more than simple survival on his mind then. He had fought to save his beloved wife. That determination wiped away panic.

The longer he thought about it, and the less he felt for Audrey, the more appealing it came to sneak up on Benedict and gun him down from ambush. Bravery and careful reflection were strangers.

"Here," he said, shoving one of his captured pistols into the woman's hand. "You probably won't need it. If you do, use it. You know how, don't you?"

"Of course I do. You showed me, Lucas, before you went gallivanting off to war."

"That was a long time ago," he muttered.

"I won't be long." She settled the slicker around her thin frame, tucked the six-gun into her saddlebags and graced him with a smile.

Sarah rode off into the drizzle. She never looked back but did start singing "Green Grow the Lilacs." He watched until he no longer saw or heard her. He gathered his gear and stowed it, checked the Schofield to be sure it carried a full load, then made certain the other pistol tucked into his belt was ready for action, too.

Firepower set for use, he led his horse around the base of the hill until he reckoned he was only a hundred yards from the camp.

"The enemy camp," he muttered. Getting himself prepared for the gunfight mattered now. Calling those two out for their actions helped. He pressed his fingers into the middle of his chest until a stab of pain caused him to suck in a tortured breath. Audrey had done more than shoot him there. She had ripped out his heart, as well.

He advanced slowly until he heard their voices. Luke sank down and tried to figure the best approach to their camp. They were close to the windward side and caught occasional gusts. He smirked. He knew how to pick a campsite, and it wasn't where the wind blew all night. Storms pounded this side of the hill. Flagging on the few trees marching up the side showed that clear as a bell. He was more skillful than the pair of them when it came to finding a decent campsite.

Buoyed by this small triumph, he crawled forward

on his belly through the undergrowth until he was within a few yards. He drew the captured six-gun and made sure the one riding in his holster came out fast and easy. If he ran through six rounds that meant he'd need six more in a hurry.

"You and Rhoades went off together. Back in Chicago. You were gone for a week." Benedict sounded close to losing his temper.

"We found ourselves a mark. It took time to fleece him out of his money so he wouldn't go to the police. That was important back then, you know? We had to keep working in one town. It wasn't like we swooped down, robbed a bank and hightailed it for who knows where."

"I know where. You don't," Benedict said. "And I was sayin' you and Rhoades were doin' more than just nobbling some fool out of his money."

"Are you accusing me of cheating on you, Malcolm Benedict?"

"I reckon I am. We were married then, but you and Rhoades were mighty close a lot of the time. He always found some chore to send me off on, like I was his errand boy. Lookin' back now, those weren't anything important but just a way to have you for himself."

"He was always a better man than you, Mal. In all ways. He was smarter, he was quicker with a gun, he was a lot better than you in—"

Luke recoiled at the sound of a loud slap. Audrey gasped. He moved forward in an attempt to find a hiding spot to spy on their argument. He had to see what went on. If he barged in at the wrong time, they both might shoot him.

He crept closer, aware of the squishy sounds he

made in the mud. When he tried to step rather than sneak, the sounds became sucking noises as he broke the seal between his boot sole and the muddy ground. The argument grew louder. The small noises he made were drowned out by the shouts as the two argued.

Crouching low, he parted a chokeberry bush and saw Audrey and Benedict standing almost nose to nose. She stood with balled fists. He reared back, ready to slap her again. Luke caught his breath. They turned into statues, a frozen tableau of anger. His heart almost exploded when he thought they had spotted him spying on them.

Instead, it was just a moment's hesitation.

"You don't deserve anything. You cheated on me with Rhoades. And I think you wanted to run off with that sodbuster. Admit it. You weren't trying to fleece him. You wanted to cozy up to him and—"

That was as far as Benedict got before Audrey punched him. She didn't even wind up. Her fist came from the side in a roundhouse punch that caught him on the temple. He stumbled and went to one knee. He shook his head to clear it as he looked up at her. The sneer on his lips became forever etched in Luke's memory. Never had he seen anything quite so cruel, even when Benedict had shot him at the wedding ceremony.

"You'll never see any of the gold. I'll make sure of that!" Benedict got to his feet. The punch he intended to deliver would stun a bull. Hitting a woman with such force would kill her. He meant to beat Audrey to death with his fists.

"I don't need you," she said, backing away. "I know where Rollie hid the gold."

"There's no way you could. He never talked to you before the farmer gunned him down."

"He told me before he robbed the bank. He told me everything, how he intended to double-cross the rest of the gang—and you!"

"I figured he wasn't playing fair. He had a twitch in his eyelid. Every time he lied, it twitched. Was it twitching when he said the two of you were going to run off together? I'll bet even money that his eye was almost squinting with that tic!"

Luke saw Audrey go rigid. Benedict had wounded her with his words. He advanced on her, ready to do more than wound her with his fists.

He never got the chance. From the folds of her dress she drew a small pistol. It was almost engulfed by her hand.

"I can't say it's been good between us, Mal."

"That toy? It's not big enough to—"

She fired point-blank into his chest. He staggered. She fired again and again until he fell facedown on the ground. Audrey kicked him once, twice, a third time.

"You died too fast, Mal. I wanted you to suffer." She stared at him as she raised the pistol to keep firing into his back.

Luke stood, his six-gun in his hand. He realized instantly the mistake he made. Waiting for her to empty the pistol was the smart tactic. When he appeared, she caught movement from the corner of her eye. Instinct rather than skill caused her to whip around and trigger off two more rounds.

Standing still was safer than moving, but lead flying so close to him sent Luke diving into the bushes. He wiggled along like a snake for a few feet, then came up to see Audrey drawing Benedict's six-shooter from his holster. The way she held it warned him she was a good shot. The heavy iron never wavered as she cocked the gun and widened her stance.

"Whoever you are, come on out."

"You don't recognize me, Audrey?" He chanced a quick look up.

The expression on her face was priceless.

"You? You're dead! I put a slug in your chest, set fire to your vest!"

"Drop the gun, Audrey. Surrender and I'll take you in. I'm taking you in and you're going to prison for a long, long time—if the judge doesn't sentence you to hang!"

Luke jerked back. He had made another mistake. In spite of her obvious familiarity with a six-gun, he dismissed it all in his rush to humiliate her for all she had done to him. He scrambled behind the wall of brush until he came to a dead one to shoot through. Luke swung his gun back and forth, hunting for a target.

Audrey was nowhere to be seen.

CHAPTER TWENTY-TWO

LUKE STEPPED OUT from behind his shrub cover, wary that he walked into an ambush. He turned his good ear toward the camp. He heard the slow rain causing a loud hiss as it extinguished the campfire. In the distance the thudding of a galloping horse receded. Audrey had eluded him.

He made a quick circuit of the camp. Benedict's gear was untouched. Audrey hadn't wasted an instant heading for the hidden gold once she killed Benedict. Luke stopped and stared at the outlaw's body. He shook his head sadly. This would have been him if he had stayed with Audrey even a day longer.

"Thanks," Luke said. "You don't know it but you saved my life." He touched the spot on his chest where Benedict had shot him. "I only wish I'd been the one to put you in the ground."

He resisted the urge to kick Benedict. Audrey had

done that for him. Truth was, she had done more than kick him. Luke paused, considering how long it would take to bury the outlaw. It was more than he deserved.

Memory of the last hoofbeats fading away decided him. Let the wolves and coyotes and buzzards take care of Mal Benedict.

"Just don't get sick on the putrid meat," he said. A quick spin oriented him. He'd have to ride through a storm, at night, following a woman whose only goal was to recover gold from a bank robbery before hightailing it north. Uncertainty and danger were going to be his trail companions, but he had come this far. Luke Hadley wasn't the kind to quit. He touched the bloody spot on his chest to reassure himself of that. Twice he'd been shot there and twice he had survived.

She had mentioned Canada, he remembered. Or one of the gang had. Rhoades had intended to go south into Indian Territory, but she had suggested the opposite direction. Once she retrieved the gold, she had no reason to follow any plan laid out by Rollie Rhoades.

It took him close to fifteen minutes to find his horse and convince it to leave a nice patch of succulent blue grama. He tugged and slapped and spoke softly and yelled. Finally the old horse gave in and let him hit the trail after Audrey.

Luke pulled down his hat and turned it just a little so the hole in the brim leaked water to the side of his face. The warm rain turned colder as he rode, and all too soon he began to ache and downright hurt all over. Worst was his half-shot-off ear. He had never been a vain man, or so he told himself, but showing his face in public now meant ridicule. Children would point and snicker and women would turn away to avoid looking at him directly. In his day he had seen enough men with wounds worse than this. A few jokes at his expense tested how he reacted. If he ever showed that it hurt him, he'd either be an outcast or have to practice his draw. Survive a few drunks insulting him, buy a few rounds, then he'd fit in.

Among those similarly shot up or deformed.

He pulled his hat down a little tighter around his head. The brim scraped the ragged top of his left ear to remind him what Audrey had cost him. Finding her and the gang had almost taken his life. When he finally caught up with her, nothing more mattered.

"There, go there," he said to his horse. The stolid animal changed direction slowly. It slogged through fetlock-deep puddles and kept moving. Luke lifted his face as a lightning bolt ripped through the sky.

In the afterimage he saw a solitary rider. Audrey? He wasn't able to tell because of the sheets of rain and the distance, but who else braved the elements this night? He tried to spur the horse to a quicker gait. It refused. Its one speed suited it, and that meant it had to suit Luke, too.

He wanted a mount that flew. He wanted this to be over. Most of all he wanted to reach a point in his life where he no longer thought of Audrey or their wedding or anything to do with her. Recovering the stolen loot from the bank robbery meant less than simply washing his hands of her.

His hand moved and touched his gun butt. How he won free of her was still something to determine. As he rode in the rain, the sound of drops spattering against his brim stole away any chance to hear her horse. The increasing number of lightning bolts and the thunder rumbling from them made his ears ring almost constantly. Worse, the flashes and noise spooked his otherwise staid horse.

Riding in his own bubble, the world of storm enveloping him, he began to dream of the map on Marshal Hargrove's desk. The marshal had been sure the Rhoades gang was planning a bank robbery, but not in his Podunk town. That hadn't stopped him from trying to figure where the real robbery would take place. Hargrove had been all het up because of the way station being burned to the ground and the deaths of three locals. In his way, he had better reason to come after the gang than Marshal Wilkes, and it had been his town suffering the robbery.

The thought of the map caused Luke to strain to remember more details. Where he had killed Rhoades had been marked with one X. Others around it had to mean something. Hiding places favored by the outlaws? He got his bearings before the heavy rain started and headed for another of the X's on that map.

Since Audrey rode the same direction, and she claimed Rhoades had spilled the beans about where he had stashed the gold, he felt more confident about continuing the hunt in spite of the foul weather.

Trying to remember the map suddenly became a moot point. He heard the spark of a horse's hooves against rock. It came through the steady drone of the rain clear and sweet. His horse turned toward the sound, and he spotted a dim figure ahead. The sheets of water and the dark prevented him from identifying the rider. He nudged his horse to a slightly faster gait, knowing this was about the maximum speed the plow horse had in him.

To this point he hadn't considered the best way of proceeding. The gold mattered very little to him. He still had a small fortune, for him, in gold dust sewn into his battered coat. What penalty to extract from Audrey tore at him, though.

"Had loved her." His words were buried under a thunderclap. He wished his confused emotions were as easily hidden. Somehow, a new crackle of lightning working its way from cloud to cloud and turning the landscape into a purpled haze decided him.

He reached the rocky patch that had betrayed the woman. Finding her trail amid the rocks proved easy, even for a novice trailsman like himself. The path through the rocks was limited as it worked higher on a hill. As he rode, he fumbled about in his coat pocket and found the fake tin star. He worked the leather backing down into a vest pocket so the star with its bullet hole rode on his chest, as if he were a real lawman. He might pretend, but for a short time he would work as a real Pinkerton agent.

Reaching the crest of the hill gave a strange view of the plains all around. As the wind whipped the clouds about, curtains of rain drew back and showed the prairie in black and white. He sat a bit straighter when he saw movement far to the north. He settled down when he realized he saw a small herd of buffalo weathering the storm, moving slowly, heads lowered and downwind.

He caught his breath when he looked along the ridge in the other direction. A horse tethered to a tree limb tugged and whinnied and tried to break free and run. The vivid bolts and snapping thunder spooked it. But its rider was nowhere to be seen.

Luke dismounted and walked his horse. For all the weather, the horse remained sedate. Not much spooked it. He swung the reins around the limb next to those of Audrey's horse and studied the ground. Footprints on a muddy trail were so fresh they hadn't even filled with water.

He rested his hand on the butt of his Schofield. Months tracking Audrey, praying she was still alive, came to a sorry conclusion now. Taking the same trail, he almost slipped in his haste. He slowed and then stopped when he saw a figure crouched ahead. Two trees bent toward each other, forming an X. Directly under the intersection someone had built a small rock cairn.

Advancing slowly, he drew his pistol and let it hang loose at his side.

"That's real smart," he said. "Hide the gold in what looks like somebody's grave. Nobody who doesn't know what's there is likely to dig it up. And it's easy enough to find."

Audrey spun about so fast, she lost her balance and sat heavily on a grassy patch. She reached for her pistol, then saw Luke raise his six-gun. He cocked it to let her know how close she came to getting plugged.

"Luke! I—"

"You didn't expect to see me because you shot me down like you did Benedict?"

"He made me do terrible things, Luke. You saw what power he had. He controlled me. I was helpless!"

He moved a little closer. She had removed the rocks

where the corpse's feet would be. A slab of wood caught the rain and sent droplets bouncing.

"You want to go on and open the grave?"

"I don't know what got into me. It's wrong to desecrate a grave."

"Stop it! I'm not that stupid. I fell for your lies. I even asked you to marry me. That's all crazy and dumb. But I'm not so dumb that I don't know what's hidden here. Rhoades told you where to find the stolen gold, and that's it."

"Look, Luke, I still have it. I'm wearing your wedding ring." She held up her left hand. A flash of lightning reflected off a tiny gold band.

He swung his six-gun around and fired. The bullet kicked up mud and grass between Audrey's reaching hand and her pistol.

"I swear, if you'd not gone for your gun, I'd have been fool enough to take you back."

She shifted her weight to her knees and knelt as if praying. Her face burned with contempt for him.

"Now who's the liar? You came hunting for me to kill me." She turned her head a little and looked at his chest, then locked her gaze with his. "That's a badge. You're a deputy?"

"It's a Pinkerton badge."

"No!"

This produced more reaction from her than he expected. It both pleased him that it agitated her so and also made him a bit sorry for her.

"What's the agency want you for? What'd you do back in Chicago?"

She spat.

"You're one of them Pinks. Allan sent you to find me, so you know what they want me for. I'm not going back. Not ever, and you can't make me." She lowered her head, then looked back at him. "No more lies, Luke. You know I don't love you. You know that me and Mal were married for more than a year and that makes our wedding a fraud."

"Why are you trying to get me to shoot you?" His hand trembled the slightest amount. The rain was slowing and the intense lightning moved farther south. In another half hour there wouldn't be any hint in the sky above that the storm had ever existed. The stars would show and the clear sky would show the best a Kansas summer night had to offer.

"I'm not. I think we can be partners—not lovers!" She looked panicked at that notion. His stomach did a flip. She rushed on with her plea. "We're survivors, me and you. I don't know how you kept from dying with so many bullets in you, but you did." She peered hard at his chest, just to the right of the star rising and falling with his heavy breathing.

Luke stiffened when he saw her look away from him and her eyes go wide. Not much, but not subtle, either. He feinted right and dived left as three shots tore through the air where his head had been.

"If you don't die with a bullet to the heart, I'll blow your fool head off!" The voice was one he recognized all too well.

More bullets sought to perforate his hide. He hit the ground and skidded along. Jerking hard, he twisted around. Pain shot through his tortured body. Then he sprawled on his back, furious at what he saw.

"Benedict! How'd you survive?"

"She shot me but like everything else, she never finished the job." Benedict kept firing until the hammer fell on a spent chamber.

Luke struggled to sit up. Waves of pain blasted through him. He lifted his six-gun using both hands and got off a shot. He missed by a mile, but he forced Benedict to look up. For an instant he stopped working to reload his Colt.

"I won't miss this time," Luke promised. "Rhoades outdrew me, but I was the better shot. And by the stars above, I will not miss you." His hand steadied and a coldness seeped into him. This had to be what gunfighters felt in a fight. No nerves, confidence, even the arrogance that they were good enough to take another man's life.

"Don't listen to him, Mal. Kill him!" Audrey scurried about, hunting for her pistol in the dark.

Luke looked from her back to Benedict and knew where the real danger lay. He fired at the outlaw again. This time he either winged his target or came close enough to send him blundering away into the night. Scissoring his legs in a powerful kick gave him enough momentum to turn over and come to his hands and knees. From there, he climbed to his feet.

"You might be a cat and have nine lives, but I'll take them one by one till you ain't got anything left!" Benedict snapped the gate on his six-shooter shut with a click as loud as a gunshot.

The threat allowed Luke to home in on where Benedict had taken cover. Bushes moved just a bit to tell him he was being gulled into thinking the outlaw was in one place when he was a yard away. But which way? If he fired, the muzzle flash would give away his position in the dark.

"Shoot him, Mal. Don't let him take the gold!"

Luke glanced at Audrey. She still searched for her gun. Of all the things she might have done, she chose the worst. If she'd kept her mouth shut, Luke would have ignored her and kept after Benedict. As it was, she goaded her husband on to kill the man who'd have let her live. Luke knew there wasn't any chance after what she'd done that Benedict would let her live. However much gold had been buried spent a whole lot better if one hand passed over the gold coins rather than two.

Moving deliberately, he tried to get Benedict to give himself away. The outlaw was too cagey for that. The bush moved again. Droplets of water from the rain cascaded off the leaves. Luke still couldn't see where Benedict waited in ambush.

The longer he waited, the more dangerous his position became. If Audrey found her pistol, there'd be two guns trained on him, and they'd have him in a cross fire. Though he knew she would shoot Benedict if she had the chance, the woman's treachery knew no bounds. Both he and Benedict—her two husbands—were corpses with a gun in her grip.

She was dangerous. Benedict was the real threat. Luke judged how far on either side of the moving bush a man might hide. He fanned one round off to the left, spun and fanned another round the same distance to the right. The second shot rewarded him with a grunt. Then Benedict blazed away. The foot-long tongues of orange flame gave him away as surely as Luke's firing had flushed him like a quail.

The difference was in mobility. Benedict had lain flat on the ground to set his trap. Luke, as painful as it was for him, moved away from his initial position. He advanced until a silhouette formed to his right.

He fired twice more. This time Benedict cried out in utter pain. Then came silence. Deathly silence.

"Mal! Are you hurt, Mal?"

Luke swung back to the woman. She had her pistol in her hand. She froze when she saw that Luke had the drop on her.

"I need to poke him to be sure, but I suspect Benedict is more than hurt. I finished off the chore you started back at your hideout."

"You got me all wrong, Luke. They held me prisoner!"

"You said no more lies."

"All right. What I was saying before is that we can split the gold. We can each go our separate way, but together we can get rich. We can use the gold as a stake to buy a ranch. Not a farm. Cattle. We can raise a whole herd of longhorns. That's where the money is, in beef. Or we can go to San Francisco. You can use the money to stake yourself in poker games. You're smart. You can clean the lot of them tinhorn gamblers out in nothing flat."

"I don't know how to play poker."

"I can show you. Partners, Luke, we can be partners!"

"That's enough of your lying, Audrey. I don't want to hear another word."

He lifted his six-gun and pointed it squarely at her. He had moved close enough so he couldn't miss. His finger had drawn back on the trigger when he heard movement behind him.

A cold voice said, "Drop the gun, Hadley. Drop it or I drop you!"

He hesitated. A single quick jerk on the trigger ended Audrey's miserable existence. What else did he have to prove?

"Luke, he means it." This was another voice he recognized.

He glanced over his shoulder. Marta Shearing stood beside Marshal Wilkes. Both had their guns drawn and aimed at him. She lowered hers. The lawman drew a bead. Luke took a deep breath, eased down the hammer on his six-gun and slipped it into his holster. He turned, hands raised.

"She's yours," he said, not sure who he directed it to. From the delighted expression on her face, Marta got custody.

"You're gonna pay!" Audrey shrieked.

Luke heard Audrey moving, then crashed forward facedown onto the ground. Her weight kept him from moving. She pinned his shoulder down with her knees. The hiss of a knife slipping from a sheath told him what was next. She had stabbed him in the back before, but not with a steel blade. This time she'd finish the job that Rhoades and Benedict had failed at before.

Fight or die. Those were his only options. He grunted as he pushed straight up against her weight. Muscles strained and popped but he wasn't going to die like this. As suddenly as Audrey's weight had crushed him, it disappeared.

For an instant he thought he listened to a catfight. Hissing and screeching and rolling around. He came up to his knees and laughed.

Sarah Youngblood had tackled Audrey from behind.

"Get off her. Take that knife away. Do it!" Wilkes motioned for his deputies to disarm Audrey. "If you don't, I'll shoot her. Then I swear, you'll all walk back to Crossroads!"

This lit a fire under the men in his posse. They rushed forward. Two of them grabbed the fighting, spitting, snapping Audrey and pulled her away. Rabid dogs put up less of a fight. Somehow they shackled her and dragged her off.

"I declare, I have to tell them boys every little thing to do," the marshal said, looking like he'd bitten into a rotten apple. He spat, wiped his mouth, then pointed to the partially unearthed grave. "The bank's gold there?"

"It seems that way, Marshal. It's all yours," Marta said. "In exchange for the prisoner. She's going back to Chicago."

"I don't want her, that's for certain sure." He took off his hat and swept it across his leg for emphasis. "The town's not got the money for a trial, and I don't need the drama. Rebuilding what got blowed up is going to provide too much of that."

Luke came to his feet. Sarah grabbed him and spun him around.

"I saved you, I saved my Lucas!" She almost squeezed the stuffing from him with her bear hug. He pried her loose.

"Why don't you ride on back to Crossroads with the deputies? I'll be there soon enough."

"You promise?" She looked up with nothing but admiration and love in her eyes. "When you find the gold, you'll come to town?"

"What's that?" Luke perked up. "We found the gold." He pointed at the partially opened grave site.

"That's not where he hid the gold. He said it was hid real good. That's not real good. Why, anybody would know to look there."

"Wait!" Luke shouted to stop the marshal from digging more dirt from the wood planks hiding the grave's interior. "She overheard Rhoades talking with his henchman. Be careful poking around."

"Miss Youngblood led us right here, Marshal. You have to think she knows more than any of us of the outlaw's scheme," Marta said.

"She's crazy as a bedbug." Wilkes still backed away a pace. "What are we going to do?"

Luke pushed Sarah into the arms of a deputy, who reacted as if he'd rubbed up against a leper. In spite of his obvious distaste, the deputy pulled her farther away. Luke picked up a long tree branch and went to the foot of the grave where Audrey had begun excavation. He jabbed tentatively at the exposed planks.

"Go on, do it right," Marta said. "Give it a real poke. Here." She reached around him, took a double hand grip on the branch and shoved.

The explosion lifted both her and Luke into the air and tossed them back to land hard. The impact stunned him. Luke wondered if any part of his body wasn't hurting. He looked, his eyes watering from fumes spewed out by the explosion. Dirt and debris still cascaded down. Marta simply stared at the hole in the ground.

"He set a mine for us, like those the Confederate Secret Service used."

Luke gaped. She looked disgusted at his lack of knowledge.

"Torpedoes. Rains patents. General Gabriel Rains?

Oh, never mind. I should have expected something like this. Rhoades loved his explosives." She helped Luke to his feet.

They edged closer to the crater.

"Rhoades loved one thing more," Luke said. "The notion of blowing people up with his dynamite. He set the trap for Benedict. That's the only explanation. If Benedict double-crossed him, both were goners. If Benedict played straight, Rhoades deactivated the trigger."

"Why bother doing that at all?" Marshal Wilkes peered into the crater. "If they stayed partners, leave the grave unopened and ride off. I reckon Rhoades had it in mind for Benedict to dig here, though. Thieves. Double-crossing thieves, the lot of them." He spat into the grave.

"That sounds like what Rhoades planned," Marta said. She peered into the cavity. "I don't see any trace of gold in there. Not one speck."

"So where's the gold?" Marshal Wilkes slapped his hat against his thigh again in frustration. "Even though he's dead, Rollie Rhoades is still causing me a world of woe. I can't go back without the loot. Everyone in town would eat me alive. And the banker? What'll he do? This is a pile of money belonging to ranchers." Wilkes sagged, a defeated man.

Luke kept himself from feeling any vindication. The lawman had tossed him in jail for no good reason. But Wilkes didn't deserve to have his career—maybe his life—put in jeopardy. Even dead, Rhoades presented a powerful adversary to defeat.

"He won't get away with it," Luke said. He thought he spoke only to himself, but the ringing in his ears caused him to talk far louder than he anticipated. Everyone stared at him.

"What're your thoughts, Mister Hadley?" Marta's expression said she expected him to return the gold. Find it, then return it.

"Why are you callin' him 'mister'?" Wilkes came closer and saw the fake badge dangling on Luke's chest. "He's one of your folks? A Pink?"

"He's one of our best undercover agents," she said loudly. In a lower voice, she added for Luke's benefit, "if he finds the gold."

Luke stepped away from the grave and stared up at the crossed trees. They formed a perfect marker to find the gold. Only Rhoades had left a trap here. He walked around, then back to use the X like he would a gunsight. The direction pointed out across the prairie. While Marta and Wilkes trailed him like baby ducklings, he went to the far side. Sighting along this line made him perk up.

"You find something? What?" The marshal started to grab him but Marta restrained him.

"Let him run free."

"I ought to clap him back in the hoosegow. He did escape, Pinkerton agent or not."

She engaged Wilkes and gave Luke the chance to follow the new line to a low hill dotted with rocks. He climbed the hill until he reached a spot directly in line with the crossed trees. A few kicks at the sod revealed a hole in the hillside lined with rocks. He started to grab, then turned cautious. Rhoades had booby-trapped one possible hiding place. Doing it twice had to appeal to the outlaw.

Finding nothing to show that another land mine had

been stuffed into the hole along with the gold, he started dragging out one bag of gold coins after another. His arms ached when he pulled the sixth bag out.

"That's it. That's all of it," the marshal said in a low voice. He had watched in mute appreciation. "You found it. Let me shake your hand, Mister Hadley."

Luke winced at the power in that grip. But Marta Shearing's approving smile took away any sting, in the hand or elsewhere.

CHAPTER TWENTY-THREE

LUKE HADLEY SAVORED every bite. The eggs were fried to perfection. The slab of ham on the side and fried potatoes went down as slick as a whistle with a draft of the good coffee. He even put sugar in the coffee, though he never drank it that way. He put the sugar in because he could. And after he finished off the delicious breakfast gracing his plate, he'd consider ordering a slice of apple pie with cheese on it. If he lived here in Crossroads where they knew how to cook such a great meal, he'd put on so much weight he'd waddle.

"More coffee?"

He looked up and smiled.

"When did a Pinkerton agent take up waitressing?" He beckoned for Marta Shearing to sit opposite him.

"My job's done, and it'll be a few days before my next assignment comes in." She settled into the chair and poured herself a cup of coffee. A quick shake of the head told him the sugar he held out for her wasn't needed. She drank it black and hot, like he did when he wasn't enjoying the decadent delights of civilization.

"I heard that three agents arrived on the stagecoach to escort Audrey back to Chicago. Why so many?"

"She's a slippery one. It took a considerable amount of resources to track her down."

"What'd she do that riled everyone up?"

Marta sipped at her coffee and carefully put the china cup into its painted saucer. Every time someone did that, Luke knew they weren't going to answer. He wasn't surprised when she looked up from the coffee and asked, "How long do you have to sit on a pillow?"

"The doc says my hindquarters are healing nicely. I don't need it now, but I've gotten used to it being between me and whatever I'm sitting on." He polished off the last of his breakfast and leaned back, considering the pie. Rumor had it that the peach cobbler was good here, too.

"You can have both, you know," Marta said.

"What?" His eyebrows arched in surprise. Then he laughed. "You shouldn't read a fellow's mind. It's not polite."

"But it can be useful in my line of work. You are healing just fine?"

"You did a decent job sewing up my, uh, backside injury." He stretched. Muscles protested and the half-dozen wounds he'd sustained all over his torso were almost healed. "That said, I'm thinking about going back to the farm where I got my horse and buying it all over again. That plow horse never goes but at one speed, but he gets me where I want to go."

"You might need to gallop," she pointed out.

"I need to learn patience, and that old horse gives me a chance. I paid good money once for him, but he's been worth twice that to me. Seeing that the farmer and his family are reimbursed for their charity is the right thing to do." It had hardly been charity, selling him the plow horse and gear, but Sven and his family could use the extra payment. A growing town the size of Crossroads could use a second fine restaurant.

Marta looked around at the side of his head and made a face. He flushed. The way half his ear had been blown off made him self-conscious. A quick movement shifted his lank hair down to fully cover the ear.

"When are you leaving?" He twisted around to hide his left ear from her and get her thinking on other subjects.

"There's someone I want you to meet." She made a quick motion. An old man at a nearby table used his cane to get upright and shuffle over. With a deft motion he hooked a chair leg with the crook of the cane and pulled it along. When he collapsed, the chair was exactly where it needed to be so he wouldn't land on the floor.

He shifted his pince-nez spectacles and leaned forward so his face was only inches from Luke's. Before Luke shied away, the cane looped out and caught his upper arm, pulling him even closer. A yank of the cane caused Luke to spin in his chair. His damaged ear almost touched the old man's nose.

"Not bad, not too bad," the old man said. "Here. Let me work a bit on this."

"What are you doing?" Luke yelped when the cane

turned in the other direction, pinning him down so he had no chance to get away. The old man's gnarled fingers worked on a bit of putty taken from his coat pocket.

"You can use this deformity. Yes, you can, but you don't want to look like that all the time."

"Stop fiddling with my ear!" Luke found the cane pressed against his throat. He batted it away, only to find the stick crushing into the side of his neck. Protesting the old man's attention any more made them the center of attention. With his damaged ear on display for anyone in the restaurant to see, Luke settled down to let this public humiliation run its course. The old man had to tire of his plight eventually.

"There, there, good. Use this to color it." The old man dropped a small tube of cosmetic coloring on the table. "A pleasure meeting you."

He pushed himself to his feet, nodded in Marta's direction and hobbled to the door. Lukc startcd to protest the man's behavior when he saw him straighten outside and walk away with as sure a stride as a marching soldier.

"What was that all about?"

Marta examined his left side critically, squirted a tiny bit of the coloring unguent onto her finger and dabbed it on his ear. Whatever she did left his ear untouched, though he felt the warmth of her hand against the side of his head.

"There. The color matches the rest of your ear." She beckoned the waiter over and spoke quietly to him. The man looked at Luke, then smiled broadly. He hurried away.

Luke hated being the butt of a joke. At least neither

Marta nor the old man had carried on about that wound.

"You're due a big pile of cash," she said. "The banker's reward was matched by several ranchers. What are you going to do with so much money?"

Luke ran his fingers up and down the seams of his new coat. The gold dust from his old frock coat had been transferred. He had spent a goodly portion of the money from selling his farm to the railroad while tracking down Audrey, but he had enough left to serve him well for a while longer.

"I told Marshal Wilkes that none of us would have found the loot if it hadn't been for Sarah Youngblood. He's arranged for her to stay with a woman and her three daughters at the edge of town. The reward money will keep her for years. She shouldn't be put in a crazy house."

"She *is* loco," Marta said.

"The difference between crazy and eccentric is a lot of money. She'll have enough to be as eccentric as she likes. Sarah saved my life almost as many times as you did. Does that make you loco, too?"

Marta laughed at that, then took a small mirror from the waiter, who stood patiently by. She held it up for Luke.

"What am I looking at? I—oh." He grabbed the mirror and moved it around to reflect what looked to be a whole left ear. He touched the top. The putty had been artfully shaped to mimic his real ear. Marta had the color a little wrong, but no one would pay it second notice. He moved the mirror all around and broke out in a broad grin. "The old man must be quite an artist. A sculptor? Who was he?"

"He's my boss."

"I don't—" Luke blinked. "That was Allan Pinkerton?"

"He made the trip to Crossroads to be sure Audrey was well on her way back to Chicago. He's quite a makeup artist. He can concoct a disguise for any job."

"From what I hear, he's not that old."

"Hardly. He's always practicing. He'll be pleased to know he fooled you. Here." She drew out a folded piece of paper and passed it to him. "Instructions Allan wrote down for you to replenish the ear when this wears out. You might be able to take a bath but only once. A second time and it'll look as if your ear is falling off. You need to learn to craft new ones for yourself."

Luke stared at the instructions, written in a small, precise hand with detailed illustrations.

"This is an ample reward for all I've been through." He tucked it into his coat pocket. His fingers brushed a strip of latigo. He pulled out the leather band with the tin star attached. He laid it on the table.

"You threw this away once. Here. You can get rid of it for good this time. I won't need it to impress people and convince them to tell me if they'd seen Audrey or any of Rhoades's gang." His fingers ran around the rim of the beaten metal star. "I never noticed 'Pinkerton' was spelled wrong. I never looked at it after I paid a blacksmith fifty cents for it. I should have asked how far he got in school." He pulled away from the fake badge but stared at it. The deception had helped him. "I hope you don't mention this to Mister Pinkerton. He might chop off the rest of my ear."

"He knows."

Luke sighed. Then something in the way she said it turned him wary.

"He knows and he's going to have me arrested for impersonating an agent?"

"Does that seem reasonable?" Her face turned neutral so he got no hint as to the answer. He had to work it out for himself.

Luke's mind raced. He quickly shook his head.

"If he knew before he gave me back my ear—and dignity—that means he's willing to forget it."

"Not that," she said.

A cold lump formed in his gut.

"What, then?"

She pushed the tin star to one side and dropped a leather case in its place. She flipped it open. Inside rested a shiny brass shield emblazoned with *Pinkerton Agent.*

"If you want to work for the agency, that's your badge. A real one."

Luke ran his finger over the lettering. It was all spelled correctly. He closed the case, held it for a moment, then put it into his pocket. "What now?"

"There's a required training period for all new agents, no matter their experience, and I need an assistant. Allan hinted at what he wants me to do next, and it will be a dangerous case. Will you work with me?"

"As your assistant?" Luke knew of worse things.

"So what do you say?" She looked eager to hear his reply.

"You talked me into it. I'll have both peach cobbler *and* apple pie."

He thrust out his hand. They shook on it.